WATERMARKED

DANIELLE BUTLER

For my family—through blood or marriage or happenstance.

CONTENTS

Chapter 1

Twenty-seven hours.

It took me twenty-seven hours of straight travel to get to where I am now. Standing in front of a cottage that belongs to my grandmother.

Three flights, two long layovers, a cab ride, one smelly bus, and finally a small boat to reach this island off the coast of Maine.

My mouth feels like it's coated with wool, and my eyes are gritty from lack of sleep. My sides hurt, and my stomach is still churning after the terrifying, white-knuckled sea crossing.

I don't do boats. I don't do water.

I am so over waiting rooms and done with trying to squash my tall self into too-small seats. But now that I'm finally here, I have no idea what is waiting for me. This wasn't my choice.

In the dusk, my grandmother's house looks like something out of a fairytale. It's made of uneven stones fitted together, compact and rustic. Moss grows on the side, smoke curls out of the chimney, and orange paint is peeling off the rough planked door. A narrow stone-lined path leads off toward another house further up the hill. What on earth will the neighbors be like? Who would choose to live here?

I turn to take my bag from Rob who is the quietest man in the world. He met me in Bath at the bus station and hasn't said much beyond making sure I was me and telling me his name. I'm not feeling super social though, so I didn't mind his silence.

I take a deep breath and smell pine and fish. I don't like fish much, but the scent is clean and somehow settles me.

"Better?" Rob asks.

I blush. I can't help it. My straight-up panic at being surrounded by so much water had soon given way to seasickness, and I'd spent most of the trip hurling up everything I have ever eaten ever. I'd like to think that I don't care what others think about me, but no one wants to be seen like that. By anyone. Even silent middle-aged sea captains.

At least he didn't try to do anything or try to comfort me. It was embarrassing enough. And he did give me a clean-ish cloth to wipe my mouth.

"I'm fine," I say although I still feel light-headed. "Thanks. For meeting me. I don't think I would have found it on my own." Complete understatement.

"No," he says and turns to go.

"Wait." I'm suddenly nervous. I don't know my grandmother, never been here before, and after the last few days I don't know what the hell I'm doing—anywhere—but especially here. This guy is the most familiar thing in sight.

Rob stops and turns to face me.

And I feel stupid. "Um…" I falter. "…Aren't you coming in?"

The big man's face freezes and then changes like something's swimming under the surface of his skin. He pushes out a breath. "No, I'll leave you here if you can manage." He is clearly uncomfortable.

"No, yeah, I'm great." I watch him walk all the way back to the boat.

The light is really fading now and with the darkness, the damp air is turning colder. I shake myself and face the door. It's open and a woman stands in the shadows.

"Grandmother?" The word feels unfamiliar in my mouth.

The shadows move, and the woman comes into the light. Her thick hair is a mixture of white and blonde. It's piled on her head, surrounding it like a soft corona. She's slim, shorter than me by a few inches, but she holds herself straight and strong so seems taller. She adjusts the large shawl she has wrapped around her and meets my eyes.

Time slows, and my head feels like it's floating, like it's going to pull me off the ground. I hear rushing water, a heartbeat, and for a moment she seems to shine. Her eyes are a mixture of blue and green—just like Mom's, just like mine.

Then she blinks and the world rights itself.

She looks me over from feet to crown. "She cut your hair," she says under her breath.

I try to smooth my short curls. They are already getting a little too long for my taste. I can feel that they're standing on end after my trip. Nothing to do about it now. I force my hand down and look back at her. I feel dirty and sore and very tired. Even my bones ache. The last two weeks have been the worst and all I want is a toothbrush, a bath, and bed. In that order. A lump forms in my throat but I don't cry. I never cry.

"Come inside," she says. I hoist my bag again and follow.

The door leads to an open room where a low couch sits next to a fire burning in the hearth. The air inside the cottage is damp and smells heavily of fish, herbs, and smoke. I switch to breathing through my mouth.

Near the fireplace is a drying rack of some sort with various colored cloths hanging on it. Off to the right, there's a small kitchen with a pale wooden table and one solitary chair. Something is simmering on the stovetop. My grandmother looks inside the pot and ladles liquid into an earthenware mug. Toward the back of the room is a closed door. I guess that's where the bedrooms must be. I hope it's not as smelly back there.

I set the bag down and stretch my hands over my head, trying to work out the travel kinks. My hand brushes something soft and I look up. It's just more of those cloths hanging from the ceiling. I reach up to touch one again when it dawns on me that they aren't cloths at all but fur... animal skins. I snatch my hand back and feel my stomach lurch as a shudder whips through me.

"Camline."

She says my name like a statement with an underlying... something. Sorrow? Expectation? She looks me over like she's weighing me or measuring my worth. Maybe I'm hearing disappointment. Before I have time to figure it out, she's pushing the mug into my hands.

"You have to be hungry."

I sniff the mug and take a tiny sip to be polite. It's a thick broth, kind of salty, with bits floating in it. Some fishy stew. She's watching me, so I take another sip. I've never liked seafood, but this isn't bad. And I love salt. The taste and texture are strange but oddly satisfying. I drink more and my stomach calms. Weariness weighs on me. I feel the days catching up.

"Sit for a moment." She gestures to the couch and sits in the chair opposite.

The couch is stiff but a lot softer than plastic waiting room chairs. I take another sip of the broth, and something squishy slides over my tongue. I bite down and brine with a sweet, rich flavor bursts inside my mouth. I swallow reflexively and try not to grimace.

"What is this?" I keep my voice under control.

"Sea stew." She seems surprised by my question. "It's a restorative for us," she continues, as if it's common knowledge.

I'm pretty sure I have had enough "island restoration" for now and set the mug down with a thud. "So, Grandmother, Gran..." I'm trying out words, but she just looks at me. "I'm sorry, I don't know what to call you. Mom—" The words dry in my mouth. I haven't even called her yet to tell her I've made it here. Guilt burns at the back of my throat. I breathe. I'll call her when I'm alone. "Mom didn't tell me much about you."

"Call me Ellie."

"Okay," I nod, taking it in stride, and wait for her to go on. But she just watches me and silence stretches out between us. I can't make out her expression. I look away, shifting my eyes around the room—the skins, the fire, and back to the mug on the table. It's too smoky in here and the light isn't good. I sink further into the couch and yawn, then cough out damp, sooty air. I don't know how I am going to get used to this. I look back at my grandmother.

She purses her lips, then gives a quick shake of her head and in clear, clipped syllables says, "You can't stay here."

I sit up, stunned, like someone just splashed water in my face. There is no one else. Where am I supposed to go? My dad is stationed overseas somewhere, and we don't even talk that much on the rare occasions that he is stateside. My mom can't even...

After the first shock, anger gathers. My grandmother, this weird woman, a stranger, has just forced me to travel all the way here from New Mexico just so she can kick me out? It's beyond belief.

Before I can say anything, Ellie continues. "The cottage, I mean. The house behind will service you."

House? I stare at her. "Who lives there?" I finally manage.

"It's empty. You will need to bring some things in, but it will be plenty of space for you."

So, *no* neighbors.

My mind reels. I'm getting a house. I'm stunned but also a little relieved. I mean, with the stuffy air and all those skins...

"We should get you settled." My grandmother—*Ellie* —stands up.

I get up too and grab my bag again.

The sun has completely set, and I shiver in the cool air. Far too cold for June but as I fill my lungs with clean air, I relish the bite. The path behind the house leads to "Windemere" as the sign outside says. It's a one-story wooden house. Ellie opens the heavy door with a key. I can't see much reason for keys on this island. For what—thieving seagulls? Still, after years in cities, I'm happy to see they exist anyway.

Inside the house is dark, and Ellie lights a hurricane lantern next to the door. "The electricity can be sorted out tomorrow."

I'm almost past caring. Almost.

The dim light of the lantern shows an open plan front room with kitchen area on one side and a dining and living room combined on the other. It's similar to Ellie's plan. But no dead animals, thank God. There's a heavy wooden table with three chairs that match her lonely chair in the cottage. She leads me past all this into the hallway and points to a closed door.

"Bathroom." She passes it, turns left into a bedroom, and puts the lantern on a dresser just inside the room.

"The other entrance to the bathroom is there." She points to another door further down the wall. "So, I thought you might prefer this room. When you wake, come down to me. There is water if you want to wash tonight, but it won't be hot. Do you want a fire?"

"I'm fine." The house feels snug if a little stale from being closed up. "I need to call Mom."

Ellie freezes. "She speaks to you?"

I am instantly, irrationally angry. Maybe it's her tone, or the simple fact that I can't even remember the last time Ellie had even checked on Mom. It's like those doctors that wouldn't prescribe treatment because they thought Mom wouldn't respond. They wouldn't even try.

"She hears. She's still there. You can't just forget about her because you think she's broken." I stop. My throat feels like it's closing.

Ellie is stationary in front of me, unmoving but trembling. Her eyes shine in the lamplight. Then she seems to vibrate and expand in the space. I'm transfixed, a deer in headlights. The air goes out of the room. I am pinned in place, caught in Ellie's stare.

She hisses through her teeth. "You know nothing. Just a child. She made her choices, wouldn't listen. Left it so late. Left *you* so late."

A band tightens around my chest, constricting my lungs. Pins and needles climb my fingers and toes. Everything narrows to just the sea green of my grandmother's eyes. The floor tilts, I hear rushing water again, and then with a pop, it stops as Ellie closes her eyes.

She seems to age in seconds; years settle back over her,

shrinking her. "There is always more to the story than the pieces you can see." She turns and walks out.

I hold on to the side of the dresser until I hear the front door close. My hand shakes as I twist the key on the lamp to get more light into the room and chase away shadows. Anger recedes to a dull burn. My head is pounding, recovering from my dizzy spell.

I must be even more tired than I thought.

I kick off my shoes and grab my toiletries bag from my duffel. The floor in the bathroom is chilly under my feet. I splash my face and brush my teeth with the achingly cold water. Back in my new bedroom, I change into my pajamas, slather my always chapped lips with balm, and pull out my favorite photo. Me and Mom before she got so sick. I love her smile in it. I place it on the side table and crawl into the bed. I have just enough juice on my phone to make a call.

A bored receptionist answers and puts me on hold while she transfers me to the east wing. The charge nurse picks up.

"Hey Maria, it's Cam. Is Mom sleeping? Can you put the phone up to her?" I wait while she transfers the call. After a few minutes, Maria picks up again and I can hear her softly talking to Mom, letting her know I am on the phone. I make myself smile, hoping Mom will hear it. Keep positive.

"Mom? I'm here. I made it. I'm okay." I strain my ears. I think I can hear her breathing. "Mom? Did you hear me? I love you."

"Cam," Maria's voice again, "she's tired today."

I say my goodbyes, turn off the lamp, and lie back on the bed. Frustration burns behind my eyes. I hate that I am over 2,000 miles away. In less than two years I'll be eighteen and can go wherever I want so no one can stop me from being there with Mom. Today though, I am bone weary. Ellie is nothing like any of my friends' grandmas. I tell myself that I don't even want to stay with her, but I actually can't believe she won't let me live in her house.

Maybe she doesn't like me.

Maybe she knows that Mom's sickness is probably all my fault.

Chapter 2

The next morning the sun wakes me. I don't even know where I am at first, but I do know it's way too early to be awake. But the angle of the sun shows me that it is later than I think. Right. Jet lag. At least now I can see where I'm staying. I dig out Mom's old iPod. Yeah, an iPod. My phone is almost out of battery, and anyway, I don't keep any music on it. I have the only phone that just works as a phone. I put my earphones in as I investigate.

There isn't much to see. An iron bedstead, plain white sheets and comforter. There's an empty dresser, bedside table with a currently useless lamp, and a closet, also empty except for a couple hangers. On top of the dresser, though, is a beautiful little wooden box. It looks hand carved. When I flip it over, something moves inside it. I pull out an earphone and gently shake the box. It rattles. There's definitely something inside, but I can't see a catch. I try to pry an end open, but it won't budge. I take it with me while I go to check out the rest of the house in the sunlight.

The hallway is empty except for an old mirror. The heavy glass subtly distorts my face and kind of freaks me out.

Across the hall is another bedroom, but this one has a bit more life in it. There's a single bed covered with a pretty patchwork quilt and a white dresser with hand-stenciled flowers and shells decorating the top and sides. In the top drawer I find a dried starfish, brittle and coarse, and some sort of dried plant. I leave them there and close the drawer like I'm trying not to disturb them.

Next is a small laundry room which will be awesome if the old machines work. No more saving all our quarters for the coin-op machines like Mom and I had to do in the last place. I fiddle around with the buttons and feel hopeful that with some power they might actually function. The kitchen has a fridge, stove, and even an old microwave. I go through all the cupboards while idly shaking the little box. The hollow rattle becomes a tiny addiction. One ear focuses on that while the other is lost in an instrumental from a movie I've never seen but heard the music and liked it. There's a basic collection of cookware and essentials in the kitchen cupboards.

In the living room, I hit pay dirt. There's a tall set of shelves full of books. I set the little box on the coffee table and check out the kinds of books that got left behind in a place like this. It's a completely eclectic array: classics, grocery store paperbacks from twenty-some-odd years ago, and a couple of heavy, leather-bound books that I have never heard of. The bottom shelf is filled with children's books, mainly mythologies and fairytales. I pick up one which makes me smile remembering the stories from when I was little, Hans Christen Anderson. Across the first page, written in looping cursive, is the name *Serena Alcott*.

"Oh!" I breathe out and then hug the book to me. This was my mom's book. It hits me then that this is where she grew up.

A dog barking catches my attention. I look out the

window and, in the distance, see a black and white dog running around, and with it is a person. Another actual person! He or she is too far away for me to guess age or gender, or see much more than the green of their jacket, but I know it's not Ellie. They are too tall, and besides, my grandmother doesn't seem to be the kind of person that keeps pets. Not ones wearing their skins anyway.

I suppose I better get on down to see her. I clean up and get dressed, gearing myself up to go down to the cottage. The wind blows softly, cleanly, and from the slab of concrete that serves as Windemere's porch, I can see all the way down past Ellie's to the ocean. From here the expanse of the ocean reminds me of nights at the sand dunes outside Yuma, Arizona, where we had lived as a family for a little while. Except all this is wet. The sight of all that water is overwhelming even from here, and I shudder. We have always lived in dry climates. Small towns, big cities, military bases when Dad was still in the picture, but never the coast.

Besides my grandmother's cottage and the path that connects it to my house, there is only one other pathway that leads down to the cove with the dock and, further to the right, a thin strip of beach. A couple of sea birds cry out as they fly above me.

To the right of the house, a clutch of pine trees blocks my view. I tell myself it's just curiosity that makes me put off heading to Ellie's and go around the side of the house instead. Opening up behind it, further south, is an open tract leading to more trees and some rocks, looks like. I can't see the person or the dog from earlier. I don't know where they could have gone.

I'm on an island. How in the heck did I get here and what the hell am I doing here? I hate water. I don't swim. Never have. Not even in the height of summer in Arizona. Dad hated open bodies of water too, and I must take after him in that respect. He always took me off to do something else when Mom insisted that we go to Lake Havasu or Elephant Butte or even Abiquiu where Georgia O'Keefe painted. Dad and I always had a great time. We would find something to do —go camping, see a movie, or explore a ghost town. Mom would take off for hours or a day, sitting by the water or swimming or whatever she did there. I couldn't understand it. Didn't appeal to me at all. She would return full of sun, hair damp and smelling of lake. She was always so peaceful after these trips.

A few times she tried to get me to promise to come back with her the next day or even later that night. She was so happy and excited that I would've considered it, but Dad had the sharpest ears. He didn't like the idea. Then they'd argue again. I'd squish my pillow around my head and try to block out the noise. The next day, without fail, we would leave and drive in silence back to the dry desert.

Then Mom got sick, and Dad started taking overseas tours.

"Camline." I jump a tiny bit. My grandmother is standing outside her cottage watching me. She's too far away for me to have heard her like I did, like she was right next to me. She hadn't shouted, I know that. Maybe I'm just hearing things now.

As I get closer, she asks, "Did you sleep?"

"Yeah, uh yes, thanks." I'm not really sure how to interact with this woman. I barely know her, and after that weirdness last night…

"Hungry?"

More soup? I wonder.

Her mouth quirks, as if she can read my thoughts. "I have bread."

In her cottage, I see that the drying rack has been moved to the side and all the skins from the ceiling are stacked up by it. Ellie motions to the one chair at the table and hands me a plate of fresh, delicious-smelling bread with a dollop of butter and honey, as well as a hot mug of tea. She pulls up a stool across from me and places a small dish of something that looks like crystals on the table between us; a tiny spoon sticks out the side. Ellie scoops up some of it and as she dumps it on my plate, I realize that it is sea salt in flat flakes. I sprinkle a liberal layer over the bread and honey.

"I learned to make bread for your grandfather. Now I have grown to like it as much as he."

Curiosity pricks my ears. As little as Mom had told me about Ellie, she had said even less about my grandfather. "I don't know much about him, except that he was a fisherman." And that he sailed out one day and never returned. Abandoning his family, or dead, but he hadn't been seen since well before I was born. Maybe I won't mention that, though.

"Today, I thought you might like to get some supplies from the mainland. You should get some food and gasoline for the generator."

"We're going to the mainland?"

"You are. Rob or one of his sons will take you. I have money." She walks to the kitchen and takes down a ceramic container and pulls out some cash. Literally out of a flour pot or cookie jar or some other household bank from another century. My gaze wanders and lands on the drying rack.

"Um, Ellie, what are the skins?"

"Rabbit, muskrat, beaver, a bobcat."

She does not give any other explanation. I change the subject. "So, my grandfather?"

"He was the handsomest man I had ever seen."

"Really? What was he like?"

"Unlike anyone I had ever met." Her voice is soft. "He was clever and so alive. He was bursting with life."

I want more. "How did you meet?"

Ellie fastens her eyes on mine, and her mouth lifts on one side. "Your mother told you nothing? Truly?"

Before I can respond, a knock at the door surprises me, and I spill some of my tea. Ellie hands the wad of cash to me.

"Get whatever you need or want. This is yours. Get enough food for two weeks."

I take it, but I am still wondering what Mom should have told me about my grandfather.

Chapter 3

Outside, Rob stands a little way down the path, not too close, not too far to be rude. At the door is a woman who looks about twenty.

"You must be Cam. I'm Jane. You know, like 'Plain Jane,'" she says. There is nothing plain about the person in front of me. She's almost my height with a toothpaste-commercial smile, bright brown eyes, and buttery gold hair. She carries herself with the easy physical confidence of an athlete, or someone who spends a lot of time outdoors. Her wide smile is infectious and, although I am confused, I can't help but grin back at her.

"I heard you'd come in and thought you could use a hand. I need some stuff too." Her tone sobers as Ellie comes up beside me. "Miss Ellie. Is there anything we can get for you?"

"No, Jane." She nods to Rob. "You should have enough time." Then they both look to the empty blue sky. Ellie guides me out with a gentle hand at my back and closes the door with a snap.

I follow Jane down toward the dock where Rob's motor-boat is moored. My breathing quickens as my heart starts to pound. For a second, I don't know if I can make myself get back on the boat.

As if he can sense my worry, Rob says softly, "Calm now." Without waiting for my reply, he heads off in front of us.

Jane smiles. "I heard about the trip in last night. No fun. Don't worry—it's calmer and we're not going as far anyway. Just to hit the stores in Williams Point."

I have no idea where the town is, but I nod anyway. Shorter trip should be okay, but I'm still confused. "Jane, not to be rude, but who are you?"

She lets out a shout of laughter that is as natural and bright as the sun. "Of course! You rode over with Rob and spent the night with your grandmother. Neither of them could ever be accused of being chatty. I'm staying on the island right now with Rob's family."

I frown at Rob's back. "Are you related?" They couldn't be more different.

She laughs again. "No, they're putting me up. I'm studying anthropology at UCLA, in California. I've spent the last year doing research on offshoot cultures. The coast of Maine is good for that because there are so many islands and contained groups of people. We live on the far side by the other houses. Your grandmother's house and cottage are the only ones on this side. You can walk to us through the woods but I think a boat is faster if you go around the north side." She finally takes a breath.

I jump in while I can. "Wait, how many people live here?"

"Right now, only Rob and Anne, his wife, and their sons, Macon and Jack. And me. And you and your grandmother, of course. There are three other houses on our side, but they only have people in the summer, usually."

We get to the dock where Rob is already prepping the boat.

I stall. "So, how big is this island?"

"I think it's about two, two and a half miles?" Jane says, looking to Rob as if for confirmation. "That's from extreme points east to west where the island is the widest as the crow flies. Or as the osprey flies, to be geographically specific." She chuckles at her own joke.

I don't know what an osprey is and don't care because Rob is motioning us to get in the boat. I swallow. The water does seem calmer than it was last night, so they were right about that, but there is just so much of it. My hands are already shaking. I grit my teeth. I'm just going to have to suck it up though and get on the boat. I can't be marooned on this island, and boats are the only way off it. I hope my stomach holds.

I step down and take Rob's rough hand, gripping it as tight as I can. The floor of the boat moves under me, and I clutch the side as well as his hand until I'm seated. Rob gives me a life jacket, and I try to put it on with one hand while the other hangs on to the side of my seat.

Jane sees me and laughs good-naturedly as she helps me with the clasp before putting on her own jacket. Rob pushes us out and starts the motor. Jane is standing, balanced and at ease, as we start off. "Don't worry, it's just water!" She shouts over the motor. "Even if you fall in, you won't melt."

I smile like I am in on the joke but just hold on even tighter.

~

WHEN WE FINALLY ARRIVE AT Williams Point, my hands are cramping and although I feel sick to my stomach, I am super proud that I didn't lose my breakfast. Williams Point is not what you would call a big town, but I have lived in smaller. It will have gas stations and neighborhoods and chain stores. Just like anywhere else. Somewhere up those streets will be my new school. I'll worry about that later. For now, I'm just really enjoying the feel of solid ground under my feet. Rob looks at the sky again and tells Jane what time to meet up later. Then Jane marches me over to a store that sells outdoor gear.

"I want another waterproof bag, and I bet you don't have anything. Trust me. You need at least one good raincoat and maybe a pair of rubber boots."

A man comes over to us and Jane greets him. "Hi Mr. Riggs, this is Camline..."

"Vale." I supply my last name.

Mr. Riggs is a stocky man of medium height with reddish-brown hair streaked with grey and is sporting the biggest mustache and beard combo. He has pale grey eyes. "What can I do for you ladies?"

His accent is strange. Well, still strange to my ears. It's similar to Rob's, I guess, but much thicker. Jane leaves me with him as she heads to the back to find what she needs. Mr. Riggs is courteous but not exactly friendly. He's more restrained than shop staff or owners in the Southwest. But we're not in the Southwest. I wonder if everyone here has this kind of reserved nature. Everyone who's from here that is. Jane is open, cheerful, and chatty but she's from California. She doesn't count.

Within twenty minutes, I am standing in front of a mirror in a knee-length coat in the most astonishing shade of yellow and a pair of thick, black rubber boots. I feel ridiculous.

I change, and as we pay for our purchases, Jane assures

me again, "You'll thank me when the rain hits; the island can get slammed in storms."

Mr. Riggs gives Jane a funny look but smiles at me, "Young lady, you are staying on Shell Island as well?"

"Ellie Alcott is my grandmother."

Mr. Riggs' smile doesn't move, but I feel a sudden coldness from him. Like all his previous geniality just evaporated. "Of course, the eyes," he says under his breath.

"Do you know my grandmother?"

"Yes." Without another word, he turns to speak with a middle-aged woman who had just entered the shop.

"That was weird," I say as we get outside.

Jane shrugs. "People can be strange here." She leads me into a grocery store. "Did Miss Ellie give you a list?"

"No, I'm just getting stuff for me, I think. I'm staying in Windemere."

"Really? In that case, you should stock up on canned goods, just in case, and some dry goods. Anything you can make easily." She leaves me to make a start while she goes to check on a special order.

My first stop is the over-the-counter medicines, but they don't have anything for motion sickness. I'll have to ask Jane where the nearest pharmacy is. I wander around pulling things from the shelves. At least I know how to shop. Mom always took me with her and pointed out things to buy and showed me how to plan meals. After Dad left, I learned about budgeting. Mom always made it like a game though, so I never felt like we were deprived. We would have competitions to find the Best Bargain of the Day and whoever won got to decide what we were having for dinner that night. After Mom got sick, I had to go by myself. I'm not a creative chef, but I know how to feed myself. But seriously, I can hardly believe that I am doing this, setting up house. What 16-year-old has to live in a house alone? I should be with my Mom. I slam a can into my basket. Thinking of Mom brings that familiar ache to the back of my throat and tightens my chest. I shove those thoughts down and grab another can as Jane appears at the end of the aisle.

"How'd you do?" she asks, peering into the basket. "Not bad, a bit boring, maybe." She turns and grabs a couple packets of cookies and holds them up. "Chocolate or not chocolate?"

I don't have a big sweet tooth, but I grin anyway. She takes that as permission and puts both into my basket. I take some salted nuts as well, throw in a Chapstick, and head to the checkout. A bored older man rings everything up and waits as I count out the cash. I still have a lot left over from what Ellie gave me.

"We have a little time before we need to meet Rob. Want to get coffee?"

"Yes, please!" I think I might love her right now. Caffeine has definitely been missing from my day. "But I need to go to a pharmacy and I still need gas for the generator."

"We can get gas at the dock as we leave. Rob will have containers on the boat. There is a little pharmacy in town but," she checks her watch, "I think they are closed for lunch right now."

I sigh but let Jane propel me and my growing number of bags into a funky coffee shop, scattered with comfy armchairs and low tables. A girl about my age with electric blue hair, an intricate tattoo on her forearm, and a pierced eyebrow is at the counter. She knows Jane and greets her by rattling off a coffee order almost as complicated as her tattoo. Jane throws her arms up in a "touchdown!" motion.

She introduces me. "Blue, this is Cam. She's living out on the island too."

I feel a little self-conscious, but I smile and tell her my order. The girl responds with a sideways glance, "So, you're out on Creeper Island, too?"

"Blue..." Jane says in a low voice, like she's trying to warn her.

"What?" Blue scoffs. "The woman is frea-ky. I should know. Super creepy."

Like a slap, I realize who she's talking about and my face goes hot. I meet the girl's eyes; she cuts off mid-laugh, her mouth still open.

"Miss Ellie is Cam's grandmother." Jane raises her eyebrows.

Blue looks uncomfortable. She closes her mouth and shrugs, setting our drinks on the counter. "Sorry. Here, have a biscotti."

I take my drink, leave the cookie, and spin away. I'm so angry, and I'm not even sure why. I barely know Ellie, and Blue is kind of right. Ellie may very well be creepy but to hear her talked about like this, it's just... well, rude. Jane stays behind talking to Blue. I tune them out and stare into the street. There are hardly any people out there, and it's starting to get cloudy.

"Oh, c'mon! That was it for the sun today?" Jane grumbles, looking out the window as she sets down her sweet-smelling coffee drink. A blob of caramel sauce falls to the table. "I guess we should get going soon. Be right back." She heads for a door marked with a crescent moon, like an old-fashioned outhouse symbol.

"Hey, I didn't mean anything by it. Seriously." I look up to see Blue standing over me with two biscotti biscuits. "Peace?" She holds out the treats. She seems genuine, and I accept the biscuits. "So, you just got here?"

"Yeah. Yesterday."

"From where?"

"New Mexico."

"Really? Like with those tall cactuses that look like they're waving?" She strikes a comical pose with her arm cocked like she's stopping traffic.

"Cacti. No, those are saguaro. They're mostly in Arizona. We're the next state over, and we were in the mountains."

"They have mountains there?" She cocks her head.

Jane comes back and takes a big gulp of her drink. "Yikes. That's hot."

"Duh. I just made it."

"Yeah, yeah." Jane sits, takes another sip and winces. She blows on the top while stirring it.

Blue sits down with us, shoving Jane over.

"Aren't you working?" Jane asks with a smile.

"Yes. This is part of the excellent customer service." She fiddles with her eyebrow ring. "What are you guys doing now?"

"Just heading back. This was our last stop."

"Cool. So, Cam, why are you here?"

"Blue!"

"What? I am making conversation."

"For the coffee," I say and take a swig of my drink. It's not too hot for me.

Jane looks from me to Blue and says to her, "Get me a to-go cup, will you?" Then to me, "Do you need one too?" I shake my head.

Blue sighs and gets up like it's a huge chore.

"We should probably get going, Cam."

"That's fine." I finish the last of my latte.

Blue comes back with a paper cup and Jane pours the rest of her drink into it. "Sorry, but Rob will be waiting for us. See you later, Blue."

"Later. Nice to meet you, Cam."

"You too."

We gather our things and leave. I'm wearing the yellow coat and as we head for the bay, I'm glad for it. The wind has picked up, and I pull it closer. Rob's waiting for us with two large gas canisters.

"Need to go." His broad face is set.

I look up and see the darkening sky.

Oh crap.

Chapter 4

I hold on tightly, clenching my jaw as Rob pilots the boat back across the water. The rain starts about halfway through the journey. Even Jane's face is grim. My coat keeps a lot of the water off, but my stomach's so not happy with me. I'm regretting the coffee now. Stupid pharmacist lunch hour. The wind whips at my hood and rain hits my face. My new boots are still in the box and my sneakers are soaking by the time we finally get back to the island. It takes me two tries to get out of the boat. My knees are rubbery and my hands slick with rain. Jane passes me my groceries and the bag with my boots in it. She tells me she'll see me soon and they head off.

Bags swinging, feet squishing, and rain in my face, I walk as fast as I can up the path. I slow when I get to Ellie's, but decide getting dry is more important than checking in. I keep going until I reach Windemere and as I shut the door, I realize I have forgotten the gasoline.

Fumbling around in the near dark inside the house, I find the hurricane lamp and the lighter and get it going, wishing I had thought to buy a flashlight. I put away the cans and dry packages and think about building a fire. I'm pretty sure I remember how to do it. When Dad and I used to camp together, he showed me. It's been awhile, but there's plenty of kindling.

I soon have a little flame going in the grate. And a load of smoke filling the living room.

Covering my nose and mouth, I find the handle to the flue and after a couple of tugs, get it open. The smoke begins to clear. I sigh and look around. My clothes are wet; I need to change. I still haven't had a proper shower, and I'm hungry. The water is too cold for a bath, but I wash my face in the sink and then slip into a pair of comfortable sweats and a long-sleeved t-shirt that my mom gave me. Mom! I haven't charged my phone. It's still sitting by the side of the bed and is now completely dead. I want to kick myself; I should've taken it with me today and found somewhere to plug it in.

I hang up my wet jeans to dry by the hearth and am reminded of the animal pelts at Ellie's house. My skin crawls. I lie on the couch, enjoying the heat from the fire. I don't even realize that I have fallen asleep until something hits the window, and I wake with a squeak. A very girlie, undignified squeak. It's dark now and I can't see much out the window, but it seems like it's just the rain. It's really coming down hard now. I add another log to the fire, glad that there is plenty of wood stacked there.

Opening a can of peaches, I drink the juice. The house seems to move all around me in the gathering storm, and there must be a window that doesn't seal because the mournful sound of the wind echoes through the house. I check every single window and they all seem to be fine. But I can still hear the sound, like wailing. It must be outside.

I am really creeped out now. Dark and stormy night, crazy Maine island. I am basically living in an old Stephen King novel. The sound swells in the house like a tangible thing, tingles the nape of my neck and, I swear, shakes the hall mirror. Then as quickly as it had built, it tapers off. I'm going to have to get a bit more backbone if I'm living here alone. I laugh at myself and head to the kitchen to forage a proper meal.

A slamming fist against the door nearly sends me out of my skin, and I drop the metal bowl I'm holding. It makes a terrible noise. I'm sure it's just Ellie, checking on me since I didn't stop there on my way back, so I open the door without hesitating. A gust of wind blows rain into my eyes, and the lamp flame flares in the sudden rush of air.

A man is standing there. No, a boy. A young man. He has black hair plastered against his hatless head and impatient hazel eyes.

"You Cam?" he asks, brushing the rain off of his face.

I nod dumbly, a machine gun fire of questions popping off in my head. Who is he? How does he know my name? Or where I live? And why would he come out on a night like this to find me?

"Look—sorry if I scared you. Can I come in?"

I finally realize that he is carrying the forgotten gas canisters. He must be one of Rob's sons. I step back as he comes inside. He's taller than me and seems to take up a considerable amount of space in the room. He sets the canisters down and looks around the dim house.

"Electricity already out?" He has a little bit of an accent. Not like his dad's or anything, but a hint of French.

"It hasn't worked since I got here."

He flicks the switch anyway like I wouldn't have tried that. Nothing happens.

"Like I said…"

He ignores me, crosses to the kitchen tracking wet, muddy steps across the floor and opens a panel on the wall that hides the breakers. He slides them back and forth, and suddenly the overhead light illuminates the room and the refrigerator begins to hum. I cannot believe it was that simple.

He looks at me with amused annoyance. "Didn't you check this?"

I feel totally stupid, and then irritated. This guy just comes in here like he owns the place, messes up the floor, and acts like he knows everything. And stands there grinning. He's almost laughing at me! I'm mainly irritated with myself though. I know about breakers. I didn't even think to check them because Ellie had told me the electricity was out, so I thought she would have tried them.

"So why do I need the gas?"

"For the generator," he says in a tone that asks if it is not painfully obvious. "In case the electricity goes out. For real."

This isn't getting anywhere. "So, where's the generator?"

"In the back." He pauses like he's mulling something over, and then seems to come to a decision. "I better show you, just in case." He picks up the canisters again and walks out the front door, like he's expecting me to follow.

I throw on my slicker and boots as fast as I can and run outside. The wind has slacked off, but rain is still falling steadily. The boy has slowed enough that I see his flashlight disappear around the side of the house. I hurry to catch up.

Behind the house is a pile covered in a dark green oilcloth tarp. I peek under it to find stacks of wood. Well, that's good to know. Next to the pile is a contraption that must be the generator. He's fiddling around with something and waves me closer. He shows me where to put the gas and how to turn on the machine if needed. When he's satisfied that I will be able to manage this basic task, he stores the gas canisters out of the way and we turn to go back inside. The rain increases, falling even more heavily, and my eyes sting with water. It must be all the salt in the air. The light spilling out of the windows is comforting and I realize that this means the water heater should be working, and I can finally get a bath.

At the porch, the boy opens the door, letting the light wash over us, and turns. For the first time, we really look at each other. He has a strong, serious face and straight black brows over his eyes. His cheeks are red from the chill, and water tracks down his face. Our eyes catch, and his expression changes as he looks at me. He looks puzzled, like he's trying to place me. His lips part like he's about to say something but just stares at me with a curious expression. I stand there for a fraction of a second too long, and I find myself wondering what I must look like sopping wet and wearing this ridiculous rain slicker. Then he moves to let me pass.

"I'm Macon," he says. His accent is more pronounced on his own name. *Mah-cohn.*

I try it out in my head. "Oh. I'm, uh, Cam."

He smiles and his face changes becoming less severe and almost mischievous. "Yeah, I figured."

"Right." He's laughing at me. Again.

He turns to go and is already fading into the night before I think to call out a lame "Thanks!" He doesn't stop. I don't even know if he heard me.

I shut the door tightly and hang my coat on the hook. Rain drips from it to the floor. The water heater will need time to heat up. The bottoms of my sweats are wet, so I hang them to dry and ferret out another pair before making myself a quick peanut butter sandwich.

I wait as long as I can before turning the water on full blast in the bath. After a minute it starts to heat up, and just the thought of getting clean and warm is almost as good as if it is actually happening. I leave the bath to fill and go to grab my pajamas. The wind is picking up yet again and flings water against the windows. I wonder just how far Macon has to walk out in the rain. I really should've made more of an effort to thank him. I could've done better than a last-minute shout that he probably didn't even hear. How graceless. Mom would not have approved.

Thinking of her, I make sure my phone is plugged in before getting into my bath. This is the way that water is meant to be enjoyed: in a tub, hot, and never too deep. As I sink down into the warmth, I relax properly for the first time in days. I stretch my arms over my head and then just go limp, resting my head against the back of the tub, body buoyed by the water. I close my eyes.

Very faintly, I can hear that howling sound again. Not howling, more like wailing. Like a cry of sadness. As I listen to it, it pulls at me, sending prickles across my skin, like threads hooking me and reeling me toward it. It's heart-breaking. I want to soothe the pain, right the wrong. I can almost make out words.

I wake up when my head hits the water and I come up spluttering—coughing, panicked. I take several deep breaths as I pull the plug on the now cold bath. My heart is pounding, and my hands tremble as I reach for my towel. It is so quiet now.

Think I might stick to showers for a while.

Chapter 5

The next morning, I kick at the dried dirt on the kitchen floor. That Macon just stomped through the house tracking mud. His footprints make a clear path straight to the breakers and then out again. I scrape the dirt into a pile with my feet. I'm still annoyed about the breakers. At least the electricity works. A little mud is worth lights and warm water, right?

I guess I should really thank him. It's only polite, but I'm reluctant. It makes me sort of nervous thinking about Macon. I don't know why. He's cute, I guess, but I have no intention of getting involved with anyone even if he (or I!) was actually interested. There's just already too much to worry about in my life. And I don't need any ties to this place.

Besides, I've seen what love can do to a person.

But I should still thank him. Mom would want that. She always said to be grateful for the little things and make sure you tell someone that you appreciate what they have done for you. Resigned, I decide to check in with Ellie and find how to get to Rob's house.

It's raining again so I put on the on the slicker and boots, and head down to the cottage. There is no answer when I knock.

"Ellie?" I open the door a crack. I hear something inside. "It's Cam." The air is damp and chilly, no longer smoky. Ellie is sitting in the living room armchair staring out the window. On her lap is a reddish-brown pelt of—something—that she's stroking. She doesn't even look up when I shut the door. I wait for a second. "Are you all right?" Ellie just continues to stare and stroke the pelt. I feel a cold prickle of fear start up my spine.

"Grandma?" I say, then louder, "Ellie!"

Her eyes snap to mine, and she looks at me for a moment like she doesn't even know who I am. Then she shifts, throws the pelt onto the couch as she stands up. Her face is more lined, and she moves slower.

"Are you okay?"

"Yes, Camline, just thinking of my sisters."

This is news. I have great-aunts out there? No one has ever mentioned them to me. Mom and Dad are both only children. So am I. I can hardly wrap my head around the idea of more family. I have so many questions but before I can ask for details, she's all business, pulling out the breakfast items.

"Did you get groceries? And gasoline?"

"I did. Thank you." I fish out her change from my pocket. "I also got this coat and boots. Hope that's okay."

"Keep the money." Ellie touches the sleeve of my coat. "Why did you need this?"

"Jane thought it was a good idea. To keep me dry."

Ellie laughs like she's unused to it. "Water never hurt us." She smiles at me like I have made a good joke.

"I don't like water," I admit.

Ellie looks at me like she's measuring me again.

I feel the need to explain further. "I know Mom loved to

swim but Dad hated it and after my accident, I guess I took more after him."

"Accident?" Ellie seems puzzled.

"When I was really little?" I'm sure Mom would have told her about it, but Ellie looks at me blankly. "I was like three or four. I fell into a swimming pool and almost drowned. Dad saved me."

"Your father. Saved you. In water." Ellie says this flatly, unbelieving.

"I almost died." I'm defensive. Sometimes I still dream about the pool—the way the water burned my eyes and throat, the fear. I shudder. "After that, I never liked it. Never wanted swimming lessons. I still can't swim."

Ellie scoffs, "Don't be ridiculous. Of course you can swim, Camline."

People never understand. Thrashing in the water, I remember thinking very clearly that I would never find the surface again. I remember the sheer panic of not being able to breathe. I was so terrified. Just thinking of it now makes my palms itch and throat close. My heartbeat speeds up.

"We will go to the ocean; I will show you."

"No! I don't like the water." My heart is going to gallop out of my chest.

Ellie gives me a considering look, wary and disappointed.

I take a long slow breath and change the subject. "Can you tell me how to get to Rob's place?"

She doesn't look fooled by my topic change. She scrutinizes me a few seconds longer, then just hands me a roll with butter and the salt pot. "Yes."

"I want to thank Macon."

"You need to thank one of Rob's sons?"

I explain about the forgotten gas and how he had shown me the generator.

"You needed the generator last night?"

"No, he showed me just in case I needed it later. It was a tripped breaker; that's why there were no lights."

Ellie shrugs and seems to lose interest in that part of the story. "Macon. He is the younger boy." I can't read her face.

It's my turn to shrug. Jane hadn't told me the family order.

"Just be careful, Camline."

I nod, but I don't get what she's warning me about. Talking about my accident and the insane suggestion of going in the ocean has thrown me off. I don't want to get into some other strange conversation with my even stranger grand-mother. I listen as she explains how to find Rob's house. Then she points to an oilcloth sack near the door and asks me if I can take it with me. I lift it and it's heavy, but I'm pretty strong. It feels dense, but it's soft enough to give under my fingers. "What is it?"

"The skins I was drying. They're ready now, and Rob can take them."

I seriously almost drop the package. My eyes shoot to the couch to the skin she had been petting when I arrived.

"Yes," she says softly, "that one too." She picks it up, pushes it under the flap of the sack, and then tightens the strings again.

I PULL up my hood and trudge in the direction Ellie told me, straight into the woods. The sharp scent of the pine trees smells great. The needles littering the floor muffle my foot-steps. I forgot my iPod, so my steps are all I hear at first. Deeper into the trees, I feel like I am somewhere else alto-gether. The light is different, filtered by the trees, and the sounds of the forest rise up around me. I keep following the beaten down path winding through the trees.

The rain stops and after a bit, the package of skins weighs on my arms, so I set it down to take a rest. Something catches my eye through the trees off to the left, like a glow or flash of color. I peer into the forest, but it's gone. Just as I think I must have imagined it, I see bright green pulse to life again. Curious, I leave the sack to check it out. Keeping my eyes on the glow, I make my way, stepping over fallen logs, leaves, and other forest detritus. My last English teacher, Mrs. Albetta, would appreciate my use of that vocab word.

The light gets brighter and fades, but I can still see where it was. I hurry and step into a small, hidden meadow ringed with trees. The moment I cross the tree barrier, I feel at peace. It is completely silent in the clearing—no rustling, no insects, no birdsong. I am entranced by the stillness. Then the sun breaks through the cloud cover, hitting the wet grass, and the whole place glows like an emerald. I angle my face to catch the sun's glow, close my eyes, and breathe in the scent of grass and pine. Warmth fills me like I'm breathing in the sun, too, until the inevitable cloud covers it. It's still unnaturally quiet, but without the sun, the spell is broken. I turn to go back to the path. For a moment I am turned around, not sure which way to go. Then I see the pack on the ground in the distance. I take one last look at the clearing and move on.

By the time I break through the trees on the other side of the forest, I'm sweating. I'm surprised to see a cluster of houses. Jane had said there were more houses over here, but I'd forgotten. One is on its own—a three-story wooden home with peeling whitewash and some purple flowers growing out front. The other three houses are connected in a row and each has shutters fastened over its windows. A middle-aged woman steps out onto the porch of the single house. She's wearing a dark, long-sleeved t-shirt and jeans, with a butcher's apron covering her down to her knees. She clutches a white hand towel and frowns at me.

I wave and call out a hello as I shift the package to my hip. The lady just steps back inside without saying a thing, banging the screen door behind her. I roll my eyes. This New England behavior borders on straight up bad manners. I'm getting tired of it. Since the three houses in a row are shut down tight, the other must be Rob's, and that woman must be his wife, Anne. Macon's mom. I have half a mind to turn around and forget the whole thing, but now I have this stupid package to deliver. And I really do want to thank Macon and Rob properly. I refuse to let East Coast "hospitality" stop me. I climb the steps, set the sack down, and knock on the door. A dog barks.

After a moment, too long for someone who literally just went inside, Anne appears. She cracks the door and looks me up and down.

"Hello," she says warily. "Do you need something?"

Her accent is like Macon's but much more pronounced. French-Canadian maybe? It's really pretty. A black and white dog huffs and tries to reach me, but the door opening is too narrow for it to get through. I put my hand out for him to sniff and he slobbers all over it.

"Uh, is Macon here?" I blurt out without even introducing myself.

Her eyes immediately narrow. "What do you want with him?"

Her apparent hostility startles me. How could I have already offended her? I open my mouth, unsure what to say, and then I am saved by Jane. She comes in from the back room, sees me and smiles.

"Hey! You found us!" At Jane's appearance, Anne opens

the door fully. The dog tumbles toward me, wriggling. "Did you meet Anne? Anne, this is Miss Ellie's granddaughter."

Anne looks between Jane's smiling face and mine. "I know." She steps back to let me through, snapping her fingers. The dog follows her.

Jane shrugs and raises an eyebrow in my direction. "What brings you over here?"

I tell her about the package and wanting to thank them for sending the gasoline. The dog comes back and pushes his nose into my hand, snuffling interestedly before moving on, tail wagging, finding something even more interesting on the floor. I run my hand down his back. We moved too much to have pets, but I've always liked dogs.

"That's Beau. The guys are all out on the boat right now but should be back for lunch, right, Anne?"

Anne is busy doing something in the sink. I see a tail fin and realize she is gutting fish. Her hands are bare. Gross. A pile of hollowed out carcasses forms a slippery stack on the side. I watch as she scoops her hand down the belly of the one she's holding and flings the insides into a bucket next to the sink, deftly shoving Beau away with one leg. She holds the empty fish body under the running water, lays it on the stack, and washes her hands. As she dries them, she turns.

"Yes, that's right. It was kind of you, Cam, to bring the skins." She's super polite now, almost formal. "Rob will take them to town with him next time he goes." She smiles a little, but it doesn't make it to her eyes. "Leave them in the boathouse, if you will. Jane can show you. I will give Macon your message." She goes right back to the next fish waiting and slices it from below its center right up to the gills. Evidently she is done talking to me.

I look at Jane as if she can answer for Anne's lack of

social skills, but she just jerks a chin toward the door. "Come on."

Outside, I heft the package again and follow Jane. As soon as we're far enough from the door, I ask, "Okay, am I imagining things, or did you see that too?"

"I don't know what's up with her. She's usually really nice. People can be cold here. When I first arrived, I could barely get anyone to say hello much less give me directions."

"Is that all it is?" I ask, looking Jane in the eyes.

She shifts her gaze. "Maybe. Probably. Or, I don't know… It might have to do with your grandmother…"

I stay quiet. There's nothing to say. My first instinct is to defend Ellie again—but why? Duty? Like I don't want anyone talking bad about my family?

After a beat, Jane moves on toward the boathouse. "I met Miss Ellie almost as soon as I arrived on the island. Rob had to drop off a pile of skins…"

I interrupt. "What is the deal with the skins; do you know?" I shudder.

Jane chuckles. "Omigod, I was totally the same way when I first saw them. So disgusting, right? Your grandmother cures them. The butcher in town, Blue's dad, collects them from people who hunt or trap the animals. He gives them to Rob, who gives them to Miss Ellie. She cures them and then sends them back. Most of these people could do the skins themselves but not like she does them. They rave about her technique. It's like some lost art or something. They pay pretty well for it, too."

I'm still creeped out by all those pelts.

Jane goes on, "I was thinking it would be a great chapter for my research. I went to see her on my own but—"

"She wouldn't talk to you?"

"No, not that. Well, I mean, she wouldn't say much the

few times I did visit, but I could tell it bothered Anne. I don't know what she has against Miss Ellie. Or maybe she doesn't like how much Rob does for her—even if he gets nervous whenever he has to make a run to her cottage or to that side of the island at all. It's crazy-town. He respects her, won't hear anything bad said about her. She's like a wise woman or something to him, but I also think he's a little scared of her."

I remember his face when I suggested he come inside the cottage. "So, why did he come pick me up in Bath? Why come get me to go to Williams Point, or send Macon last night?"

Jane shakes her head. "I don't know. She asked him to. She doesn't ask a lot but if she does need something, Rob always helps out. It's respect, I think, or maybe he owes her something, or just has a reverence for her. Maybe that extends to you? And getting here from Bath is impossible if you don't know where you're going. As far as why Macon came to you last night, he lost the draw."

"What draw?"

"Well, we didn't notice that you had forgotten the canisters until we were back on our side. Then when it started storming so hard… These island people are pretty tough, but no one wanted to go out into it. Rob was afraid the electricity would go out, and you'd be without power if you didn't have the gas for the generator."

I don't tell her that I had already spent a day and a half without power.

"Jack and Macon drew straws. Anne didn't want either of them to go. She insisted that Macon come back as soon as possible. She paced the entire time he was gone. I guess she was worried for her little boy." Jane laughs.

So that's why Macon had been so irritated. Of course—I was a chore, and he resented me for it. I feel a bit bad he had to walk through the storm. Staying to show me the generator and all of that just added time onto his trip. That's probably why his mom had been so cold to me.

Jane pushes the door to the boathouse open. Inside, the dark room smells of oil, damp, and the pervading scent of fish. Broken lobster traps (as Jane identifies to me) and unraveled nets lay waiting to be repaired. I thunk the package down on a workbench and check my watch. It's almost noon. I don't want to leave without seeing Macon.

To thank him.

Just to thank him.

It's polite.

That's all.

"Let's go down by the beach," Jane says. "I need a break anyway, and that way we can see when the guys come in."

The beach is just a narrow strip of sand in the cove, smaller than what we have on our side, but like ours, it is surrounded by rocks. They lead out to the span of ocean on this side. I hesitate at the sight of the waves, my pulse already thrumming. I take a deliberate, slow breath and follow Jane as she climbs up onto the rocks overlooking the cove and pier. It's not that close to the water here. We scramble up to a flat rock and settle down. The sun is out, and I drink in the light. I lick my lips, taste salt, and put on some Chapstick.

"The water is always cold here. Always. Even in July and August on the hottest day of the year. They say the Atlantic isn't even that much colder than the Pacific, but I don't believe it. If you want to swim, you have to ease into it in stages and come out when your lips turn blue." Her gaze is wistful as she stares at the water.

I make the same noncommittal sound I always use when people talk of water sports. They may not understand me, but I don't get why they would purposefully put themselves in the water like that. The thought of being in the waves makes cold sweat break out across my skin. Who knows what's really underneath the surface? It could hide anything. And how could you be sure that you wouldn't just float away into the distance and never come back to dry land? Or be sucked right down to the sandy bottom in the dark of the deep?

"Where were you before you came here?" Jane taps my arm. "What's your story?"

"Albuquerque." I say, and nothing more. The sun is out, and I don't want to cast unnecessary shade.

"Oh! I've been there," she says with enthusiasm.

"Really?"

"Yeah, a few years ago, with my mom and dad. We went to Santa Fe and Acoma and Taos, but we spent a night in Albuquerque, near the airport. So how did you end up here? Where are your parents?"

I wonder how much to get into it with her. You never know how people will react, but she seems genuinely interested and she's so easy to talk to. I give her the short version. "My folks split up years ago, and I don't see Dad much anymore. He's overseas. Like on a continual basis. I don't think he wants to live here anymore." I try to laugh that off. It's better than admitting that he doesn't want me anymore.

"What about your mom?"

This is harder. "My mom is sick. She couldn't take care of me anymore. Can't take care of herself. She lives in a facility back in New Mexico." I pause.

"Wow. I didn't realize all that was going on."

I shrug. "When Mom started to get bad, social services got involved. They helped us when she had to go into care. And of course, they were real interested in me since I'm underage. Mom had insisted I come here. To my grandmother."

"I guess that makes sense."

"Why?"

"She's your family."

"Yeah. I guess. I don't know. I was actually surprised. Mom and Ellie had some sort of fight ages ago. She hasn't been in our lives. I don't know her at all. The last time I saw her—or she saw me, I guess—I was a baby. But Mom had set it up, so, here I am."

I keep my tone light. It had been a massive fight with my mom. It's the only time I ever remember shouting at her. We're close, like friends—especially since Dad left. I relied on her and she on me. We stood up for each other, had each other's backs. I would never have left. I would have preferred to be in foster care if it meant I would be near her. But she wouldn't budge. She organized it all. Wrote Ellie, bought the one-way ticket with a flexible departure date. Told the social worker. Arranged everything. I thought I would eventually talk her out of it, but she made me promise that if it came to it, if they were going to take me away, I would do as she asked. This was before she lost the ability to speak.

A crease forms between Jane's pretty eyebrows. "What does your mom have?"

"No one knows." My voice catches, and I feel the pressure in my chest build. Talking about mom always does this. Guilt pulls at me. "Keep positive," Mom always said. "Focus on the good; don't give in to the bad." It's so hard to do though. I swallow and continue. "She started to get sick a few years ago. She had trouble with her legs. She went from leaning against walls, to a cane, to a chair, and now a bed. They tested here for everything—MS, Lou Gehrig's—nothing came back conclusive, and she just got worse. Now she needs twenty-four-hour care. She can't feed herself; she doesn't talk anymore. But her eyes are still alive and bright, and I know she's still in there." I stop. I have said way more than I intended. My throat feels like it's closing up; my chest is tight. I breathe in and out, measured and slow.

Jane is quiet, her eyes shining with tears.

Mine are dry.

We hear a shout, and I see a fishing boat pulling up alongside the pier. Rob, Macon, and another older boy, who must be Macon's brother Jack, are working together. It's almost like a dance the way they coordinate and move, all working toward a common goal. Macon jumps easily from the boat to the pier, and Jack throws him a heavy rope as Rob maneuvers the craft.

Jane squeezes my hand. "I'm really sorry about your mom." Then she lets the matter drop and recovers her usual cheer. I'm grateful. It's hard enough to manage my own feelings about my mom and her situation without trying to deal with how other people take it. No matter how nice they're trying to be.

We make our way down toward the guys coming up from the pier. Jane calls out a greeting, almost bounding down the path in front of me. She introduces me to Jack, who's big and broad like his dad. He smiles shyly and actually shakes my hand. He looks me in the eye, and I think he might be the friendliest person I have met here. Besides Jane. He looks a lot like Rob, but I can see Anne's dark eyes in his. Macon doesn't really look like either of his parents. Jane is telling Rob about the bag of skins that I brought and asking Jack about the trip. He asks her about her research, and they fall into an easy camaraderie. Rob walks silently ahead of them. I turn to Macon. I am suddenly, acutely, totally self-conscious.

"I wanted. To thank you. Properly? For coming by. You know. In the rain." Oh my God, what is wrong with me? I can't even say one normal sentence. I feel my cheeks warm.

To make matters worse, I swear he is fighting a grin. "I mean, I know it was a pain. You didn't have to— Well, you did because you lost the draw, right?" I snort. "Still." I stop and mentally center myself and choose my words. "I just wanted to say thank you for bringing the gas."

He's grinning outright now. He has even white teeth and a nice smile that softens his serious expression. "It's fine, really. Did the power hold?"

"Yeah, I finally had a bath."

"Okay... good to know." I feel myself blush again.

"Why are you in Windemere on your own?"

I smile at his accent on the house's name but don't how to answer his question. I suppose it's weird that Ellie makes me live by myself in a whole separate house. Maybe it's my fault, or there's something wrong with me. "Umm, more space? I don't think Ellie's place is big enough."

"I see. She uses the cottage for tanning, I guess?"

Ugh. "I don't know."

"She's amazing."

"Ellie? Yeah..."

"I mean her work with the skins."

"Right, I think Jane said something about that."

"So, are you all right there?"

"With Ellie? Well, she's not going to skin me."

"You sure?" We both laugh.

He continues, "I mean, are you all right at Windemere on your own?"

I search his face to see if he's making another joke, but he seems to be asking for real. My mind touches on the wailing sound in the storm.

"Yeah, I'm fine." I smile to make it true.

Anne is on the porch and calls out in French. Rob answers her as he climbs the stairs. He's as terse in French as he is in

English. He follows her back into the house. She looks back and frowns in my direction. I try not to take it personally, but it slows my steps. Jane and Jack have stopped at the bottom of the stairs, laughing together. Macon is smiling at them. Jane is so easy to like. She probably gets along with everyone she meets, and they all say nice things about her. I have no idea what it would be like to be so comfortable in my skin.

When we reach the others, Macon asks, "Are you staying for lunch?"

"Yeah. You should," Jack agrees.

They are being nice, but I can't imagine that would go down well with overprotective Anne. Besides, I don't think Macon meant it as an invitation, just a question. "Uh, no," I say, "I have to get back."

"We're making another trip to the mainland tomorrow if you want to come," says Jane.

"That'd be great. I need to do a few things, and I need to figure out how to get mail." I wonder what my address would be: Tiny Weird Island, Maine, USA. "I want to find somewhere to check email."

"Can't you just get it on your phone?" Jane asks.

"It... No, I can't." My phone only works as a phone. People understand this less than my water phobia. I only pay the very basic phone service. She doesn't press the issue. We make plans for tomorrow and settle on a time as the guys go inside.

At the door, Macon flashes a short smile and says, "See you," before disappearing into the house.

I take off and as Jane closes the door, I hear easy family laughter from inside. I can't help feeling a little bereft.

Chapter 6

The walk back is easier without the bundle but still takes me longer than expected. I move slowly, lost in thought, remembering when I lived in a house filled with laughter. Missing my mom hits sudden and sharp. You'd think I would get used to it.

I also miss having good friends. My circle had dwindled as Mom got sicker. It was hard to stay in the mix when you never knew when you would be needed at home. My school attendance last year was less than stellar. I had barely scraped by.

I chide myself for thinking this way and feel the familiar burn of anger rising. Anger and guilt, they are my BFFs now, I guess. I don't even look for the clearing again and am tired and hungry by the time I finally get back. In the house, I add salt to a bowl of already salted almonds and munch them while I make a peanut butter and honey sandwich.

Afterward, I head down to check in with Ellie. She's standing by her front door like she's expecting me. She hands me a tightly woven basket with a hinged cover and handle. She carries a similar one with a red checkered tea towel wound around the handle. She doesn't say anything to me but starts walking down the path, just expecting me to follow. I laugh under my breath, wondering if I will ever get used to this way of communicating, but I go after her.

She leads me down toward the coast, off to the side away from the pier. The tide is out, leaving a great reach of rocky terrain leading out to the ocean. I start to feel the first twinges of worry when Ellie leads me off the path, and we start to pick our way over the rocks. I slow my pace, careful with every step, as we get closer to the water and pass little nooks and crannies of tide pools. We reach a large pool, and Ellie stops and sets down her basket. She takes out two short-handled, sharp-looking knives and hands one to me hilt first. Then she toes off her shoes and steps down into the pool. It has to be freezing. I'm afraid she's going to ask me to get in, and I start swallowing reflexively, flipping through a million excuses wondering which one will work. Before I try one out, she holds up a hand and says, "Stay there for a moment."

Fine with me. I put the knife down.

Ellie is sure-footed in the pool. She winds a cluster of seaweed around her wrist, cuts off great handfuls of the stuff, and brings them back to me.

"Line the baskets with these."

I plant my feet and stretch my hands out for the seaweed, trying to keep the rest of my body away from the lip of the pool. The seaweed is slick. I have never touched it before like this. Mom used to get dried seaweed from the natural food store for snacks. It was dry and salty and tasted green. This is cold and leathery as it almost slips from my grasp. I lay it inside the baskets like Ellie told me. She is leaning over a batch of sea creatures that look like pin cushions. She slides her knife under one round body, starts to toss it up to me but then stops.

"Take the towel," she instructs.

I pick up the tea towel and turn just in time to catch the creature in the towel. I hold the circular-shelled creature; it is spiky, colored deep green. "What is it?" I ask with wonder.

Flicking her eyes to me, Ellie pauses and says, "Urchin." I can tell she is suppressing disbelief but doesn't say anything. I am fascinated by the thing I'm holding, and just as I touch my bare finger to one of the spikes, Ellie says, "Watch the spines."

Too late. It stings like mad and I drop the urchin, shaking my whole hand.

"Did it break the skin?"

"I don't think so. It hurts."

"No blood?"

I examine my fingertip. It's red and a little swollen but not bleeding. I shake my head.

"Just rub your finger on the seaweed."

I do, and the ache disappears. "Seaweed fixes that?"

"The salt will help you." She tosses another urchin, and I fumble but catch it in the towel and put it in the basket.

"They don't hurt you?"

Ellie spreads her hands. They are unmarked, unaffected by the urchin spines. "I do not feel them."

I look in the basket. "They're moving." The creatures shift along the bottom.

Ellie throws another. "They will stay alive for a while. They are surprisingly fast in the water." She works quickly, removing creatures and tossing them to me. She moves onto another section and throws a reddish, gelatinous blob. "Anemone."

Next is a five-pointed starfish. As I catch it, it wraps a thick scratchy leg over my hand. "I know this one," I mutter.

Ellie's mouth widens and her eyes crinkle. A smile?

Really? I watch her for a moment. She is completely at ease, not even noticing the cold water or the fact that her pants are getting soaked. Her face is flushed, and her hair is coming loose from the complicated knot at the nape of her neck. Her eyes are bright and alive. She is more spry, seems younger, as she almost skips to another pool.

When her back is turned, I throw the starfish back. I have a good idea that most of the creatures are going to end up in the stew pot. But come on, starfish? I move the baskets and Ellie's shoes to the new pool. Her focus is completely in the water, plucking snails from the rocks, like berries from a bush.

"I begged your mother to leave you with me when you were born."

I am speechless.

"She wouldn't hear of it," she continues. "It wouldn't have been so sad if she could have been close to the sea, to teach you. Show you things, the way things are. But your father… She had to follow him. She loved him. Such a selfish man. A scared little man."

I am as shocked by Ellie's revelation as I am by the fact of anyone calling my dad a coward. He's a real live hero with medals and everything. The military told us all the time. I can't remember the last time someone said something bad about him, out loud. Mom always saw him in the best light, even after he left.

"Dad's serving our country," I defend by rote, without feeling. "He risks his life every day." I haven't seen Dad in years. Haven't spoken to him in months and the last email I had received contained no details of what he was doing, or where. Totally normal for a man on duty, right?

"Courage comes in many guises. Your father wears his like armor, polished bright, shiny to distract. But he was not brave enough to see your mother fail. Or let his daughter be true."

I shift in place. I don't know what she means by me "being true," but her take on Dad is too close to fears I can barely acknowledge myself. I want to argue with her words. I don't want them to be true. My Dad and I were so close when I was little, but that disappeared when they split, when Mom first got sick. He signed up for an overseas tour and effectively disappeared from our lives. Mom always said he was saving the world, but if that was true then he destroyed ours to do it. I don't say anything.

"How's your finger?" Ellie asks. "Come down here and wash it in the water. It will help."

"No." I say it too quickly. "It's fine. I'm okay."

"Come down. I can show you—"

"No." I don't care what island thing she wants to show me. "Thanks, I'm fine here." We catch eyes, but I'm not going anywhere.

Ellie sighs and climbs out, and we go to another pool. We continue until the sun slants low, and the baskets are almost full. Ellie takes another handful of seaweed and spreads it over the tops of the creatures in the baskets, still shifting in their algae-lined prisons. Ellie grabs her shoes and, without putting them on, picks up one of the baskets and walks back toward the cottage. I follow her straight back and keep my thoughts to myself.

At the cottage door, Ellie takes my basket. "I will show you the preparation later." She searches my face. I'm not sure what she sees but she says, "You must have some stew."

She leaves me on the porch and returns with a covered bowl. As I walk back to Windemere, I can smell the stew and my stomach growls. I warm it and eat it bite after bite without focusing too closely on the bits floating in it. It tastes even better than the other day. I scrape the bowl completely clean and just stop myself from licking it. I feel great, and I wonder if there is something to this "restorative" island concoction after all.

I check my watch and count back to New Mexico time. If I remember her schedule right, Mom won't be back in her room for at least another forty-five minutes. My evening stretches out before me. I pick a book from the shelf, Greek myths, and settle down to read.

LAUGHTER WAKES ME. Outside it's still light. I step out and see something happening down by Ellie's cottage. The clouds are racing across the sky, but there's no wind. The air is balmy, warmer than it's been since I got here. Ellie is standing on the path. Her hair is loose, shining as it snakes away from her head, as if caught by the nonexistent wind. She's facing the coast, walking toward the ocean. I call out to her, but she doesn't answer—doesn't even pause. I hurry to catch up gripped with the sudden knowledge that I have to stop her before she gets to the sea. I run, the ground hard on my bare feet. I don't stop, but I can't catch up.

Then like a jump in film, I am almost at the little beach. Ellie's pace remains steady, always in front of me, never faltering. I call to her again; my voice cracks with fear. I push myself, running faster, and finally reach her. I grab her arm, spinning her toward me.

But it's my Mom standing there.

All the air leaves my lungs. How is she here? How is she on her feet? She smiles her beautiful, knowing smile and beckons to me. She isn't just standing but *walking* backward into the surf. I'm struck dumb for a moment watching her, graceful and strong, as she moves away from me. I run toward her but stop when I get to the water's edge. Little waves reach for my feet. I step away from their touch. Mom's up to her calves, still smiling, beckoning. Still walking backward, she's up to her thighs, her hips. I stretch my hands to her, crying out for her.

The world tilts, and suddenly I am far above looking down from the edge of a cliff. Mom, up to her shoulders now, her face turned up toward me, still smiling as the water closes over her face. I scream for her, but she has disappeared. Cold seizes me, and I feel every hair on my body stand on end. I am not alone. I whip around to see Ellie standing there.

"Don't be a coward," she says and pushes me off the cliff.

I WAKE for real this time, gasping. It is full dark and dead quiet in the wooden house, except for my own noisy breaths. I need to call Mom. When I stand, I wince. My feet ache. I run my hands over them and they come away sandy. I stare at the grains on my hands for five full seconds before wiping them quickly on my pants. I must have gotten them dirty at the tide pools.

Chapter 7

I oversleep the next day, so I'm standing at the sink brushing my teeth and wearing only a T-shirt and underpants when there's a knock on the door. Of course. I wrap my towel around me and go to let Jane know that I need a couple more minutes.

Jane looks me up and down when I open the door, "Toga is not for you. Come on, I know we're early, but let's go."

I then notice that Jack and Macon are standing there too, both averting their eyes. I'm immediately blushing. I shoot the traitorous Jane a look and mumble, "Be right there," and shut the door. I didn't know the guys were coming. I'm flustered, wondering if I want to wear what I had already picked. Then I'm annoyed with myself for even hesitating. I throw on my jeans and pull a light sweater over my head. No time for make-up but I wet my hands and finger-comb my hair into some sort of presentable mess. It's getting too long already. I just had it cut, it seems, but of course that would have been before Mom took this last turn. I grab my wallet and scowl at the yellow slicker before deciding it's better having it than not if the rain comes again.

As the others head toward the pier, I stop at Ellie's. She opens when I knock.

"I'm heading to town. Do you want anything?"

Ellie glances over my shoulder to the others and then studies me. "I don't need anything. Be careful with those boys," she says, looking into my eyes.

I cut my gaze away, embarrassed. Nothing was going to happen with the guys. Ellie spends too much time on her own. I may not know them well, but I feel safe with Jack and Macon. And besides, Jane will be there. I'm more worried about getting sick on the boat and humiliating myself. She finds my eyes again. "I'll be careful," I promise and feel about twelve years old.

At the boat, I see a familiar parcel. "Is that... Are those Ellie's skins?" I ask no one in particular.

"Yeah," says Jack. "We're taking them in for Dad. He's fixing the traps today."

I wonder if that package is going to follow me all of my days.

The ocean is calm as Jack maneuvers out of the cove and heads toward the mainland. Macon is sitting next to his brother, faced away from me. He has a knife and a piece of wood and is shaping it. I can't see what he's making.

Jane smiles into the spray. "I love it when the sun comes out," she shouts over the motor.

I smile tightly, holding myself rigidly in the seat. I can feel the blood leaving my face.

"You really don't like boats, do you?" Jane teases me.

Macon looks over his shoulder at us. I feel exposed.

"I'm fine." I look into the distance, willing the land to appear, and try to relax.

When we finally pull into the bay, the tight coil of apprehension eases some. My stomach is only a little riled, and I am absurdly grateful to my body for not getting sick or having a panic attack on the way over. Macon jumps out and secures the boat, while Jack cuts the engine and Jane clambers over the side. I follow her. As I'm crawling onto the pier, I slip. I throw out my hand to catch myself, grabbing the side of the boat. Pain lances through my hand and I gasp. Macon takes my other hand and helps pull me to the warm wooden boards of the deck, and I sit down. Jane's brown eyes are wide, and I can see white all the way around her irises. Then I shift my gaze to where she's looking. My hand is full of blood and as I see the wound, it starts to throb. There is a slice right across my palm. I am shaking and my chest contracts and my throat closes.

Jack kneels by me. "I'm sorry, Cam, we keep meaning to sand that metal down." He turns my palm toward him. "Deeper than I thought. You'll probably need stitches. You okay?"

I can't answer him. I can't speak. Air rushes out, and then I suck it back in. Then out. I can't get my breathing right. I am pretty sure I saw the white flash of bone in my hand.

Macon jumps down into the boat and comes back with a mostly clean rag and a tin cup full of seawater. He splashes it over my hand and I gasp again.

"The salt will help clean it." He holds up the cloth. "Put this around it, and we'll take you to the clinic." He winds the cloth across my palm. I hiss through my teeth as he tightens it.

Pressure builds behind my eyes, and I press the heel of my right hand against my brow bone. If I could get my breathing right, I could calm down. Jack tries to help me to my feet but the world is turning too fast, so I have to sit right back down again. It hurts so much, and I'm stupidly embarrassed. Especially when I open my eyes and see Macon looking at me like he's trying to calculate the distance to my home planet. I glance away. Why does he get to witness my epic fail moments?

It finally starts to dawn on me that Jane is freaking out. She has tears in her eyes and is speaking in a high, rapid voice, "Oh my God, I don't even know how you cut it—what did she cut it on, Jack? Are you sure you're okay, Cam? There's so much blood. Are you sure you're okay? We have to take you… I mean…"

I almost smile. Her freak-out helps me calm down a bit, to at least focus. I know I need a doctor. I don't know how I'm going to pay, but I'm pretty sure they won't turn me away. At least they can bandage it. I have insurance through my dad, but I don't know where the card is or how it works. Mom's care is now state-run. I wish she was here, wish she could take care of this. Macon is looking at me again, head cocked to the side.

"Can you walk?"

"Yeah, I didn't hurt my legs." I try to joke, but it even sounds weak to my own ears. I get up again and make it to my feet this time. The rag is soaked through, dark with my blood. The front of my slicker looks like I dumped ketchup all down it. I start forward, then sway. Without a word, Macon slips an arm across my shoulders. He smells of sea spray and pine, and something else that I can't quite identify. Like sawdust, or maybe even oil. He is warm and solid next to me. Jane is saying over and over that she is fine. Jack gets a bucket of seawater and helps me rinse the blood from my coat. He then sluices the water over the blood on the planks, washing it over the pier. Then he and Macon exchange a couple of quick sentences in French.

Macon moves with me away from Jack and Jane. "They'll catch up."

I cradle my left hand close to my chest and hang on to Macon with my right, as another wave of dizziness crashes into me.

"So that's the tackle shop," Macon says, gesturing across the street. "And over there is where you can get seventeen different kinds of twine. For your twining needs."

"My what?" I stumble, and Macon adjusts his grip, one hand slipping to my waist, taking more of my weight.

"Yeah, you never know when you'll need twine. Useful stuff. Look at that." He points out a V of birds flying overhead. "Those are Canada geese. Those two," he eyes a couple of black birds on a rooftop, "those are crows. Or ravens, maybe. And those over there, uh, those are grayish-brown birds."

I laugh a little.

"That shop there sells handmade toys that tourists like to buy, and in the back, you can get retro candy." He speaks to me low and soft like he's gentling a spooked animal as we wind our way through the streets.

I'm aware that I'm being handled, but I don't care. I'm glad he's here. I half-listen, paying more attention to the resonance of his voice that I can feel through his body. Rib to rib.

Just as my busy mind goes back to insurance information, Macon stops in front of a tall narrow house. I feel stronger and drop my hand from his waist. His arm falls away from me. I am suddenly much colder.

"Where are we?"

"This is the clinic. Doc Mercier will help you." He offers his hand as if to help me up the steps.

"I'm okay, thanks," I say, but grip the railing as I climb up after him. I have never heard of a clinic being run out of a house. We enter into a converted reception room. It looks like any other waiting room, with chairs and outdated magazines.

A plump, business-like woman sits behind a counter at the back. Behind her are doors leading to other parts of the building.

"Hi, Mrs. Burke. This is Cam; she needs to see Dr. Mercier."

The woman takes one look at my soaked bandage and nods briskly at a clipboard. "Fill that out. The doctor just got in and doesn't have any appointments until this afternoon." She picks up the phone.

A doctor's office without a huge wait? That's new to me. I fumble with the clipboard as we sit.

"Do you want me to do it?" Macon offers, reaching for a pen.

"No— I have it," I say, balancing the clipboard on my knees. Sitting in this room, I feel totally fine and a bit embarrassed that he had to walk me here like a little kid. I don't get much past my name and basic information—I have to leave the address blank—when a woman around my mom's age appears from the back. She speaks with Mrs. Burke for a moment and then looks straight at my hand.

"You can finish that back here," she says.

Macon picks up a magazine. "I'll wait."

I'm glad he's staying and doesn't have to witness whatever uncomfortable conversation I have to have about insurance with the doctor. I walk through the door to the back.

"I'm Dr. Mercier," the woman says as she closes the door and motions me to the paper-covered table. "Now, what did you do to yourself?" She takes my arm and unwinds the cloth.

"Cut it on a piece of metal or something. Dr. Mercier, I— I don't have my insurance card with me. I just moved here; I don't even know my address on the island."

She looks up. "Shell Island? Are you related to the

Stones?" There is still a little trickle of blood coming from the cut in my hand. I avert my eyes.

"No, I'm Ellie Alcott's granddaughter." I brace for the tension that seems to follow my grandmother's name.

But Dr. Mercier's face breaks into a smile. "You're Serena's daughter! I should have guessed. I see it now—those eyes. Here, we need to wash this." She pulls me across to the sink and turns on the faucet. She runs water into a jug, adds iodine, and pours the mixture over my hand.

I jump as the liquid hits my hand but ignore it because I am riveted by my mother's name. "You know my Mom?"

"I didn't know her well. She was ahead of me at school. She didn't socialize much, living on the island, but you couldn't forget her. She was so beautiful. Everyone thought so. I'm sure she still is." She opens cabinets and pulls out clean cotton bandages.

"She is."

"I heard she was sick."

I don't want to talk about that. "My insurance…"

She holds up a hand. "It doesn't matter. You don't need stitches, and I won't charge you for the Band-Aids."

I'm confused. I had seen the cut across my palm… but now as I look at it, I see she's right. It's much shallower than I thought. I want to laugh at the panic I had felt. A flash of bone! What a drama queen. I'd barely cut myself. It doesn't even hurt that much now. Then I see the cloth that Macon had wrapped around my hand. It's soaked through. I didn't imagine that, at least.

Dr. Mercier swabs the wound and fastens three butterfly bandages to keep it closed and then covers it with another swatch of gauze. "Keep it dry and come back if it swells or you get a fever."

When I get back to the front, Jane is waiting with Jack

and Macon, looking sheepish. "I am so sorry. I am so totally not good with blood."

"It's okay. It wasn't that bad after all."

Jack scoffs, "Look at who's being brave. Come on, how many stitches did you get?"

"None."

"You're kidding. I saw the damage."

"I know, I thought it was bad too but really it's fine. Hardly hurts now." They are all looking at me, and Macon is giving me that funny look again. Jane breaks the tension with the suggestion of caffeine and food.

We go to the same coffee shop. Blue is at the register and greets us with a cheeky smile. We order sandwiches and coffee, then find a large L-shaped couch with a table. Jane gets a call and goes outside to take it, and Jack gets up to go to the bathroom. I settle into my seat and am distinctly aware of Macon's eyes on me.

"What?" I blurt out.

He blinks. "Can I ask you a question?"

"Yeah, I guess."

"Why didn't you cry?"

"What?"

"I saw your hand, and I saw you after you cut it. You were in a lot of pain. It had to be killing you. It wasn't a clean cut, couldn't have been. You bled a lot. I thought you were going to pass out. You were shaking. But no tears."

"I don't cry."

"Never?"

"Not since I was little."

"That's crazy."

Being the center of attention bothers me, so I don't like it when people point out anything different about me. A caustic retort forms in my head, but Macon doesn't look like he's trying to be mean or tease me. His hazel eyes are unguarded and curious. I finally say, "I just... don't cry."

His eyes now look puzzled. There's a lot of green in them, and they are fringed with long dark lashes that any girl would kill for. His black brows are pulled forward in concentration, waiting. I don't know what to say. I remember Dad hated any show of big emotion. Never liked to see Mom or me cry. Ever. Sad movie, fell out of a tree, stung by a bee—it didn't matter why there might be tears, he just didn't want to see them.

"My dad's in the military."

He chuckles. "That's why?"

"No." I flush. "He just taught me to be tough?" I hear the question in my own statement. Truth is, I'm not sure why. I remember my mom, tracing around my eyes and singing to me to calm me when I was really little. She never cries either. Maybe we can't. Maybe we unlearned it. Except that's not actually true. Last time I saw my mom and said goodbye, her eyes were glittering with tears.

Macon studies my face until Jane plops down on the couch next to me, and Jack comes back and shoves Macon closer to me. He bumps my shoulder. "Sorry," Macon says, resting his hand on my arm for one, two, three seconds.

When he moves it, I have the absurd desire to reach for his hand. It's so strong that my fingers twitch before I will them to be still. Oh my God! I don't even know this guy. And it doesn't matter because I don't want any entanglements here. Maybe even never. My face goes hot as if anyone else could guess the thoughts in my head. To cover, I say, "Uh, thanks again. For taking me to the doctor."

"Of course. That's what friends are for." His voice is quiet; he's not looking at me now.

Our food arrives. The meal is uneventful and doesn't

include Macon shooting me strange looks or me blushing for no good reason.

JANE DESCRIBES to me where the post office and library are. They are both close to the main street, and I assure her I can find them. I go to the post office first. The white-haired man looks at me twice when I tell him where I live. Then he doesn't look at me again, even if he remains courteous. I set up a post office box filling out the form, listing my cell phone and the complicated address that the man gives me for Shell Island. Nothing is delivered out there, of course. I'll have to come here to pick up mail or send anything out.

I don't expect anyone to write me, but I feel more settled with an address. Each time we moved with Dad's job, in every new town, even before we had an apartment and were staying in a Motel 6, Mom always made sure we had a PO Box address. She called it getting the new roots started, with a smile and a wink.

At the library, I sign up for a card and book time on an ancient but net-connected computer. I log onto my email account and check my messages. I weed through spam that made it past my filter and find a mass email for "Nikki's Super Sweet 16 Surprise Party!" Nikki's mom had apparently invited Nikki's entire contact list. I laugh to myself. What I would give to have seen my old friend's face when she realized that her mom had been messing around with her email account. The party happened two weeks ago, but it probably didn't matter that I hadn't RSVPed. Nikki hasn't spoken to me since I canceled going to her fifteenth.

She had been so pissed when I backed out at the last minute. A small group of us were going up to Santa Fe for the weekend. Nikki's mom was renting a two-room suite at a hotel downtown just for the girls invited, and she was going to stay down the hall. Close enough for adult supervision to count, but far enough away for us to feel like we were on our own. There was going to be horseback riding and hiking during the day, but Saturday night we were going to a concert and Nikki's publicist mom had scored us backstage passes. She was footing the bill as well. I'd helped Nikki research and plan for weeks, but the day before, Mom fell down. Her legs just gave out. Although she said she was fine and told me to go, I knew I couldn't leave her.

I tried to explain all of this but as soon as I said I was canceling, Nikki stopped me. She didn't want another "lame excuse" and I could "just 'eff off" until I figured out what "being a real friend" meant. It hurt but I let it, and Nikki, go. I didn't know how to explain the mounting terror of watching Mom get sicker and sicker. Nikki had been the last close friend to get fed up with my unpredictable unavailability. I can't believe that was over a year ago.

I delete the message and search for anything from Dad. There's nothing except an automatic message from my bank, notifying me of a deposit into my account. I guess I should be happy that at least those are still going through. There isn't that much deposited into checking, but my cell phone bill is directly debited from there.

A few years ago, Dad gave me his old—and very basic —phone and set up my own account with the direct debit. He didn't pay for any extras on it, saying that it was "just for emergencies." A month before I left New Mexico, my mobile company upgraded me from the old-fashioned clamshell to a smart phone. But without changing the plan, it is still just a phone. That's why I can't get email on it. Sometimes I think about joining the twenty-first century and adding data, but even with the most limited plan, I would still have to transfer money from my savings account.

I never touch that account. My dad's parents opened it for me when I was a baby and put a little in to start me Saving for My Future. I only remember them a bit, but their legacy has lasted. As soon as I was old enough to understand, I would deposit a little here and there. Since my dad left, I have squirreled away a little money every month. It's my emergency fund. A little buffer in case I needed it for Mom. We'd had some lean times and although Mom never wanted to use anything from it, knowing it was there made me feel more secure. Even now that Mom's in the facility and the state funds her care, I still like knowing the money is there. You never know. If anything were to happen with Mom's care, at least I have this bit.

Dear Dad, I hope you're OK. The deposit came through, thanks. Just wanted to let you know I'm not in NM anymore. I'm in Maine with my grandmother. Mom is—"

My fingers falter.

"Hey guess what? Mom can't walk or talk anymore and since you effed off and won't come back, I had to leave her and come live in the middle of nowhere in the most bizarre place ever with a creepy lady and the rudest people on earth. Hope you're awesome! Write soon! Kthxbye."

The librarian gives me a look and I realize that I have been banging on the keys. I tamp down my anger. I thought I had made peace with this. Once upon a time, our family had been really tight. I always felt close to both my parents when I was little. But I loved the adventures that Dad would take me on when Mom would go to the lakes. Then those trips ended when I was about twelve or thirteen, like as I got older, he just didn't want to spend time with me anymore. And he didn't take Mom's illness well at all. He was impatient with it. With her. With me.

Then he was just gone. Off to serve. She couldn't take it. She was so sure that he would come back "soon." The divorce papers came through the mail. Mom went downhill even faster. Like she had lost the will to get better.

I highlight all the text and delete everything. Screw it. If he wants to know where his daughter is, he can write to me every once in a while.

I leave the library, wander down the street in the general direction of the harbor, and stop to look inside the window of a restaurant. Old fishing nets and a few dried starfish decorate the window. There are also clam shells and strange spherical shells, each the size of a squashed tomato, like pin cushions. They're purple and green, their surfaces pebbled and striped. Then it comes to me, this must be what the urchins look like without their spines, after they've dried out. The window dressing reminds me of Ellie's baskets of creatures and the stew she would certainly make from them. My mouth waters, and hunger hits my gut. It has barely been two hours since I last ate, and I don't really even like fish! At least I didn't before. I can almost smell the stew right now. My stomach growls.

I tear myself away from the window and continue down the street. I see a group of boys around my age, hanging out in front of a store. They're joking around and laughing. With a start, I realize that Macon is there too. Next to him is an oil cloth sack larger and lumpier than the one from the boat. With everything that's happened, I'd forgotten all about that. When I look back up, Macon is staring straight at me. The others follow his gaze. I hesitate and then wave.

"You get everything done?" he calls out to me as I get closer.

"All set."

"How's the hand?"

"Fine." He doesn't seem convinced. "Really. Only hurts if I press on it." I laugh. Not my usual dry chuckle, it comes out in a trill, a musical riff. I stop abruptly, surprised. The other boys are staring at me.

There's a brief pause and then Macon clears his throat, gestures to each pointing them out, "Luke, Diego, and Wolf, this is Cam." They mumble hellos. They seem both curious and guarded.

The closest boy to me, Wolf, is my height, slender with dark hair and light brown eyes, and looks lost in thought. He shifts toward me and opens his mouth like he's going to speak. His eyes grow soft and unfocused. I wait but he just raises his hand, very slowly, like in a dream, and reaches for my arm. I flinch at the contact as his hand closes on my wrist. I jerk, and Macon claps his friend on the shoulder. "Wolf?"

Wolf jumps like he's been shocked and snatches his hand back, reddening. His mouth opens and closes, and there's a pause like a held breath. Then one of the other boys laughs and the circle breaks. The others dissipate, saying "later" and "nice to meet you." Wolf doesn't meet my eyes again.

What the—? I shake myself and turn to Macon for an explanation, but he looks as confused as me, brow furrowed, watching the retreating backs of the others.

"Friends of yours?" I ask dryly.

"Known them all my life." He's focused on the sack now, tightening the straps. He picks it up easily. "Well, since I started school." He nods toward the harbor. "We should get back. I guess you'll go to school here in the fall?"

It's another thing on my list. "Yeah. I have to work out getting my records transferred. And sign up."

"You have all summer. We just finished. Will Miss Ellie take you in?" He asks this last like it's incomprehensible.

"I guess so. I haven't talked to her yet."

"It's just... she doesn't really leave the island."

"Not often?"

"No. She doesn't leave it. Ever."

I stop in my tracks. Of course. Ellie is some sort of recluse. I should have figured it out when she didn't come pick me up or take me to buy groceries. I knew she was eccentric, but maybe there's something really wrong with her. "I'll work it out." I'm trying to convince myself. Then changing the subject, I ask, "What's in the sack?"

"Ah—that's for you."

"Me?"

Macon chuckles. "It's your grandmother's next batch of skins to be treated."

"Oh. Ew."

JANE IS WAITING for us when we get to the dock. She has more groceries. White, puffy clouds are high in the blue sky, but I wonder when the rain will come again.

Jack arrives. He's been to a hardware store of some sort. He's carrying four long planks wrapped in the middle with brown paper, tied with rope, and a roll of something that looks like fencing wire. He settles all of this along with the groceries and the bag of uncured pelts into the boat and helps me climb into it telling me to mind the side where the metal sticks out.

"You cold?" he asks when I shiver.

"No, all good." I grit my teeth and draw my lips back into what I hope passes for a smile. The boat rolls as Jane puts a foot on the side, and my tummy does a slow somersault. I forgot to try the pharmacy again. I shiver once more.

Jane steps gracefully the rest of the way into the boat while Macon busies himself with untying the craft. He climbs in and shoves his leg against the dock to help push us out. I brace myself for the crossing.

"How's your hand?" Jane asks me.

"Fine," I choke out as we hit a wave hard, and I bump in my seat.

"You check your email and all that?"

I give her a short description of my afternoon, leaving out meeting Macon's friends. I am still unsettled by the glassy look in Wolf's eyes. Jane chatters on about what she did. I cut my glance to Macon. He's in the front of the boat, whittling a piece of wood again, as the spray hits his face. I still can't tell what he's making, but it looks more complicated than I first thought.

When we reach Ellie's dock, Macon passes me the bag of pelts. It's soft and heavy like an overripe melon. I wince as I unthinkingly tighten my left hand on the strap and a tingle shoots through my palm. It's still a little sore.

"Do you have it?" Jane asks, doubt clear on her face.

I'm a little dizzy from the crossing but reassure her. I thank Jack for the ride and ask when his next trip to the mainland will be.

"Actually, tomorrow, right?" says Jane as Jack nods. "We're going all the way to Bath. I have a bus to catch."

"Where are you going?"

"Quick trip for my research. I'll be back in a few days, maybe a week, maybe less. Depends on what I find."

I'm disappointed but try not to show it. I like Jane. She's the nicest person I know here, but she's older than me and has her own life, her own priorities.

"The guys will be here." She looks back to them and says, "You'll have to check on Cam while I'm gone. Keep her out of trouble." She laughs.

Jack grins. Macon lifts a hand and says, "See you."

I smile a little to myself as I head to Ellie's. One thing I know is that despite all the strangeness and my own reservations, I would like to see Macon again.

Chapter 8

A cloud of steam carrying the unmistakable scent of spices and savory goodness comes out as Ellie opens the door.

"Good. I want to show you something," Ellie says, eyes fixed on the sack. She switches back the cover to see the contents before pulling it inside.

It's so damp in the cottage that I feel like I have to adjust my breathing to filter the water out. How Ellie can live like this is a mystery to me. How is the cottage not overtaken with mildew? Even in the arid climates I have lived in my whole life, we'd sometimes get mold in the shower. Ellie has created the most humid atmosphere possible. It reminds me of the indoor rain forest at the Botanical Gardens we went to once on a school trip.

Ellie has a stockpot already going on the stove. One side of the double sink is filled with some of the creatures we collected, the other side has discarded shells. The baskets are stacked on the floor. Ellie works quickly with one of her short-handled knives. I watch in mute fascination, glad I had saved that starfish.

"You cut here," Ellie says as she makes a neat slice from

the underside of a sea urchin to about an inch in and then begins sawing a large circle out of the shell. Then using a spoon, she deftly scoops out pale segments, almost like an orange, and places them in a bowl. She flicks some black goo into the sink. "You can discard this if you want."

"What is it?" I wrinkle my nose.

"What it was eating. Here." She hands me another knife and points toward the baskets. "Chop a bit of the seaweed."

I take the knife and open the top basket. The smell of the sea is strong but not unpleasant. I must be getting used to it. I pull out a couple strands of the rubbery seaweed and clear a space next to Ellie so I can chop it.

"I prefer these raw, but it isn't to everyone's taste." Ellie picks up another urchin.

My stomach rolls a little at that idea, and then I have a thought. "Ellie, do you have anything for seasickness?"

Ellie tosses another segment into a bowl and regards me with interest. "For whom?"

"Me."

"Camline." Ellie sighs. "You must embrace the ocean. You must learn."

I suppress an eye-roll. "Well, until that happens, do you have any Dramamine? The trips across the bay make me sick."

"What happened to your hand?" Ellie snaps hold of my wrist and turns my palm upwards. Without waiting for a reply, her knife flashes and in two strokes she skillfully cuts the top bandage off. She ignores my intake of breath. "This was very deep, Camline."

"Actually, no. I thought it was at first but really it's just a shallow slice."

"It may be now, but when it happened, it was bone deep."

I laugh breathlessly remembering the phantom white flash. "It wasn't. Look at it."

"You have treated it." She states like it's a matter of fact.

"I went to Dr. Mercier."

"You bathed it in the water."

"She washed it with an iodine water mixture."

"You used seawater."

"No, I don't think so—" Then I remember. "Well, Macon rinsed it with a cup of water from the bay first."

She finally releases me. "Macon did well." She seems proud. She turns back to the shellfish.

I fumble with the cut pieces of bandages trying to figure out how to cover my palm again. I reposition a piece of tape to hold the gauze.

Ellie stops what she's doing, stares at her own hands. "Your mother didn't have to suffer like she did. Not in the beginning. She needed to return to where she came from. If she had come back…"

"She didn't get sick because she left home, Ellie."

"Didn't she?" Ellie looks directly in my eyes, and I feel a spinning sensation as I wonder what she isn't saying.

"What is that supposed to mean?"

"People make their choices. No matter who else it hurts."

In a flash, anger hits me squarely in the chest. "She didn't *choose* to be sick. That's like saying that she made herself sick… like it was her *decision*. It just happened, and the doctors don't know why, *I* don't know why…"

I falter. Sometimes I think I do know why. So hard to "keep positive." I shove the thought away.

"You don't know either," I finish. Guilt and anger spreads, filling me from my fingertips to my toes. My chest tightens, and the cottage closes in around me. I just want to speak to my Mom. Not just call her, but have her respond—talk to me.

"You don't understand." Ellie's sympathy is laced with impatience.

"I understand just fine," I shoot back. The room is stifling. I'm choking on the air. "I have to go." I grab my coat and fly back to Windemere.

Inside I go to the little bedroom, my mother's old room. My heart is pounding. The helpless frustration of watching my mother get sicker and sicker in front of my eyes crashes me flat onto the bed. I bury my face in the pillow. How dare Ellie suggest that it was something that Mom *created*. If anyone is to blame, it might be me. I didn't do enough to help her; I should have done more! I scream until my throat is raw.

My breathing calms a little, but I can't stop my brain from rehashing everything. Mom got worse when she started fighting with Dad. Or did they fight because she was sick? It's all intertwined. I do know that the worst came after the divorce papers arrived in a thick, anonymous, manila envelope. But Mom didn't give up. Did she? And coming back here to her only remaining family wouldn't have made that much of a difference. It couldn't have, or she would have tried it. Of course, she would have. Because if she didn't try, then that's even worse.

It's too much. It's all too much. I wrap my arms around the pillow and miss my mother. I want her here, to kiss my hurt hand and make it better. To pick me up and tell me to be strong, to think positive, like when I was little. *Show* me how you keep the positive thought in your head. I want her to be strong for me. Tell me it's all going to be fine. I am exhausted. My eyelids are heavy with hurt and spent anger; I close my eyes.

THE WIND IS BLOWING AGAIN, and the wailing noise is coming from every corner of the room. It has to be outside. I open the side window in Mom's old room and put my head through, trying to figure out where the sound is coming from. It's in the air. I climb onto the ledge and stand. The ground is wet and dark beneath me. The sky is amazing, full of colors and swirls, and on the ledge, leaning my body outside, I want to dive right into the night. My heart speeds in anticipation; I *know* I could do just that.

I *know* all I have to do is just jump.

I bend my legs and launch myself straight into the sky. Above my house, toward the forest, the mournful cry slips like ribbons across my face and down my back. I open my mouth and swallow; the noise disappears as I absorb it. I swim through the sky, like I never could in water, rushing over the trees, dipping close to run my fingers through the pine needles. I'm closing in on the other side of the island and then in a breath, I'm there, outside Macon's house. I'm buoyed by air, holding me like an embrace. I peer into a window and see Jane sleeping with the light on, curled on her side, book forgotten in front of her. Another window: Anne and Rob, his hand on her hip, asleep. Another: Jack, snoring, his head half under the pillow. Finally, I am at Macon's window.

He looks like he's dreaming, sweat on his brow and covers tangled around his legs. His chest is bare, breathing shallow, muscles moving under his skin as he shifts. I want to put my hand out and feel the rhythm of his heart. I open my mouth and the swallowed sound flies out, through the glass and into him. Eyes closed, he reaches blindly toward me. I pull the sound back to me, drawing him with it; he's on his feet. I feel triumphant, gleeful. There's a clatter on the stairs and Beau bursts into the room, barking wildly. Macon's eyes open and he looks straight at me.

I WAKE in the dark and have to take a moment to get my breath. The dream is fading but I feel like I just lost something, like it was cut away from me. I'm cold and uncomfortable on the small bed. My throat hurts.

It's the middle of the night. Too late even to speak to Mom, but not too late to ask the duty nurse how she is doing. I tap in the number, and when the night receptionist picks up, I try to speak but no sound comes out. I try again but only breath passes my lips. The other woman grumbles something about perverts and hangs up.

I clutch my throat. No sound but I feel my pulse kick under my fingertips. I try to swallow, but my throat is too dry. Freaked out, I run to the fridge and grab the first thing I reach, which turns out to be a mug of Ellie's stew. The salty broth hits my throat and I cough. "What the h—?"

When I hear my own voice, I relax. I wonder when Ellie left this stew for me, and I laugh at myself. Dry throat now causes panic in my world. Silly. But my heart is still pounding, and as I drink the rest of the stew, I smell pine.

Chapter 9

I lie in bed while the sun tries to tell me it's morning. Job done, it hides behind a cloud, and rain starts to fall. The rest of the night was uneventful, but my dream of Macon unsettles me. I push all thoughts of him to one side. I feel... odd. Jane will be gone by now, and I'm disappointed I won't see her cheerful face for who knows how long. I don't want to see Ellie at all. I'm not privy to everything that happened between her and Mom, why they were estranged, but I always thought it had something to do with Dad. I don't want to talk about it. Ellie's disapproval grates in my memory. She doesn't understand.

Four days down. A little less than two years to go. I have no clue what I want to do with my life except get back to my mom. Maybe I could go to college somewhere out west. Make a base in New Mexico and be close to her. Make sure she's cared for and comfortable. When I'm an adult, they have to let me have more say about Mom's care.

I don't let myself think about a cure anymore. It's not being negative; it's just too painful. In the beginning, we just waited for the doctors to figure out what was wrong and then fix it. That's what they did, right? That went on for years and even now, they still know nothing. I'm afraid sometimes that they never will. Or if they ever figure something out, it will be long after it could have done her any good.

No. I cannot go down this path. Mom always said you have to keep positive. Keep focused on what you want, don't get bogged down in the "what ifs" and "maybes" of what you don't.

I shower and get dressed. My hand looks all right. It's a little sore to the touch and it itches, but it's healing really well. Crazy fast, too. I pour dry cereal into a bowl and choose a book off the shelf to read while I pick at it. I'll buy some milk next time I'm in town. Maybe some fruit and one or two vegetables, too. I suppose I should eat more than dry cereal and sandwiches and stew. The thought of stew, even this early, makes my mouth water, but it's the thought of Ellie's fresh bread that actually makes my stomach growl. The dry cereal suddenly tastes like sawdust.

Better breakfast is tempting, but I don't want to go down to the cottage after yesterday. Part of me, the I-should-keep-the-peace-part, thinks I should apologize for running out. But Ellie was the one who was wrong. She doesn't know the situation like I do. She doesn't know Mom like I do. Yeah, I know Mom is her daughter, but they haven't seen each other in years. Ellie hasn't lived the excitement of the small victory of a good day or the despair of yet one more thing going wrong.

I toss the unfinished cereal back in the package and carefully re-wrap my hand. I rinse my bowl and call Mom, hoping that she'll be up. I lean a hip on the counter and trace a pattern in the water on the tiles. The receptionist answers and transfers me back to the nurses' station. Maria isn't on today, but Suzanna or Lupe are also happy to help me speak to Mom if I ask. As Suzanna holds the phone, I talk brightly to Mom for the few minutes we have.

I'm not a coward. I just need to hold my ground with Ellie. I pull on my slicker and boots, and it's now raining hard enough that I pull up the hood to protect my face. I feel sorry for Jack and Jane in the little boat on the way to Bath on a day like today.

Ellie opens the cottage door as I approach. She says nothing as she trades me my coat for a roll. I say nothing about cereal and take a bite. It's warm and soft and tastes like heaven, the top studded with salt crystals.

"Thanks," I say. Ellie turns back to the kitchen, busying herself with pots and bowls on the counter. I lift my head and square my shoulders. There's no time like the present. "Ellie. About yesterday."

She stops moving and swivels her head to the side without turning around. She is silent.

"I'm sorry I shouted. And left like that."

After a moment, Ellie gives a short nod.

I squeeze the roll in my hand. I'm not mad anymore, but I have to make this clear. "But, Ellie, you haven't been there. I have. Every time something changed, something new went wrong. It's not... She isn't... This isn't on purpose. It's not something she's doing to spite you. You can't—" I stop because my chest is so tight, I'm not sure I have enough breath to make more words. I concentrate, breathe in and then out. "You can't blame her."

She rounds to me. Her words sound careful. "I hear you, Camline; I do hear you. I just want her to be safe, to be well."

"I do too."

She touches my cheek. "Leave it for now."

I hear the finality in her voice. I don't know what—if anything—I have accomplished. "I should probably go."

"I could use your help."

I stop.

"Please bring the bottle by the door."

The large glass bottle is filled with water. Ellie lays a porous cloth over a pot on the stove and carefully tips the bottle over it. The strained water fills the pot with a hollow splashing. Ellie puts the burner on high and stirs the water. Then she turns to the other pot on the stove, turns the heat off that, and drags her spoon through the contents. It sounds like sand. I peek over her shoulder to see that the bottom of the pan is covered with an inch of flaky white crystals. Ellie scrapes her spoon across the bottom again and hefts the pot, dumping the contents into a flat rectangular pan. She pinches a bit of the flakes and holds it out to me.

"Taste that," she says, dusting her fingers into my palm.

I smell it and gingerly touch my tongue to the white. Recognition floods me. "Salt! You're making salt."

"I am not making it, only uncovering what the sea offers."

I'm impressed. It makes sense, but I'd never thought of how to make salt from seawater. Now that I look at it, I can see that it's very similar in texture to the sea salt you can buy at the store. Just coarser.

"You can help me today."

"Okay, how?" With our newly brokered peace, it has to be better than moping around Windemere.

"First, I will make bread."

Excellent, this is a skill I would love to have. Ellie moves around the kitchen "activating" the yeast with warm water and sugar and mixing the dry ingredients, all while she keeps an eye on the boiling pot on the stove. She directs me at intervals to reach for the oil or to measure out the damp salt in the pan. With the oven on, the kitchen is drier than usual, and as we work together, I feel the earlier tension evaporate, replaced by the honest scent of flour.

Ellie shows me how to knead the dough. The repetitive motion is relaxing. I have to be careful of my bandage and pick off stray bits of dough from it. As I fold and press the dough, a subtle ache of pressure and electric tingling shoots through my left palm.

"Don't overdo it. Just until it's elastic," Ellie says, poking the dough.

I rest my hands on the supple mass in front of me. It feels alive. Ellie greases a bowl, puts the rounded lump into it, and then flips the ball over. She drapes a cloth over the bowl and sets it to the side.

"Wash your hands. That needs to rise. It will double in size." She turns the heat off the second pot of salt and scrapes the contents into the cooling pan.

I rinse my hands in the sink and dry them on a blue checkered towel hanging on the handle of the oven. Ellie goes to the other room and picks up the oilcloth sack. I recoil at the sight.

"They won't bite," she chides. "Come with me."

This cannot be good.

I follow Ellie outdoors. It's misting now, but since she walked out without a coat, so do I. She has the sack of pelts in one hand, carrying it easily. She must be stronger than she looks. Around the side of the cottage is another tiny structure made of stones. Inside the room, there are racks down one wall and large tubs along the other. In the middle at the back is a deep double sink with an old-fashioned hand pump and spout over the end. I've never seen one of these in person.

"I like to get to these sooner, but we didn't have time last night."

Ellie opens the bag wide. Each pelt is rolled with the fur-side out. She unrolls a large dun-colored hide, places it in the sink, and pumps the handle until water splashes over it. Then she gently squeezes the excess off and places the pelt into a tub. She motions to me to join her as she reaches for the next pelt.

I hesitate. This is definitely a skill I *don't* want. She can't really mean for me to help her with this. Ellie runs her hands through the fur-side of the skin. I glance around for gloves but don't see any. Ellie's not using any. If she can do it, so can I, right? But my body refuses to move. I don't want to touch the skins, afraid of how they will feel. Or smell. I have been breathing through my mouth since we walked into the shed. I stand there until Ellie glances back to me.

"Feel the skins, Camline. I want to see how you work with them." Her expression brooks no argument.

I sigh and, using just my fingertips, I take hold of a skin from the sack and flop it into the sink. It unrolls as I pump clear, cold water over it. Bits of debris wash down the drain. Ugh. The skins make me sad. Using as little of my hands as possible, I press out the excess water and put it into the tub. Fine. I did it. It wasn't so bad. If I don't think about it too hard.

She motions to the next one, and I swallow my disgust to do another. Then another. After a few, I stop using just my fingertips and we get into a rhythm: rinse, press, put in tub. When the first container is full, we move onto the next tub.

"The base is seawater, but there isn't enough salt in the water to make a difference to the hides. You must add more." Ellie takes a large canister down from the shelf above the tubs and shakes crystals into the tub without measuring. "Stir that. It's better to start this process straight from the animal's back, but the butcher that collects them gets them to me as soon as possible."

We continue until the bag is empty and all the pelts are submerged. I push the last one down into the water. My bandage is wet through and falling off.

Ellie must notice it because she says, "Clean that in the house. We'll leave these for a day or so. The dough should be ready now."

Inside, Ellie tells me where the bathroom is and as I head there, I see the door opposite is partly open. It leads to Ellie's bedroom, and I can't resist having a quick look at where my grandmother sleeps. The bed is... Well, unmade isn't the right word for it. There are sheets and blankets twisted around, haphazardly thrown over the bed until it resembles a nest. Two low shelves made of pale wood line the walls. There is something strange about their softly curving lines. I open the door a little more and see that the shelves are made entirely of driftwood. Crowded on them is a jumble of shells. There are large ones, pearly pink and white inside, and some tiny curlicues wound tight. There is a dried starfish like the one in Mom's old room and several urchin skeletons. There are also a couple of small carved boxes like the one in Windemere. The windows are wide open in here and the air is cool and damp. Rain has dripped inside the far window and covered that whole area with a thin sheen of water. I can't believe that Ellie sleeps in here. I pull the door until it is just as I found it. I feel a little bad for snooping.

In the bathroom, I unwind the medical tape with trepidation. My cut doesn't hurt at all anymore, but it probably needs serious disinfection after this morning's work. The wet mess of gauze falls away, and I catch my breath. Only a dark red line crosses my palm. The wound is completely closed. I stare at it, and run my finger over it. There's a little tingle, but it is definitely closed. I can't understand it. I have never healed like this before.

Ellie calls for me, and as I go back to the kitchen, I run my thumb across my palm, wondering at it. "Look at this," I say, and hold out my hand.

"Good." Ellie has the bowl of dough in her arms. It expanded while we were outside. "Poke the dough to test if it has risen enough." She presses two fingers into it, creating a hole. "Then you punch it down," she says, whacking a fist in the center. The dough sighs as Ellie beats it down. Then she tips the contents onto the flour prepped table and splits it into two.

"Wait— Ellie, did you see my hand? This is incredible."

"I see it. The water must have helped it." She works her knuckles along the length of one of the pieces of dough, pressing out bubbles. "Pay attention now; you don't want trapped air inside the loaf."

"But— I mean, this is amazing, don't you think?" I stretch my fingers back. It has fully closed.

"Camline." Ellie is waiting.

I try to focus, but I still can't get over my hand. I have never had a cut heal so fast. I keep sliding my thumb across my palm. The only thing that makes any sense is that it was even shallower than I thought in the first place. There was so much blood, though. But Dr. Mercier wasn't fazed.

Ellie raps her knuckles on the table.

I jump. "Yep, what's next?"

She rolls the dough out, patting the rolling pin with flour when it sticks. She forms the dough into a long oblong shape and, working from the short end, rolls it tightly, pinching the seam at the finish. She presses down the ends and tucks them underneath before setting the form into a loaf pan. "Now, you can do the other half."

The dough is resilient and seems to move under my fingers as I press out bubbles and begin to give it shape.

When I finish, my loaf isn't as perfect as Ellie's but to me it's beautiful. I set it gently into the other pan. Ellie covers them both again with the cloth.

"They need to rise again," she says as she wipes down the work station. "Your grandfather loved fresh bread, and I would bake it for him when I was feeling generous." She smiles, a different one than I've ever seen.

I don't say a word. I don't want her to stop.

"When I was not pleased with him, I would give him old bread to take out on the boat. He said he knew my moods by the lunch he was packed. When I first came to be his wife, I hated bread. Like eating waterlogged wood. Now when I bake it, it brings him closer."

These are the most words I have ever heard Ellie speak at one time.

"Hungry?"

I am. I offer to wash up while she lays the table. She sets out two bowls filled with thin green strips. Between them she puts a plate with a cut orange, two apples, and a few plums. Next to my bowl is a side plate with a hunk of white cheese and another roll.

"What's this?" I ask, prodding the greens.

"Seaweed salad. You may have had something similar to this with sushi."

I laugh. "We never had sushi. I lived in the desert, remember?"

"Your mother never made it for you? From fresh fish?"

"No, we didn't eat a lot of seafood."

"Oh." Ellie murmurs, taking a slice of orange. From her slightly downturned mouth, I know she disapproves. It sets me on edge. I don't want to discuss my parents' supposed failings. But Ellie doesn't say any more.

The salad is surprisingly delicious even if the texture is

bizarre. The seaweed is tougher than a salad leaf, and looks nothing like what we collected in the pools. I tear the roll and spread some of the cheese on it. It's pungent but very good.

"It's goat." Ellie tells me when I ask.

I've had goat's cheese before but it didn't have this flavor. "Where's it from?"

"The fruit and cheese were a gift. I thought you would enjoy it."

"Yeah, it's great, but where can you buy cheese like this?"

Ellie shakes her head. "Anne's sister made it."

I don't know anyone who can make their own cheese. I remember Anne's coldness to me. "I don't think Anne likes me much."

"She has two sons," Ellie says, as if that should explain it all.

"So, she's protective of her kids? That has nothing to do with me."

Ellie spears me with a look as she reaches for an apple. She peels it with a knife and is halfway done before she speaks again. "Anne is afraid for women like us to see her sons."

"See them? Women like us?" What is she talking about?

"*See* them," she says again, stressing the word.

"I don't understand what that means."

"I know. You know nothing. But it's your birthright, Camline, to have a certain allure for men."

A laugh explodes from my mouth. "Trust me, that has never once been an issue in my life."

"You have never focused on a boy?"

Macon's face flashes in my mind, but I shake my head. "I have friends, I had friends, at school in New Mexico. Boys, but not a boyfriend." Last year, one boy, Michael, had shyly asked me to the midwinter dance. I hadn't really thought of him like that, but it was nice to be asked and he was cute. But Mom was scheduled for tests that day, and I said I couldn't make it. He took it like pure rejection and avoided me completely after that.

Ellie reaches across the table and traces a finger across my eyebrow. "You have your mother's eyes, only more settled."

I am still, transfixed by her touch. Then Ellie's comment filters through... Settled?

Ellie clears the lunch plates and checks the bread pans. The loaves have swelled above the edges. Mine is totally lopsided. She puts them both in the already warm oven. "Make sure the pans are in the middle. It will help them bake evenly. The hot air circulates."

I rinse the plates and when I finish, Ellie calls me to the living room.

"I thought you might like to see these," she says handing me a large photo album. Leather bound, oversized with a heavy cover, it's stuffed with pictures. Loose photos are stuck between the later sheets, and I am careful not to let them fall as I open it to the beginning. Each page of thick paper has pictures held in place with adhesive corners. The first page is a small baby cradled by a solid looking man in a cable knit sweater and dark pants. His smile is wide across his face. Below, in a delicate scroll, is written *Serena and Oscar*. My breath catches.

"Your grandfather. And your mother."

Another photo of the baby but this time with a woman—it has to be Ellie—leaning over the crib. Her long curtain of hair hides her face. The next shots are of Mom as a chubby baby and then as a toddler at the beach. She's holding a starfish and smiling, her curly hair standing on end. On her it looks adorable and not the crazy mess that mine always seems to be.

"I've never seen any of these." It's a window into another world, insight into another time. A later photo shows Mom running through the surf. In all these shots, Mom is moving. There isn't one of her still unless she was sleeping. She gets older. Oscar disappears when Mom is around fourteen or so. There's a gap in the pictures then. She never talked to me much about this time in her life, but she must have been around the same age as I was when Dad left.

The next photos are Mom, older, about my age now. She's in the ocean and caught in the process of turning. Away or toward the shooter, I can't tell. In it, her hair swims around her head, and I think of my dream. Mom has an enigmatic twist of a smile on her mouth. But it's her eyes that stop me. They are untamed, like a wild thing. I stare at my mother's photo.

"Bread should be done." Ellie walks into the kitchen.

I shift the album and a picture falls out. Ellie's wedding photo. Her hair is fastened back off of her face but falls loose. It hangs past the waist of her simple pale dress. Oscar has one arm around her back, the other hand on her elbow, eyes fastened on his bride's face. But Ellie stares straight into the camera, a satisfied smile playing around the corners of her mouth. Her eyes are almost feral.

"This is beautiful," I whisper and then louder, "Do you have any pictures of your sisters?"

Ellie barks out a laugh. "No. You can't—" She stops. "There were no cameras. There are no pictures."

Chapter 10

As I head back to Windemere, I protect both my misshapen, still-warm loaf and the photo album that Ellie let me borrow from the light rain. Ellie also sent me with some stew in a covered bowl in a bag. I'm already looking forward to it. It's amazing how much I've come to like it, crave it.

Inside, I lay the photo album on the coffee table, gently wiping away stray raindrops. I light a fire and pick up the bread, knocking on the top to listen to the hollow sound that Ellie told me is how you know it's done. I slice off an end and boil water for tea, anxious to get back to the album.

There's a soft knock at the door, and I'm surprised to see Macon. My heart stutters. "Hi," I breathe and then clear my throat and try again. "Hey."

His eyes are shadowed. "I've been on the boat all day with my dad."

"Yeah?"

He runs a hand through his wet hair, and it falls back on his brow. He looks confused. My mind jumps to the dream of him, and my face flames as if I'd actually been caught spying on him. Silence stretches out between us.

"Do you want to come in? I— Do you want some tea? And look, I baked some bread."

His eyes move to the lumpy loaf and he chuckles, breaking the awkwardness. "Nice."

"Hey! It was my first try!"

Macon's smile spreads across his face but still holds hesitation. "I just wanted to stop by…" he says, as he steps inside. I am reminded again how tall he is in this house—like his presence fills it up.

He looks around. "Um, everything good?"

"Fine." He's being weird. "Do you need something?"

"I… I just wanted to be sure that you were okay." It seems hard for him to admit.

"Why?" He thinks I can't even manage one day alone?

"I don't know." He looks lost. "I was thinking of you. I… I, well, I thought I should check." Faint color stains his cheeks. He can't be blushing. Probably just the chill from outside.

"Oh, okay. Um, I'm fine. I've been with Ellie all day." I don't know what else to say or do. "Do you want a drink?"

"Sure. Coffee?"

"I don't have any."

"That's okay. Whatever's fine."

"Tea?"

He nods. I take the kettle off the stove and take down a couple of mugs. I drop tea bags in them and pour out the hot water. "There's sugar or honey but no milk, though. It's just regular black tea."

"Plain's fine. Do you have butter?"

I make a face. "For your tea?"

"I thought there was bread." He looks like he's fighting a smile, laughing at me again.

"No butter, sorry."

"I'll take honey, then, for both."

I make the tea and slice another piece of bread. I slather the bread with honey and then automatically salt both pieces.

He takes the plate and one of the mugs and heads to the living room. As he puts the cup and plate on the coffee table, he snags a quick bite of the bread. He chews, brows furrowing.

"Is this... salty?"

"Oh. Yeah, I like it that way. Do you want me to make you another?"

"No, it's great. Just surprised me." He snatches something off the table. "A puzzle box. Cool." He's holding the little carved box I found in the bedroom.

"A what?"

"A secret keeper." He gives the box a shake and plays with it for a second. It pops open with a click.

"Hey..."

"Oh sorry. I just love these." He hands it back to me.

"No, it's fine. But how did you do that? I kept trying to open it."

"There's always a hidden catch. What's in it?"

"I don't know..." I tip it over and a round, curled, purple snail shell bounces out.

Macon catches it before it falls and holds it out to me flat-handed. It's purple, darker underneath and lighter on the top, almost two-toned. I pick it up. His palm is dry and warm. I feel a little thrill in my fingertips. The shell is so delicate that I can't believe I haven't broken it by shaking it around in the box. "I've never seen one like this. It's so pretty."

"Well, you wouldn't normally find this kind around here. It's a violet sea-snail. They're usually in warmer and deeper waters, far away from land. I wonder how this little guy got here?"

"It seems so fragile."

"They have to be light. They float." He takes it carefully back from me. "Not by themselves though. They create a kind of raft out of bubbles."

"Are you serious?" It sounds like science fiction—floating snails.

"Yeah, really. Can I borrow this?"

"The shell?"

"No, I wouldn't want to break it." He sets it gently on the mantle above the fireplace. "I mean the box."

"I guess. But it's not mine."

"I'll bring it back." He smiles.

"Okay." I smile back.

Macon takes another bite of bread. "The salt is actually good. It would be even better with butter." He picks up the album, and a few loose photos fall to the floor. "Is that you?"

I follow his gaze. "Oh, wow, yeah it is." I pick up the fallen photos. There are several of me as a kid. Mom must have sent them to Ellie. One is of me on a bike that my dad took when I was just learning to ride. I remember the day, but not the picture. The photo is in motion. I'm facing Dad; Mom's holding the seat behind me, running. My expression is a mixture of fear and exhilaration. I'm laughing, and my long hair is streaming behind me. Mom is smiling at the camera. She looks happy, but there's something about her that is different. I flip back to the picture of Mom as a teenager at the beach and compare the two. It's her eyes. In the picture with me, they are no longer wild but muted, like a banked fire.

"This bread is great," says Macon, peering over my shoulder, surprising me. I was so lost in the pictures. Now I am suddenly hyper-conscious of the heat from his body next to mine. His smell fills my nostrils and, for a second, I am unable to concentrate on anything but that.

"Thanks," I say, and step carefully away. No entanglements, I remind myself.

"Sorry, I didn't mean to be nosy. Is this your mom?" He taps the teenage picture of her. "My parents knew her." He sits down.

"Really? What do they say about her?" I ask, and drop down next to him. I feel his warmth again. It makes me heady, and I scoot a fraction away.

"Not much, really. I think my mom was afraid that Dad would run off with her." He laughs.

"With Rob?" I can't picture Mom with him. Can't even imagine it. "Mom met my dad when she was really young. *They* ran off together."

Macon doesn't say anything, still looking at the photos. "She's really beautiful. You look like her."

I go still.

"You have your mom's eyes." He reaches across the small space and touches his fingers lightly to my temple.

I shiver. There's a knock on the door. Macon pulls his hand back, and I let out a breath I don't even know I'm holding. I answer the door to find Jack, his face annoyed.

"Hey Cam," he says, looking past me to Macon sitting on the couch. "Mom's in a mood. Let's go."

"How'd you know I was here?"

"I didn't; she sent me to check. You didn't take your phone. I didn't need the hike, thanks. No offense, Cam." I shake my head. "I don't know what you did, but she's spitting nails," he continues as Macon shrugs on his coat.

A flurry of barks comes from outside, and Jack goes out to see to Beau. At the door, Macon stops in front of me.

"Thanks for the bread and tea. And for lending me this."

He tosses the box in the air and catches it. He seems like he wants to say something more. I wait. Jack calls from outside. Macon turns.

"See you."

"Bye." I watch him through the sliver of the door as I close it. Jack and Macon are chatting as they walk away, but I can't hear what they're saying. Beau is jumping around them but then, almost as if he knows I'm watching, he stops and faces me. He stares at me for a moment and then lets out one sharp bark and runs after the boys.

I go back to the living room and lay out the pictures of me. Mom must have been sending these for years. She never said much about Ellie. I knew they used to talk sometimes, but I didn't know that she was sending her my photos. The most recent one is at least a year or so old, but I don't remember it being taken.

It's in Albuquerque, and it's after Dad left because I'm on the porch of the apartment Mom and I had to live in. I'm in profile, and the hot New Mexico sun takes focus so that I am in shadow, facing toward the Sandia Mountains east of the city. I have one foot up on the chair with my arms wrapped around my bent knee, and the other leg stretches in front of me. I've never seen this picture before and although I can't properly make out my features in it, I just look sad.

I drop it back to the table, and it flips on the way down. I recognize the handwriting on the back as Mom's. It looks like she was writing quickly because the words are smudged, and the sentence descends at a sharp angle. As I read it, I go cold.

He's gone. You win. I will send her to you.

Chapter 11

This is exactly what I didn't want.

My mind keeps bouncing back to Macon. I tell Mom about the funny floating snail, and almost tell her about him. About how he seems like he's always on the verge of laughing at me but never in a mean way. I like that he knows so many weird little interesting facts. And how his smile completely transforms his face.

As I get dressed the next day, I find myself thinking about the color of his eyes and how the green stands out when he wears his jacket. I think about the tingle in my fingertips when I touched his palm.

This is not part of my plan.

I don't want to obsess over some boy. I never want to let someone have so much power over me. When Mom and Dad fought, it was like a piece of her was lost in each fight. Every argument chipped at her. When he left on the first tour, Mom didn't get out of bed for two days straight. When she did, she showered and said we were going to get back to normal and "keep the home fires burning" until Dad came back. When the divorce papers came through, she left them half opened on the table for weeks before she signed them. As she wrote her signature, she told me that it was "only for now," but I don't know if she believed it even then. Maybe she did; maybe she still does.

I don't want that.

And besides, I don't know if Macon even likes me. A whole unrequited situation would be even worse. But I can still feel his fingertips on my face. You don't touch someone like that unless you like them a little, right?

I really haven't had that much experience with boys, but I have seen the way people act when they like each other. And before it got tense between Mom and Dad, there were small touches between them when things were quiet and peaceful. Mom's hand on Dad's shoulder, him brushing her hair back from her face. There was definitely touching.

I want to see Macon again. I hate this. I want to know more about him. It's tempting to walk right into the woods and go to his house, but I don't relish another run-in with his mom. Especially after Anne sent Jack out to find him last night. I mean, c'mon, it's ridiculous how protective she is. What did she think was happening here?

Oh.

My face heats as I realize just what this might have looked like from the outside—girl alone in the house, boy visiting, no parents. Right! I can be a little naive. Ellie's cottage isn't that close, and she hasn't been to Windemere since my first night. I guess if I was a more experienced girl and if Macon really was into me, Jack could have rolled up on a very different scene. In my mind's eye I see Macon's grin, the way his hair falls over his brow. I wonder what would have happened if Jack hadn't come when he did.

Nope.

I cannot be thinking like this. Easier said than done. Especially because I open my door and walk straight into him. "Oh!" I say, unable to stop a silly smile from breaking across my face.

He's grinning too. "I have to go to the mainland. Do you want to come?"

Another boat ride. "Uh, I don't know…"

"Come on, I know you need butter." He grins wider.

I can do another boat ride. "Yeah, okay, I should probably check with Ellie. Is your dad coming, or Jack?"

"They're out with the traps. I got out of it because my mom needs oil and milk." I wonder if his mom knows where he is right now. I decide not to ask.

I find Ellie in the tanning shed leaning over the first tub, humming. When she sees me she says, "Another day, I think."

Great. "Okay… I was going to go into town."

She straightens and looks down the path to where Macon waits for me. He waves, and she gives me a considering look. "Is he taking you? On his own?"

"Yeah… is that okay?" Maybe I should have asked her first. It's not like it's a date. If it had been, it would be a pretty strange one. I stifle a laugh at the thought.

"Camline, you really must be careful." Ellie's voice is quiet, but I can feel something behind her words.

"It's just shopping. I'll be back soon."

"Shopping." She pauses as she shakes the excess water from her hands. "Will you get some things for me?" she says finally.

"Sure. What do you need?"

Ellie leads me out of the shed and steps inside to get some money, even though I tell her that I still have some. I wave to Macon. "It's all right!"

"I'll meet you down there," he calls back to me.

Ellie returns with some cash, a short list, and a cup. "There is an herb section in the natural foods store. I need these things—fresh or recently dried. Ask for Lila. She can help you with it. There is money for you as well."

"I told you, I still have…"

"Take it." Then she hands me the cup. "Drink this."

I sniff it, smell salt, and sip. It is salt—salty water. "Really?"

"Trust me. Finish it."

I slug back the rest and run my tongue over my teeth. It was really salty, even for me. "What is that?"

"It will help your…" she pauses and nearly smiles, "seasickness." She shakes her head as if she can't believe what she's saying.

"Okay. Thank you." I can't believe that a salty drink is going to stop my seasickness, but I'm definitely willing to give it a go. I mean, with my diet, if salt were the answer, I would have never had a problem. But I'll take whatever help I can get; my stomach is already full of butterflies from Macon. The very last thing I want to be doing is getting sick on this trip. Definitely not a side of myself I want to share with him.

I'm about to take off down the path when Ellie grabs my arm. "You heard me. You will be careful."

I am at a loss. Her hand kind of hurts.

"Say it."

I pull my arm away. "I'll be careful." I'm unable to hide the first twinges of anger.

Ellie looks me up and down. "You are so like your mother sometimes." She says it like an accusation.

I look her straight in the eye. "Thank you," I snap, and walk away without glancing back. I'm flooded with anger at Ellie's tone and words. My steps are hard on the path, like I can push the anger through the soles of my feet. I have to

make a conscious effort to relax my jaw. I take in a breath—
one, two, three—and out in measured time. Little by little, I
push down my annoyance.

Macon has the boat ready by the time I get down there.
It's the same boat that Jack took the other day, so I look out
for sharp edges as Macon helps me down into it. He catches
my left wrist and the boat rocks. I grab his shoulder to steady
myself. He runs a finger across my left palm, sending shivers
skittering up my arm.

"That's incredible. I didn't see this last night. You heal
fast." Then, as if noticing my tremble, he asks, "Are you
cold?"

I shake my head. I lift my hand from his shoulder as he
releases me. He had distracted me from thinking of the water,
for a moment. Now I'm wondering what kind of fool I am to
get on a boat. On the water. Again. I balance carefully as I
make it to my seat and strap on my life preserver. I anchor my
hands around the edge of the seat while Macon starts the
engine. As we leave the cove and head out over open water, I
realize I don't feel the slightest bit sick. Maybe there is something to Ellie's drink after all.

Today my water phobia is making me a little giddy, and
the wind blowing back my hair feels great. Spray hits me, and
I laugh. It comes out like a musical trill. Macon glances at me
and then quickly looks again. He cocks his head at me, like
he's trying to place something.

"What is it?" I ask.

He brushes his knuckles across my cheek, leaving another
invisible mark on my skin. "You're all wet."

I lick my lips. Salt water. In fact, suspiciously like the
drink Ellie gave me. I don't even care. I refresh my Chapstick. I feel good and expectant, like on Christmas morning
when I was a kid. Anything could happen. Good things could

happen. The boat's motion isn't bothering me, the sun is cracking through the clouds, and a really cute boy keeps touching my face.

"I thought you didn't like boats?" he says over the engine.

I just smile and change the subject. "So how long have you lived on the island?"

"My whole life, pretty much. It was only your grandparents out there on the island for years, but then they sold the east half to develop. My dad's parents, and him, lived in our house. Between your grandfather and mine, they built those vacation houses. The extra rent can be helpful."

"Your dad has lived in the same house his whole life?"

"Not really. He went away to college and met my mom. They lived on the mainland after they got married and Jack was born there. They moved out to the island when he was little, after my grandparents died. Dad took over the traps and the vacation property."

"You were born on the island?"

"No, I got there when I was a few months old."

"What do you mean? You said you parents were already living there."

"They were. I'm adopted."

I feel stupid. I guess that explains why he's so different from the rest of his family. "I'm sorry," I say.

"Why? I'm not."

I flush. "I don't mean I'm sorry you were adopted. I just didn't know."

He laughs. "Don't worry. I don't ever think about it. It's not a secret, but we don't really talk about it. My parents are my parents. Jack is my brother."

"That makes sense."

"Anyway, I thought you of all people would know about it."

"Me? I just got here. Why would I know anything?"

"Because of Miss Ellie. It's because of her I'm still alive."

We hit a wave and I am jostled in my seat. My heart leaps. I hang on tighter. "What do you mean?"

"I was sick as a baby, and she took care of me. Dad says I wouldn't have survived without her."

I have no words. Ellie doesn't strike me as a healer. Though her seasickness drink seems to be working. Maybe this is what Jane meant when she said that Rob might feel like he "owes" Ellie something.

Macon goes on. "I thought Miss Ellie might have mentioned it to you. It is not a topic of conversation in my house. Mom doesn't like any of us to even bring it up."

"Noted. I won't say anything." I like knowing this story. It's almost like we have a secret. I close my eyes and turn my face to the sun.

"How about you?"

"What?"

"The reason you live here. Your mom's sick?"

"Did Jane tell you that?"

"No, my mom and dad were talking about it."

I don't say anything, but he must see something in my expression.

"Hey, sorry I brought it up. It has to be hard."

"It's okay. I was just thinking of something my grandmother said." The anger smolders a little inside me. My throat constricts.

"Well. I am sorry. I'm sorry it's happening. But, and this is totally selfish, of course..." He trails off.

"Yeah?"

"I'm glad you're here, Cam. I'm glad we met. You're just so different than anyone here."

He says it so nicely, I don't even mind he's basically

calling me strange. He touches my arm, just for a second—another shiver, another mark. Then he breaks out that smile that softens his whole face.

"Thanks." I can't help but smile back at him. "I'm glad we met too."

"Yeah, or you would still have no electricity."

We both laugh.

I am still grinning when we reach William's Point. Macon tells me to be careful as I get out of the boat, saying, "I don't have time for another trip to the Doc's."

I roll my eyes, but am mindful of where I place my hands. I scramble out as he secures the small boat to the dock. There's a petite, brunette girl waiting on the dock. She has sky blue eyes and long, straight, glossy hair pulled back from her heart-shaped face. I'm happy and smile at her, but she's looking past me to Macon. When he sees her, he stops.

"Bridgette. I… When did you get back?"

The girl, Bridgette, walks up to him and wraps her arms around his neck, snugging her body next to his and pulls his head down for a kiss.

Chapter 12

It feels like the pier drops beneath me. I am such an idiot. Of course. Macon has a girlfriend. He has been being nice to me because Jane asked him to. So stupid!

Macon pulls away, taking Bridgette's wrists in his hands. He gently unwinds them from his neck but doesn't drop them. She smiles up at him. "Surprise!" she says. *Suh-preez* "I came back this morning. Your mother told me you were coming in, and I waited for you." Her accented voice is beautiful. She leans into him and speaks rapidly in French.

So, everybody speaks French. Everybody has a pretty little accent. I don't want to watch this. "Macon," I say and then have to clear my throat because somehow his name had come out in a squeak. "I have to get some things for Ellie."

Bridgette turns her blue eyes on me as if noticing me for the first time. Her left arm slips around Macon's waist. "I'm Bridgette." She says it with a hint of challenge.

"This is Cam," says Macon, stepping toward me a little. "She—"

Bridgette interrupts with a cold smile. "I heard about you. You are Miss Ellie's granddaughter with nowhere else to go."

I shoot Macon a look, wondering what he has said about me. My situation is nothing to be ashamed about, but Bridgette's tone makes it seem like it is.

"Bridge—" Macon starts but the other girl just laughs prettily.

"I'm sorry, was that rude?" She looks steadily at me. She is *not* apologizing.

Anger, white-hot and immediate, sparks in me. Macon's friend—*girlfriend*—or not, she has no right to judge me. I smile and say, "That's right, I'm here with my grandmother." I turn my angry eyes on Macon. "You can call me when you finish." I pat my pocket for my phone, and realize with embarrassment that it's not there. "Uh, I forgot my phone. Fantastic. I'll just meet you back here in a couple hours?"

"Cam, I thought—"

"That give you enough time? To get caught up?" My brittle smile hasn't moved.

He glances at Bridgette and back to me and nods once, eyebrows set low over his eyes. I check my watch. "Right. Okay, see you then." I set off. Fury, with an icy ball of misery, centers in my middle. I am so stupid. I walk like I know where I am going, up a street I don't know. Too late I realize that I'm wandering blind. I stop, humiliation making my face burn. I obviously misread Macon and his attention. Not surprising. I don't know anything about all of this. It's uncharted territory. Besides, I wasn't even looking for any entanglements. I'm extra mad at myself because I knew all along I shouldn't be thinking about some dumb boy.

I think of his fingers on my brow, him saying I was beautiful...

No. That's not right. He didn't say *I* was beautiful; he said Mom was.

He just said that I had eyes like hers. I stare into a store window at my indistinct reflection in the glass. My unruly hair is standing on end after the boat ride. I look electrified. I smooth it the best I can, and transfer my gaze to what's behind the window. Cuts of meat lay wetly in rows and, hanging from above, the sad headless carcasses of poultry. I'm primping in a butcher shop window. Manic laughter bubbles in my throat and I turn away, catching the butcher's puzzled look.

"Cam!"

At the sound of my name, I look back. Blue is standing at the door of the shop, her unmistakable cobalt hair shining in the sun. Oh my God. Seriously? Someone I know just saw all of that? I blush again.

"Hey! What are you doing? Need a steak?"

"Uh, no, I was just…" I don't know how to finish that.

"Kidding. My 'rents own this shop. I saw you passing. Where are you going?"

"Oh. I have to go to the natural foods store, but I don't know where it is."

"Grass Roots? I can take you there." She falls into step with me. "Are you here with Jane? I thought she was out of town."

I say with an ease that I don't yet feel, "No, I came over with Macon. But he met up with his—with Bridgette?" I hate the question in my voice.

"Oh great. So, she's back." Blue's voice is flat.

I can't stop my curiosity. "You know her?"

Blue grins. "Cam, I live here. I know everyone near my age and then some. We all grew up together. There haven't been a lot of additions and subtractions over the years."

I wonder what that must be like. To see the same people year after year—all the school functions, their parents' parties, dance recitals. Moving as much as we did, I've only known certain people at specific times of my life. The longest place I've lived is Albuquerque, but even then, after Dad left, Mom and I had to move within the city and I had to change schools. No one besides my parents—and really just Mom since Dad took off—had been around my whole life.

I want to ask about Bridgette. I'm not proud of it, but I am curious. I'm just not sure how to start. "People aren't friendly here. Except for you. And Jane and... the guys."

"Well, you know, you're new. Things don't really change around here and 'new' isn't always a good thing." She grins. "Jane's almost new too, and hardwired to be friendly or something. Jack is always nice to girls. Macon has his moments, I suppose. As for me... well..." She sweeps her hand in a gesture to take in her appearance. "New and different appeals to me."

"Ha ha. Do people call you Blue because of your hair?"

She screws up her face. "It's my real name. Shortened version really but blue just happens to be the color of my hair at the moment."

"What's your full name?"

"Some things are better left to the imagination."

"Come on!" I laugh, but she holds up a hand. We're stopped in front of a quaint window with a flowered awning.

"This is it. Only one in town," she says.

We enter the dry, fragrant air of the cozy store. Lined on one wall are bulk bins of dried beans and nuts. On another, is a small shelf of refrigerated items and an even smaller freezer. Blue heads toward that. I get directions from the placid man behind the register, and walk past the natural soaps and shampoos to a section devoted entirely to herbs and spices. A sturdy woman with shoulder-length, iron-grey hair is measuring out tiny, dried white flowers into a small sack for an old woman. I wait until she's finished and ask her if she's Lila.

Her broad face is puzzled. "Do we know each other?"

"Not yet. I'm Ellie Alcott's granddaughter." I pause for her reaction, but she just smiles as if waiting for me to go on. "She sent me in here for a few things." I brandish the list.

Lila takes the paper, picks up the glasses hanging from a cord around her neck, and peers through them without putting them on. Her face is so open, I can watch her mentally tick through each item. When she finishes, she begins filling little paper sacks. I know "tarragon," but have never seen arrowroot or a whole vanilla bean, which Lila puts into a slim jar.

"How is she for lavender?"

"I have no idea. It's not on the list."

"I'll give you some anyway. Have more dried than I know what to do with." She hands me two ribboned sachets. "You keep one. Put it under your pillow. It's good for nightmares."

I find Blue near the checkout, drinking from a large bottle. "Kombucha," she says, raising the bottle like a salute. She holds it out to me, but one whiff of the vinegary smell and I recoil. She laughs.

"What is that?"

"Fermented tea. It's actually really good. Jane got me into it." She holds it out again.

"I'll pass."

The man behind the counter rings up my purchases without comment. A box by the register holds a pile of different colored flashlights. I choose a small black one.

"What do you have to do now?" Blue asks as we leave.

"Just get a few groceries." I check my watch. "I should do that last, I guess, because I want to get some cold stuff. I still have time before I have to go back to the boat."

"Cool. You want to eat?" I nod and she grins. "Good, come with me." She tugs my sleeve, and I follow.

We walk further along the shoreline than I have been before and continue until the stores and houses thin. She leads me to a clapboard structure with a cartoon cutout of a lobster wearing a chef's hat and waving a spatula. A counter faces the street.

"This. Is. The. Best." Blue says, spacing each word and waggling her pierced eyebrows. Then without even asking what I want, orders two lobster rolls and two bowls of clam chowder.

A few makeshift tables are scattered around in front of the shack. A group of boys, faced away from us, are at one and Blue takes another. I sit down, my eyes drawn to the boys to make sure Macon isn't one of them. I don't see his jacket.

The man behind the counter calls Blue's name and she returns with a tray. She hands me a plate with a roll stuffed with "lobster salad" and a bowl of chowder with a few packets of hexagonal crackers on the side.

"DJ's is the best. It's delicious," she says, tucking into her lunch.

I take a bite of my sandwich and close my eyes in sheer pleasure. "You're right. It's fantastic." I have only had lobster once that I can think of, but it wasn't this good. I would have remembered. The soup is thick and creamy, studded with clams and potatoes. I shake some salt on both and after a few bites, I say with conviction, "This is hands down one of the best meals I have ever had."

Blue does a mock bow from her seat. "I aim to impress. It's a popular place. And all they sell are soup and lobster rolls. Oh, and blueberry pie in late summer. It's all fresh, even the blueberries."

A shadow falls over our table. It's one of Macon's friends

who I met the other day—Diego or Luke—I'm not sure which. The other—Luke or Diego—and Wolf, stand to the side. Wolf's gaze is focused on the table between us, but he keeps bouncing his eyes to my face.

"What's up, D?" says Blue.

So that's Diego. His dark hair has reddish highlights in the sun.

"What are you guys doing?" he addresses us both.

Blue swallows a bite of sandwich and gestures to our plates. "As you can see."

"We're going to Brookland Cove later. Luke's brother's friend is having a party."

"I'd be up for that. What about you, Cam?"

I try to mask my disappointment. A party sounds much more fun right now than going back to the island.

"I don't think I can. I came in with Macon."

"I can take you back tomorrow," Blue says. "Call Macon and tell him."

"I told Ellie I would only be a few hours."

At the mention of my grandmother, the boys exchange glances with each other. Except Wolf, who is staring at his shoes.

"Well," Blue interjects into the pause, "surely she'd be happy that your new friends are offering you a break from your almost deserted isle and getting you out of her tiny cottage."

I'm wondering what Blue knows of Ellie's place but correct her without thinking. "I'm not staying at the cottage. I'm in the other house."

"Miss Ellie moved back to Windemere?" pipes up Luke, curiosity lighting his face.

"No," I say, now wondering how everyone seems to know

more about where I live than I do. "I'm there, but she's still in the cottage."

Now all four of them are staring at me. Even Wolf.

"Because of the space," I add lamely.

"You live in Windemere. By yourself," Blue says.

"Yes." I shift under their collective gaze.

"Alone?" asks Wolf.

Luke lets out a low whistle and runs a hand through his dark blond hair. "I have three brothers. A house to myself sounds incredible."

Diego agrees. "I have a house full of sisters. I'd sell one of them for my own space."

"At least you never had to share a bedroom with three guys."

"Try sharing a bathroom with all those girls," Diego shoots back, and then to us, "No offense."

Blue punches his arm lightly and says, "I'm an only child and I'd kill for it."

They are impressed. They aren't treating me like a freak. They think it's a good thing.

"We should go there!" Blue says. Her eyes spark with anticipation. "Add a little life to your world on the island."

I try to picture this group traipsing through the wooden house. I don't know if Ellie would mind. I don't know if I would. Before I can say anything, Luke and Diego are nixing the idea.

"My mom would explode if I took off to the island like that." Diego is laughing, but there is a serious note running through the mirth.

"Mine too," says Luke.

Wolf studies his shoes some more.

"Why?" I am fed up with the looks and innuendo.

"Just got to keep on the radar," Luke says, and Diego nods.

"Loser," teases Blue.

"Maybe another time, Cam," says Diego, like I was the one suggesting this field trip. "So, you two in for later?"

"Come on, Cam. You can stay over. And I'll lend you a shirt, if you want to change."

It just sounds so normal and fun, and I wouldn't have to ride back with Macon. Except I have no way to clear it with Ellie. But why should I have to? She doesn't care. She doesn't even let me live with her, so she wouldn't even know I was gone. The anger I have been holding in check resurfaces. She can stay out there on that stupid island on her own with all her judgement and stupid warnings. It's one night.

"Why not?"

Chapter 13

Blue lends me her phone to call Macon. He is already at the dock waiting for me.

"What am I supposed to tell Ellie?" he asks.

"You don't have to tell her anything."

"You could just come with us now, and I'll bring you back later."

There's no way I am signing up for more boat rides than necessary, and I can hear Bridgette in the background so I guess I don't have to wonder who he means by "us." I try not to care.

"No thanks!" I say brightly and hang up.

Blue asks if I still need to go to the grocery store. I think of the butter I was going to get. "Nope. I'm good."

As we head toward her place, I think about the furtive glances of the others when we talked about Ellie.

"Blue, when I first met you, you called my grandmother creepy. Why?"

She shifts her eyes away from me. "I said I was sorry about that."

I can't let it go. "I'm not mad. Look, I barely know Ellie. I just want to know why you said that."

"It's… I don't know. She has all that crazy hair. She skins animals, or treats the skins. Whatever."

"She keeps her hair long and is the go-to person for curing pelts. That's it?"

"Yeah. No. I don't know. The pelts come back different. I mean, no one can do what she does. The fur is so fine, and the hide… I don't know."

"What do you mean? Come on. She's good at her job? That can't be it. People freak out when she's mentioned. Not everyone, but enough. I just need one person to tell me why."

Blue sighs and stops. "Okay, I really don't know for sure. I have known her as long as I can remember. We go out to the island sometimes. Taking pelts or just to visit. My family has stayed in the vacation cottages when the 'rents wanted to get out of town, and they'd drag me along. Miss Ellie has always made me feel weird."

"How?"

Blue screws up her face. "When she looks at me, I feel like she isn't just seeing me—my hair, clothes, whatever—but sees my insides, blood and bones, or maybe what I am thinking. She always looks at me like she's sizing me up."

"Okay." I've definitely felt that before.

"And then sometimes I look at her and I feel like I'm not looking at a real person. Like she's wearing a costume of an old woman but one day she's going to throw it off, and there will be some alien creature, and she'll boil all the children or something."

I splutter and then laugh.

She winces. "I don't really think that, about kids. She is just different. Maybe even too different for me."

I have to take a moment to try to form a reply. I barely

know Ellie, but I do know history and how witch hunts got started. She makes me furious, but I definitely know what it feels like to be the odd one out and not fit in. I can almost feel a little kinship with Ellie right now. Some of this must show on my face.

"Look, I'm sorry. I'm not trying to piss you off. You asked and I'm just telling you."

"You're right. I did ask. It's okay; she can be really critical for no reason." I think of something else. "What do your parents say about her?"

"Oh, uh, well, you know those skins? They come from my dad's shop, most of them anyway. He collects them for her."

"All right, but you didn't answer my question."

"I told you, the skins come back different. Somehow better than they were before. Well, before they were taken off the animal, I guess. But Dad says they are even improved. You can feel it when you touch them." Her voice drops. "And then my grandmother used to say that men had to be careful around her."

"What?" I wasn't expecting that.

"Like she could steal their souls or something." She must notice my shocked face because she rushes on, "It's total nonsense, but I think people just remember your grandfather."

"What about my grandfather?"

"I don't know a lot, but I know this story. Your grandfather, Oscar…"

"Alcott."

"Yeah, well the Alcotts were very well known here. They used to be a really prominent family here for years and years. You can still see their name, like painted on buildings, faded. Haven't you ever noticed down by the dock? Didn't Macon point it out?"

I shake my head.

"Well, anyway, your grandfather was the only son. He was supposed to be really hot and everyone liked him. Tons of girls wanted to marry him. But he shows up with your grandmother—like from nowhere. He never looked at another woman again. He was completely focused on her. He built that house out there that you're living in. They had your mom and the Stones moved out there, and then he went out on the boat one day and never came back."

I nod as if I know the whole story and not just the part about his vanishing act.

"So, they never found any sign of him, and people... people began to talk about how maybe *she* had something to do with it. You know, his disappearance." She hurries on again. "I don't think that, and my parents don't say that either. Maybe it was jealousy. Miss Ellie never remarried, but I guess there were a lot of men who wanted to. One guy drowned around that time, and there was a rumor that he was on his way to the island when he died. Maybe some guys didn't get over the rejection."

"Maybe..."

"Then your mom was really beautiful too, and there were guys around town that wanted to be with her—pined over her. But your dad showed up and she ran off with him. It was a bit of a scandal at the time. So I was told."

I'm listening, fascinated. "What scandal?"

"Just that it was so fast, she was so young, and your dad was a stranger. I told you, people don't like change."

"Huh." I'm lost in thought and overwhelmed by this information.

"So... well, that's it really. If people act strange, I am sure it's just that old drama or whatever. I don't know. I'm sorry I said anything."

I rouse myself and at her anxious face say, "No. Don't be. Thanks for telling me all that. I guess it's the power of small-town gossip, right?"

"Yeah…" She looks miserable. "I feel like I should give you another biscotti."

I huff a sort of laugh. "I'm not mad at you for telling me. Honest." I don't add that I just can't believe that I've ended up in a podunk backward town like this.

BLUE'S HOUSE is a three-story wooden home with a peaked roof and attic windows. As we climb the steps to the front door, I ask Blue if she has internet.

She gives me a funny look. "Seriously? We're not living in the Dark Ages here. Not all the time."

The house is quiet as we enter. "Is anyone home?"

"My folks will still be at the shop. Don't worry, I'll text my Mom. She won't care if you stay."

She leads me to the very top of the house. Her room is a converted attic with sloping walls running the length of the house. It's like being in a massive wooden tent with carpet. There are two beds at opposite ends of the room. One is a mass of tumbled covers; the other is neatly made with a striped cushion for decoration. There isn't much else at that end of the room, but the other side is all Blue. The walls are papered with posters, pictures, drawings, and notes, like a multicolored lichen slowly taking over the room. A vanity table's covered in various bottles of makeup and nail polish. A large rack of CDs sits next to a box full of old vinyl albums and a stereo system that has everything from a turntable to a dock. My old iPod wouldn't fit on that even if I had remembered it.

"Nice!" I say, impressed.

"It's not my own house, though. But it does have something that yours doesn't have."

"What's that?"

"Proximity to civilization." She sticks her tongue out at me.

I don't mind. She's right.

"You can just put your stuff over there. That's for guests." She points to the pretty, made-up bed.

Oh right, of course we would be sharing a room. I hope I don't have any weird dreams. Maybe I'll try Lila's sachet.

Blue pops her phone onto the dock and sets it to play one of her "amazing, awesome, incredible" playlists.

"We'll meet up with the others in a little while. That cool?" She sits in front of the vanity and begins to apply more eyeliner.

"Yeah, whatever's fine."

"You're just excited to be in an actual town."

I laugh. "I've been in a town before, Blue. I've been to cities even. But, yeah, the island is definitely the smallest… community."

"Well…" Blue pauses as she lines her lips. "You have some people out there." She meets my eyes in the mirror.

"Yeah."

"They're cool. The Stones, Jane."

"Jane's great."

"You don't like the Stones?"

"No, I don't mean that. I like them. Rob's quiet. Jack's nice… and Macon. Anne is… Anne doesn't like me."

"Hmm. Okay." She goes back to doing her lips.

"Maybe it's just Ellie," I say, half joking but with a sliver of bitterness.

Blue looks up quickly but doesn't comment. "You want to get online?" she says instead.

She sets me up at her desk and turns on her sticker-laden laptop. I listen to Blue's playlist and check email. There's not much there, except my bank has noted a new deposit. I shouldn't have another one for a few weeks. The email doesn't mention the amount. I log onto my bank and stifle a gasp. The money is from Dad's account but more than the usual monthly amount.

Way more.

I click through trying to see if there are any notes to explain this unusual generosity, but there's nothing. Maybe it's my birthday present. Four months late. Maybe he's trying to make up for completely missing my sixteenth.

I should be excited about the sudden influx of cash, but I'm just uneasy. I don't like the unexplained when it comes to Dad. I don't trust what will happen next. I don't know if it means something bigger—a message, a payoff—and now there will be no more deposits. Maybe he decided that sixteen is old enough to find a job and pay for my own cell phone. That would suck, especially as I have no idea what kind of job I could have while living on the island. I'll just have to wait until next month and see if any more comes in. But if it doesn't, I won't ask him about it.

A song catches my ear and I close Gmail. Whatever Blue calls this playlist, it certainly is eclectic—alternating old punk, classical, and newer almost-pop songs with the occasional truly random selection. I love it. The song playing now reminds me of Nikki, so I log on to Instagram. My account is so neglected. I haven't posted in ages, and hardly comment on any posts either. Without data on my phone, I never bothered to download the app, even when I had Wi-Fi at home. I closed my Facebook account years ago. It all just seemed so pointless when Mom was getting sick.

I scroll through and see that Nikki's party was a hit, judging from the pics she uploaded. She got blond highlights, and seems really friendly with a cute guy who sort of looks familiar, but I can't place. I have nothing in common with these people anymore.

"Wow! Is that *all* of your followers?" demands Blue, peeking over my shoulder.

"I know, right? So popular." I log out quickly.

"Wait! You should've followed me."

"I just never use it."

"Fine. I'll find you and add you later. Here, try this eyeliner. I think it'd look great on you."

I look at the dripping brush in Blue's hand. I have never used liquid eyeliner, but might as well make a bit of an effort today and give it a go. I swipe down my eyelid making a bloated, jagged line. I try to wipe it off and get it all over my face and hand. I reach for a tissue and leave a streak across the table. I groan.

"Let a professional help you," Blue says, laughing.

She dabs a cotton ball over my face and hand, cleaning off the black. Then she takes the brush, dips it carefully, and twirls the bristles into a point.

"Look down. The trick is a steady hand. It took me forever to work it out."

I stay still, eyes downcast while Blue fusses. She decides I definitely need eyeshadow as well, and spends several moments with brushes of various sizes blending and shading. She reaches for blusher but stops, studying my face critically.

"Actually, I think my work is done. You don't need blush, and I don't even think you need lipstick. Maybe just some balm. Your lips are just a little dry." She sweeps a lip balm across my mouth and moves so I can see the mirror.

It's a huge change from my normal understated style. The dramatic shading and dark eyeliner make my eyes look bigger and the color really pop. My lips are soft and plump. "Wow."

"Right? I'm a wizard. Try this shirt…" She rummages for a moment and hands me a stretchy black knit top. It doesn't look like anything special, but I put it on anyway. Although Blue is shorter than me, the shirt fits well. Almost too well—skimming over my curves, closer fitting than anything I own. The neck is wide and shows my collar bones, and the black looks good with my dark jeans.

"What else? Here, these would look good on you too." Blue holds out a pair of silver and black pearl earrings. They are an unusual design, a continuous piece of silver in an inverted V shape that comes down long on both sides. One end, the plain one, slides through my ear until the crux of the V fits snugly in my lobe. The other end hangs down, cradling the dark pearl, and ends just below my jawline. They are gorgeous. I run a thumb over one pearl and feel an electric pull in my belly, almost like a shock. My breath catches; I touch the pearl again, giddy and almost… hungry. I touch it one more time. An echo of the first jolt shoots down my middle. I've never really had a lot of jewelry, but I have had some. I've never liked anything to this degree before, though. I don't understand it, but I love these earrings.

Blue hasn't noticed my reaction but says, "Much better with short hair. You know, I never wear those. You can have them if you like."

Mine.

I trill my fingers over the pearls. "Yes. I want them. Thank you."

A text pings on Blue's phone, and she pulls it from the dock. "You ready?"

I nod. "Who is that?"

"Just Diego."

I smooth my hair one last time.

Diego is finishing a phone call but waves when we come out the front door.

"You guys clean up good." He says it like he's teasing and addresses us both, but his eyes are on Blue. She scoffs but flushes slightly.

We climb into Diego's beige four-door sedan that I am sure must be on loan from his parents. Blue sits shotgun. We drive around to another part of town that I haven't been to yet and stop in front of another three-story house. Wolf is waiting outside. Blue and Diego shout out greetings, and he hesitates only for a moment when he sees me before climbing into the back seat.

"Hey," he says, but doesn't meet my eyes.

"Hi." I look out the window. Everything looks different here. Different colors, the way people dress, and the way the houses are built.

Up front, Diego is joking with Blue about her hair color. She retorts that at least she's not boring, and he reacts mock-wounded. I smile at their flirting. Some things aren't so different after all. I catch eyes with Wolf and we both laugh quietly. The shared moment breaks the tension.

"So, Wolf, huh? Is that a nickname?"

"Wolfgang. Like Mozart." He's not looking at me again.

"Are you a musician?"

"Not like Mozart. Are you Cameron?"

"Camline. But no one calls me that except my grandmother." At the mention of Ellie, he looks straight at me for three full seconds. In a row. "You know her." It's not a question. He nods, eyes down.

"She's actually really interesting," I say. I feel like I'm defending her again.

"I know. Miss Ellie is fascinating. Fascinating and daunting. You know?" He gives a sudden laugh, but his words land with me.

"Yeah. I know." I wonder if she's heard yet that I didn't go back to the island.

Chapter 14

The party is already going when we arrive, and cars are stacked up and down the street. We park and hear a shout as Luke calls us over. There are a few people out front and many more stuffed in the sparse living room. Most of them are at least five or six years older than us. The music is pumping, and someone hands me a drink as I walk through. I sniff it and set it down. I've heard enough cautionary tales; I'm not accepting an unknown drink from a stranger.

A guy with the same shaggy, dark blond hair as Luke waves to us through the crowd. Luke introduces me to his older brother, Alex, who is standing at the entrance of the kitchen. There's another guy there as well, with dark hair and a devil's grin.

"I'm Theo," he shouts over the music and actually winks at me.

I toss a look at Blue, but she's not paying attention. She heads into the kitchen toward the keg. I go after her, and as we pass, Theo stares at me with a slight smirk. I just keep on following Blue. She is already pumping frothy beer into a red plastic cup which she hands it to me. I look around to see where the others have gone. Luke is talking to his brother, and Diego and Wolf are still by the door. Wolf is smiling, chatting easily with a couple of people there. He must not always be as shy as he is with me.

I take a sip of the beer. I've tried it once before when a kid brought some to a party, a rare outing back before the divorce papers had come, before Mom needed me all the time. Before everything changed. I hadn't liked the taste then, and time hasn't improved it. Blue swallows a great gulp of her beer.

"C'mon, let's go see if we can change this music!"

"I'm going to get some water. I'll be right there."

Blue makes a funny face at me and tells me to hurry. There's a couple making out next to the stove. I slip around them, dump my beer and then fill my cup from the faucet.

"Not drinking?" Theo slides in next to me. His eyes crinkle when he smiles. "Or just not beer?"

I shrug. He is about Alex's age, kind of cute but maybe a bit too convinced of his own charm. The music stops and then comes back on even louder. Blue must have found the stereo. Theo leans in to speak to me.

"How do you know Luke?"

"Luke?" Theo is too close, and I half step to the side.

"Isn't that who you came with?" He leans in again.

"I guess… We're in a group." I take another step away. He follows.

"You live in Williams Point?"

"Close enough."

"What is that supposed to mean?" He laughs and pokes me lightly in the side with his forefinger.

I jerk back and bump into the couple. "Sorry," I say, but they are too wrapped up in each other. I can't see anyone I know now. Theo is all charisma and white teeth. I'm in the spotlight of his attention.

"Why so jumpy?" He grins and leans over me. Maybe it's more like the cross-hairs.

"I should go find my friend."

"I'm sure she's fine. So what do you mean close enough to Williams Point?"

"I live on one of the islands off the coast." I move again and he follows me, clearly unaware of what personal space means.

"Island girl…" He strings out the words, lacing them with some sort of implication, raising his eyebrows. I smell alcohol on his breath.

"I just moved there." I shift, and he puts a hand to the side, leaning on the fridge and bracketing me in between the kissing couple and him.

"You have amazing eyes." His gaze seems to look through me, blurring and out of focus. He raises a hand toward my face, but I block him. Some of the water in my cup sloshes out onto his arm.

"Hey now, watch yourself. Thought you weren't drinking."

"Excuse me," says an annoyed voice that I recognize. Macon stands behind Theo, his eyebrows pulled low as he gestures to the refrigerator. "Hey, Theo."

Theo moves, and I sidle out and break for the living room. It's so much louder in here. I'm threading through the press of bodies and, just as a quieter song comes on, I run into Bridgette. Literally. She looks me up and down and then over my shoulder, looking for Macon, I guess. Then she smiles at me. "We missed you on the trip this afternoon," she says and then adds quietly, "I really wanted to talk to you more."

"Hey!" Blue shouts a little too enthusiastically from

where she is perched like a happy gargoyle on the arm of a couch. "Come here!"

I shrug an apology to Bridgette and make my way toward Blue.

"Where have you been?" she asks when I reach her.

She's tipsy enough that I wonder how many beers she could have had while I was in the kitchen. Then I see that she has moved onto a different drink, something that smells a little like paint thinner.

"Where's your drink?" she asks me with genuine concern.

I raise my cup. "Cheers."

I slide in onto the couch next to her. From here I can see the room. It's full of people, but they are all strangers. I sink back into the couch and close my eyes. I feel like I'm outside of it all again. Always watching from the sidelines. I stare without seeing, listen to the music, and let my mind wander. I think of when I'll be able to make all of my own decisions.

With a sinking feeling, it comes to me that with everything that was going on today, I haven't called my mom. I wonder if she's waiting for me. It's really too loud to talk, but Blue and Diego are good-naturedly battling about some movie, shouting to be heard. I have no idea what they are talking about.

"Can I borrow your phone?" I interrupt Blue.

"'Course!" She pulls it out of her pocket, nearly dropping it as she passes it to me. I'm getting a headache, a sharp spike in my right temple. I motion to Blue that I'm going to go outside. Fresh air will help. I slip through the crowd and make for the door.

No one is outside now, and I sit on a stump near the house, trying to remember the number for Mom's facility. I try one combination but am told that the number can't be reached. I check the time. It's way later than I thought. It feels like we just got here, and it feels like we've been here all night. The music changes again to something quieter, and I take a deep breath of salt air and feel myself relax for a moment. And a moment is all I get as the door bangs open, and Theo comes through.

"There you are. We didn't get to finish our conversation." He is still smiling, but there's something different in his eyes now—a predatory gleam. I pocket Blue's phone and stand up to go back inside, but he blocks my way, placing his hands on the wall on either side of me. "No running off now."

"I just want to go hang out with my friends."

"We're friends, aren't we?"

I try to laugh it off. "I don't know you."

"You could get to know me."

He moves closer to me, and I put my palms on his chest to push him away. He grabs my right arm just below the wrist. I twist to break his grasp, but he hangs on and pushes my arm back against the house.

"Come on now, don't be unfriendly," he says, his smile cracking.

I don't want to make a scene, but I don't want to be manhandled either. I move to my left, but he counters by slamming his palm against the house, bracketing me in again. Anger bubbles, spiked with fear. His smile is becoming more of a grimace, and his grip doesn't falter on my wrist. I can't move my right arm. I hear the door open, but I don't look. I don't know what Theo is going to do next. He reaches up to touch my face and I move to block him. As I do, my hand grazes the pearl earring and an electric charge travels from my belly up my spine as something *shifts* inside me. I go still and calm.

I look Theo full in the face and feel time slow. I hear my heart beating, and I press my left palm to his shoulder and push very slightly. "Let me go." His face goes slack, and he drops my wrist and rocks back. "Walk away." He turns abruptly and wanders off.

I look up and see Bridgette staring at me.

Macon comes up right behind her. "What's going on?" he asks, as Theo shuffles toward the door, looking confused.

"I... need..." Theo's eyes slide past me, like they can't take hold. "I need to go. Something..." Theo trails off and goes inside.

I don't know what Macon sees in my face, but he walks down the steps to me and asks, "Are you okay, Cam?" Bridgette stays by the door and doesn't say anything.

My breath hitches. I don't know what just happened. My anger is leaking away and the fear is lifting, leaving me exhausted.

"Wow." Macon is staring at my arm. I look down and see that there are shallow indentations on my forearm where Theo had gripped me. White impressions surrounded by red. "Did he do that? What happened?"

Wish I knew. "I think he was drunk."

"Yeah, he definitely was but..." He's looking at my wrist again. "Can I see?" He moves to touch my arm. I let him. "Did he *hurt* you?" He asks it like he can't believe it's possible. He runs his fingertips lightly over the impressions, soothing and sending sparks at the same time. I break out in goosebumps and see Bridgette watching with sharp eyes.

"I'm fine," I say and brush my own hand over my arm, erasing his touch.

"You know, girls usually love Theo, but I have never seen him act like that. I mean, you guys seemed to be getting along in the kitchen... but this... the expression on your face." He clenches his jaw. "I mean, I'm sure you can take care of yourself. But he really isn't *that* guy."

Is he kidding? Theo is exactly *that* guy. He just proved it.

As if guessing my thoughts, Macon continues, "I know how that must sound right now, but I just wanted you to know that I have never seen that side of him."

"Glad I could be just the jailbait to bring it out." Maybe not all the anger is gone.

"I'm sorry. There's no excuse for anyone to grab you like that."

"No, there isn't. But I'm all right. He left me alone when I told him to."

"Hey! There you are!" Blue shouts as she barrels through the door, bumping Bridgette and running up to me. "What are you doing?"

I reel at her breath. "I— What have you been drinking, Blue?"

She laughs. "Just a little of this and of that."

"She had to try that killer punch. It's death," Diego says, coming up behind her.

"It was blue. It stood to reason," Blue says, dead serious. Diego hands her another red plastic cup, and she takes a huge swallow. "Oh! What is this?"

"Water."

It doesn't seem like he's been drinking, at least. Blue makes a face at him but takes another drink.

"What are you guys doing out here?" Luke says as he stumbles out the door half-lidded and smiling. He probably had the punch too.

"Taking in the scenery," Diego says with a straight face gesturing to the empty yard and broken fence.

Blue and Luke laugh simultaneously, stop as if surprised, and then turn to each other pointing, laughing again in unison. I wish I was in on the joke. The music rises. Bridgette hasn't moved from the porch, and Macon is still standing next to me.

"What did Ellie say?" I ask him.

"Nothing."

"You didn't tell her?"

"I did. She kind of nodded, but she didn't say anything."

"Right." Dread settles in my gut. I'm regretting my impulsiveness. I don't know what I'm going to have to deal with back at the island. Bridgette is still staring at me. I suddenly just want to leave. Blue stumbles, and Diego catches her.

"Maybe we should go?" I ask.

"Nah!" says Blue.

"I can take you," Macon says at the same time.

Diego agrees that we should leave and starts to talk Blue into it.

"I'm staying at Blue's," I say to Macon.

"Are you sure?"

I am almost tempted to get away from this stupid party and find out how mad Ellie is sooner rather than later.

"I need to make sure she gets home."

"Okay. We'll do that first. Hang on." Before I can say anything, he disappears back inside.

"Where's Wolf?" I ask Luke.

"Inside hiding from the soul stealer." He winks, screwing up half his face to do it. "You can't catch him if he doesn't look too long." He breaks into a loud laugh.

"What?" He's acting like I should know what he's talking about.

"Scary, scary island girls…" He waves his fingers like he's trying to hypnotize me.

I remember what Blue said about my grandmother and

even my mother. I keep my voice light. "What is it they say again?"

"Got to be careful of girls who live on islands. His grandma told him stories, and she's super superstitious." He giggles. "Super-super-super."

"That's it?" I ask, trying to get him back on track.

"Oh yeah, she said that your grandmother only had to look at a man to get them to fall in love with her. And your mom. No sleep, no food. A guy could just waste away, all for the love of the unattainable girl." He shakes his head and says as if imparting a sad, serious truth, "Now you're here with those eyes."

I burst out laughing. This is the most ludicrous thing I have heard. Especially lumping me into the whole package. "Was this before or after they lured all the children to their gingerbread houses?"

"I want gingerbread. Wicked idea, island girl." He claps me clumsily on the shoulder.

"You really want to go?" Blue asks, half pouting.

"Maybe it's for the best? Your parents…?"

"No, they'll be asleep. It's fine."

Macon comes back out and hands Blue another plastic cup. She drinks.

"More water?" she grumbles, but takes another swallow.

Bridgette finally comes down the steps and stands close to Macon. "Are we leaving?" she asks him, only him. He nods, but he's looking at me.

"Blue?" I turn to her.

"I'll make sure she gets home," Diego says.

I like Diego. He seems nice, but I don't know him well enough to send my new and very drunk friend off with him. Maybe it's the aftereffects of Theo, but I'm not going to do it.

"We'll all go," says Macon. "We'll follow you to Blue's,

and I'll take you back to the island after, okay?" He turns to Bridgette. "You can drop us at the pier?"

Everyone seems happy-ish about this, although Bridgette gives me a cool look. I'm quiet on the way back to William's Point. Blue chats with Diego in between trying to get me to change my mind about staying.

Her house is dark when we get there, and she tells me to be quiet as we enter and climb the stairs. "My folks get up early. I don't want to wake them." She seems like she really cares more about their comfort than not getting caught. I get my things and tell Blue I'll call her tomorrow.

Outside, I climb into the back of Bridgette's decked-out economy car. She speaks in French to Macon, but he only answers in monosyllabic English. When we stop at the pier, Macon mutters a thanks at Bridgette, gets out, and makes for the boat.

I get out but as I pass Bridgette's window, she grabs my arm. I'm so surprised, I stop.

She bares her teeth in a smile and stares at me with the same wild intensity that she had on the porch. "I saw what you did," she says. "You leave Macon alone. I know about your family. I know about you." She releases me and with another sharp, knowing glance, drives off before I can respond.

Chapter 15

I try to shake off the chill hitting the back of my neck as I walk to the boat. I manage to get on it without freaking out. Being on it in the dark is disorienting; I can't focus on the horizon. At least the ocean is kind of calm. I put on my life jacket and settle my bags near my feet. Macon turns on lights, unties the boat, and we push off. The wind slicks my hair back; I pull my jacket closer and hold on tight as we bump over a wave.

Macon is silent at first, and I'm replaying what Bridgette said and Luke's ramblings during the party. Luke was just drunk and silly, but Bridgette's tone made it seem like we were murderers or something.

"Is she going to be mad?" Macon asks suddenly.

"Who?" I ask, still thinking of Bridgette.

"Miss Ellie."

Oh right. "I have no idea. Probably not. I don't think she cares what I do."

Macon glances at me like he's even less convinced of this than I am. The lights above throw shadows across his cheekbones. We hit a wave, and my heart jumps in my throat as I hang on tighter. I face forward into the spray and darkness and concentrate on breathing. This works for a while but then, smack in the middle of the sea, Macon cuts the engine. We roll with the motion of the boat, and I grit my teeth.

"What are you doing? Why're we stopping?"

"It's clear tonight. I want to show you something," he says and turns off the lights. Darkness drops swift and sudden, and for a moment I can see nothing. The water sloshes against the side of the boat. I shudder. Then my eyes begin to adjust, and I can see Macon with his face turned to the sky. I look up. The stars spread across the black of the sky like a spilled diamond heist hoard.

"Amazing." I mean it. There are too many stars to count. Only when camping with Dad have I seen so many, but they're different somehow above the sea instead of the desert.

"That's Saturn," Macon says sitting down next to me and pointing to one particularly bright spot. I can feel his body heat through my sleeve. "And that is…"

"Venus, I know," I finish. "Where are the Pleiades? That's my favorite."

"She's not my girlfriend," Macon says, still focused on the sky.

"What?"

"Bridgette. She's not… my girlfriend."

"Does she know that?" I say without thinking.

"She should. She's been gone."

"What does that even mean? You guys seem… more than friends."

"We used to date, I guess. I've known her forever. Her mom and mine are really good friends, and her family stays in the summer houses most years."

"Okay." I don't know what else to say.

"Yeah. But we're not dating now. We haven't been for a while."

"You don't have to tell me all this."

"I want to explain because…"

I don't take in what Macon says next because in the water past him, there is a flash. It looks like gold. Or silver, maybe copper, like a new penny. Then it's gone. It's like I almost recognize it. My breath quickens, and a buzz tickles my skin.

Macon has stopped speaking. "It's fine," I say into the lull.

I hear a tiny splash behind us and turn. Nothing is there, just dark water. Then on my side of the boat, there is another wink of silver. I slide closer to the rails to see better.

"Fine?" Macon asks, but I'm not paying attention to him.

I'm staring at the water. There is movement there, a ripple, under the surface. Macon says something else but his voice is muffled, far away. The flash appears again and it's beautiful, like the stars just dropped into the sea for a swim. It calls to me, pulling me toward it. I can't describe the feeling. Like music. The best music. I know it but have forgotten the words. Another flash, closer now, and I reach for it, stretching my hand toward the light. I can almost feel it, almost reach it; I am completely unafraid.

And then my face hits the water.

I sink forward and something pulls at my ear, jerking my head. Fear rocks me, and I scream—which starts as bubbles and ends in a hoarse yell as I'm hauled back onto the boat. I am soaked and terrified, my mind scuttling to figure out what just happened. Salt water stings my eyes and Macon must think I have straight up lost my mind. Maybe I have, because he's holding my shoulders asking me something, but I'm completely distracted by his face. It's like he's glowing within, like someone lit a lantern inside him. Like he swallowed a star.

"Cam!" His face seems twisted with surprise and worry. "Are you…"

He doesn't finish because before I know what I am doing, I press my lips to his. My mouth is cold, but he is so warm. I taste salt and smell pine. The buzzing under my skin is back and ricochets through me until a shock, like static, hits my lips.

I jump, and Macon pulls away an inch, studying my face. I can't make out his expression. My breath catches, and I'm conscious of breathing the same air as him. I can feel my pulse in my neck and fingertips.

"Your eyes. They are amazing… like a storm."

Then he's kissing me again, soft at first and then with an undercurrent of urgency. I am caught up, lost in the kiss. I am transported like no one and nothing else exists. His hands move to my hair and I curl mine into his jacket as I pull him closer. There is only the sensation of his mouth on mine, his hands tangling in my hair. My skin is electric. Then something bumps the boat and we jostle into each other, my tooth clips one of his, and he laughs as we break apart.

"I didn't mean to do that." He says it so earnestly that I think he regrets it. "Is it all right? That I kissed you?"

"Actually, I think I kissed you." I'm in a daze. My mind can't catch up.

He cups my face in his hands. "You're so beautiful." He leans forward, and I move to meet him, wanting nothing more than to sink back into that kiss, but he stops. "You're shaking. You must be freezing."

The boat rocks sickeningly as he moves to switch the

lights back on. In the stark light and away from his embrace, the cold sinks into my bones. I feel like I've just woken from a dream. What am I doing? The water is black around us, no flashes, nothing but dark waves. He pulls out an old blanket from a water-tight bench and wraps it around me.

"Macon…"

"Okay, we should get you back. You'll freeze." He is flicking switches, prepping the boat. "Do you want my jacket? My shirt?"

"No, I'm fine," I say, embarrassed. "But…"

"You lost an earring."

My hands go to my ears and find the right one is gone. I rub my thumb over the pearl on the left and a jolt zings through my middle.

"Cam, what were you doing? Why did you fall in?"

"I don't know. I thought I saw something. In the water."

"What did you see?"

I don't know how to answer. It feels far away, like a dream. "It was just—" A flash, a song, *something*. "I don't know. It was nothing. I'm sorry."

He laughs. "No need to be sorry. Good thing I have fast reflexes." Then his tone sobers. "Cam. I can't stop thinking about you. I wonder what you're doing, where you are. I know we just met, but I *dream* about you." His face is open and almost pained as he tells me this. "I'm freaking you out."

I'm staring at him, my mind reeling, but a warmth spreads through me better than any blanket. I grin. "You aren't."

He looks relieved, gives me another quick heady kiss and starts the boat.

I huddle in the blanket vacillating between shivering and feeling like I have a fever. My lips burn. Macon steals glances at me. Every time he looks at me, I feel like I'm flying. He doesn't look like he's glowing or anything weird, but he is wonderful. I watch him as he pilots the boat. I don't think about Bridgette. I don't worry that it's too fast or that I don't want any entanglements; I don't care. I ride the wave of his kiss and his confession all the way back to the island.

And then I see Ellie waiting for me.

Chapter 16

Ellie stares at us while Macon secures the boat and helps me to the dock.

"Do you want me to come with you?"

"No. It'll be fine." I tell him and start to give the blanket back.

"Keep it. I'll get it back from you later." He holds my hand for a moment and squeezes it. "I meant what I said, okay?"

I nod.

"See you, Cam."

I wait until the boat disappears into the dark before I walk up the pier. Ellie watches me the whole way.

When I get closer she asks, "What have you done, Camline?"

"Nothing. What do you mean?"

"I told you to be careful."

"I am careful!" I'm annoyed. I made sure Blue got home. I didn't even drink.

"You left."

"I told you where I was going."

"You said shopping. You didn't come back. You send that boy. And then I get this." She holds out her palm, and lying in it is my earring.

Cold climbs up my spine. "How do you have that? I lost it." I snatch the earring back and slip it into my ear.

"You went into the water."

"I didn't mean to. I slipped." It sounds ignorant and comes out defensive.

"You do not understand. You know nothing and play with fire."

Like tinder catching, anger flames and I lose all patience. "Then tell me! What don't I get?" I'm shouting.

Ellie doesn't respond but turns her back and starts walking toward the beach. I only hesitate for a second and then follow her. I am tired of her evasiveness.

"Talk to me! Come on, Ellie, why is everyone afraid of you? Why do they tell stories? What did you do?"

She looks at me sharply but doesn't stop. The tide is high, and when she reaches the water line, I hang back. I don't know what she's doing, and my feet don't want to move. I look to the stars, but they are cold and distant now.

The ocean is black stretching out behind Ellie. She turns to face me and walks backward until a small wave breaks around her calves. I think of my mother in the dream.

"I will speak with you here. If you are ready to listen, come to me."

I tremble. But I'm not a coward. I drop the blanket and bags, kick off my shoes, and roll my jeans up to my knees. There's enough starlight that I can see Ellie in the pale light. I advance; she retreats further into the surf. Anger carries me forward until the first wave brushes my toes, and I jerk. It's so cold it hurts. Ellie is up to her knees in the water. Another wave breaks around her, but she seems unfazed by it. I'm shaking, with cold or fear or anger, or maybe all three. I steel myself. I walk forward until I reach Ellie, the water pulls at me as waves recede. My feet go numb.

"What, Ellie?" I spit the question.

Ellie bends to cup the water in her hands and raises them to wet her face. Her hair is coming loose from its binding, long strands hanging down her back. Her face is alive, lips drawn back in a feral grin, and her eyes… I can't stop staring. They are like a storm.

I freeze, then flinch as she traces her cold, wet hands around my eyes. My breath is sharp and fast. I can't stop staring at her. The sea pulls at me and my feet sink deeper into the sand.

"Your eyes… What's happening?"

"I am showing you what really is. The seawater reacts with them. We are seen as we are, and we can see true."

"I don't understand!"

Ellie flings a handful of water at my face. I gasp as it hits my eyes. I close them to the sting of the salt. It only lasts a second. I move to wipe my face, but Ellie grabs my hand.

"Open your eyes, child."

I blink. Ellie's hair has come unfastened and spreads out around her. Her eyes shine with a myriad of colors—blue, green, grey—chasing through her irises. Her skin is luminescent like the inside of a shell or the sheen of a pearl. Her smile shows very white, sharp teeth. I try to pull away, but Ellie holds me fast. She points out to the ocean.

"Do you see? They are here, but you know nothing and need the push."

"What are you talking about?" All I see is the darkness of the water.

In response, with a single motion, Ellie grabs me by the back of my neck and shoves me face first into the sea.

I fight, panic taking over as my useless hands scrape the sand. Ellie is terribly strong, and I am going to drown. Every fear I have had since I was a child is coming true. I try to scream and choke on salt water. Then Ellie lifts me up. I am gasping, water streams from my hair and face.

"What the f—?" Before I finish, Ellie grabs my chin and points my face out to the ocean.

"Look."

In the dark, I see something there. Dancing in the waves, sparking through the water are colors. Red, gold, emerald, and silver. Each time a wave rises, I see more. There are faces in the waves. Iridescent skin, stormy eyes, and hair all shades, shining metallic in the surf. I forget I'm standing in the ocean, forget the water. Forget that Ellie just tried to kill me. I am mesmerized, pulled toward those faces. My ears fill with the sound of wind, what I had thought was wind. Now I hear a cacophony of voices calling, laughing, crying, singing. I step forward. The water snatches at me. I continue toward the voices. Ellie is saying something, but I can't hear her over the sound. The next wave hits at my waist and knocks me a step backward. The return sweeps my feet from underneath me, and I sit down hard. It breaks my gaze from the faces. Another wave rushes at me, and Ellie is there pulling me to my feet as it crashes into me.

"What is happening?" I cry out over the noise of the voices. Another wave breaks around us and yanks at me as it retreats. Ellie half drags me back toward shore, but the water loops around my legs and the sand sucks at my feet.

"Wait, I can't take you there; you might get lost," Ellie says, voice raised, her eyes multifaceted and wild.

I blink, and we're back above the surf's reach and where I left my things. Ellie scoops them up and, still holding my arm, starts back toward the cottage. I blink and we're in front of the door.

"Take those off," Ellie is saying to me.

I must have blinked. We're inside the cottage. With a detached certainty, I realize I am in shock, pure and simple. I am also completely soaked. My jeans are caked with mud and sand and my hair hangs in front of my eyes. I try to push it back. Ellie's dress is so wet it looks black. She has a towel. Water pools around our feet.

"Camline," she says and motions to my clothes.

My cold fingers struggle with the buttons on my jeans, but after a couple tries I get them undone and peel them off like shedding a layer of skin. My legs, mottled with cold, shine with iridescence. Not as bright as Ellie's but it's there. I scrub my hands across my thigh but nothing changes.

"It's not on you," Ellie says, wrapping the towel around me. "It's in you."

I can't take in her words. "I thought I saw something. There were people. How?" My voice raises a little at the last, and I feel like I'm falling. I pull the towel closer.

Ellie moves me gently to sit and crouches down so that her face is level with mine. I look away; her eyes still swim with colors, and they give me vertigo. "You saw true. For the first time in your life."

"I don't know what I saw."

Faces. I shiver even as a sense of longing comes over me.

"You saw through to the others. My sisters."

"What?"

"The first time I saw your grandfather, I thought he was the most extraordinary creature. He was strong and warm and so alive."

"My grandfather?" I can't believe that she's choosing now to reminisce.

"You need to understand, Camline. You need to know who you are." She stands up, goes to the stove, and ladles her stew into cups. It's the middle of the night, and she has stew on the stove. She continues, "I watched him. He fished and laughed and lived. He was so vital. He sat on the rocks in the sun. I had never seen anything like him."

She hands me a mug and I wrap my fingers around it for warmth. I shake my head to clear it, and when I look up, Ellie is watching me.

"I called to him and he heard me. But his call was even stronger. Eventually, I left with him." She looks down into her mug. "My sisters were so sad. They wept and pleaded, but I could not stay. I made my choice to live my life here. Then your mother came. Part of him and part of me. An extraordinary creature in her own right. It was good. We were close to the sea, and she grew strong. I could go to the mainland with Oscar. People there are so staid, so caught in their own lives like crabs in their shells. But we… We were happy."

I'm hardly aware of my wet shirt and underclothes seeping into the towel as I listen.

"It was a Friday. He went out in the boat, and he didn't return." Ellie stops. She looks out the window toward the coast. "I waited. No one found his boat. No one found his body. They said he had run away. They said he was dead. But I could not believe either could be true." She takes a sip from her mug. "How could he be gone? He burned so bright. How could he be gone from the world?" She looks younger and more vulnerable, her voice laced with pain.

"If the sea had taken him, it would have given him back to me. They declared him dead. They whispered that I'd done something to him." Her eyes fierce. "Stupid people. One by one they came to me, to try to capture something of me. To own me. But I still love your grandfather."

The naked admission touches me.

"I can see the ocean better from this cottage, and Windemere was too empty after your mother left."

"When she met Dad?"

"Your mother grew—strong, beautiful and untamed. She is my daughter." She says the last with obvious pride; then her face changes. "These land boys loved her. They didn't even know why. But she saw your father and gave her heart to him." Her voice turns bitter. "He couldn't see her. Not all of her. He was afraid of her power and took her to live in the dry desert." She tilts my chin to meet her gaze. "And scared her daughter from the water."

"I— Me? Dad didn't scare me... He *saved* me..."

"As if a granddaughter of mine could drown."

"I did. I almost drowned. I told you."

Ellie shakes her head with a sad smile. "Chemicals. The chemicals they put in water."

"Chlorine? What do you mean?"

"Tell me what happened to you then. What frightened you?"

I don't like to think about it. I remember I couldn't breathe and that my eyes and throat were on fire. "It was agony. It hurt so much." I hate having to relive it.

"The chemicals burned you. You would be more sensitive to them."

"But Dad pulled me out..."

"Maybe."

"There's no 'maybe.' I was there. He saved me from that pool."

Ellie's voice hardens. "I am saying he made you afraid of what you are."

"That doesn't make any sense. And what do you mean, 'what' I am?" We're just going around in circles. *She* tried to drown me. There were faces in the water. My head is spinning. The room is spinning.

"Drink that."

I'm still holding the mug. I don't know why I obey her but I do, and after one swallow, I feel calm. For a minute.

"What are you telling me, Ellie?"

"You are your mother's daughter. You are my granddaughter. You are of the sea and of the land. Of two worlds. You should have been taught. Your father was afraid. He was scared of your mother's power and what you might become. He kept you from water, kept her from the sea."

I stand up. I can't take it all in. She can't know all of this. But Dad never would let me go with Mom when she swam. And we were only ever near lakes or rivers. Never the sea. I had never even seen the ocean with my own eyes until Rob collected me the day I got here. I remember arguments between my parents. Always something unsaid.

"Who are you, Ellie? *What* are you? What am I?" I can't keep the horror from my voice, afraid of answers.

"Our kind has been called many things—ondines, sea nymphs, sirens."

My legs give way, and I sit down hard. "*Sirens*? You mean— mermaids?" I laugh, and it comes out high pitched. Visions of Disney characters and sad fairytales flit through my mind.

"Don't be ridiculous. We are not fish. There is no grand city built on the ocean floor. The sea is the passage. A portal, connected but separate. We live within the water, part of it, but elsewhere. Land people can only see in if they have been called. If they listen to our song."

"You mean siren's songs? Ships breaking up on the rocks?"

"It is not like that, Camline. It's not so simple."

Simple? None of this sounds simple. My grandmother is telling me that she's not human. "So, you are—"

"I am not from here. I'm a creature of another place, of ocean, come to live here on the dry earth. You are part of me. But part of your grandfather and your father too. Of two worlds but…" She taps me on my brow. "Watermarked."

Chapter 17

Watermarked.

I've had enough. This is crazy. I didn't ask for this. I didn't ask for any of this. I can't even sort through my emotions. I down the rest of my stew like it's medicine and struggle to pull my wet jeans back on. I gather my things, leaving Ellie's herbs from the natural foods store. She doesn't say anything more and doesn't try to stop me.

Outside the cottage, I peer into the distance at the ocean. I can't see anything in the dark. It just looks empty and black. I walk back to Windemere. All I want to do is talk to Mom, but it's the middle of the night there. And she can't talk to me.

I shower, standing under the water until it runs cold and all the sand and salt wash down the drain. I regard my reflection in the mirror. How can I not look any different when everything has changed? I wrap myself in a blanket and start a fire in the grate, staring at it with hands outstretched until warmth returns to my fingers. I can't sleep. I wait until the sun is up before I decide to call Mom. I know she won't be awake yet, but I can't wait any longer.

I find my cell phone forgotten on my bed. There are

messages. The first is from a nurse I don't know asking me to return the call. The second is from Maria. I play the message from Maria three times trying to gauge her tone. I dial the facility in New Mexico with my heart in my mouth. Reception transfers me back to Mom's wing and Suzanna answers.

"Cam. Good, you called back." She says it with her Very Professional Nurse voice. "One sec." She puts me on hold.

I don't know if I can handle bad news right now. I don't know if I can handle it ever. When Suzanna comes back on, I try to keep my voice calm. "What's happening?"

"Everything is fine now. We just had a scare with your mom's temperature. It spiked yesterday and was a bit high for a few hours. It's down now. Gosh, what time is it there?"

"It's early. Why did her temp go up?"

"We aren't sure, which is why we wanted to call you and keep you in the loop, not to alarm you. We don't have a number for your grandmother or your dad."

"They're divorced and Dad's still overseas. Ellie doesn't have a phone." I'm furious at myself for forgetting my phone.

"I see."

I feel like I have to explain more. "You can reach Ellie through this phone. I was away from the house and didn't have it. Don't worry, it won't happen again."

"Okay. As I said, her temperature dropped back down now. Last check it was 98.9 degrees and that's within acceptable range. Not perfect since she usually runs cooler, but not where it was at 102."

"102?" My breath leaves me.

"Yes, but we have it under control. Cam, look, it's fine. We didn't mean to scare you."

We speak for another minute and Suzanna's no-nonsense voice calms me down. I hang up. I'm still bothered by the fever. Mom's illness isn't like a normal sickness. She doesn't have sniffles or coughs or fevers. Besides whatever is happening now, she never got sick, not the way other people did. I can't remember her ever having a cold, even when I was little. This is new. I try to hang on to Suzanna's reassurances as I press the heels of my palms into my eyes. I feel so helpless. And I'm so far away.

I CHARGE my phone as I tidy up haphazardly to keep my hands busy. I'm tired, but I know there's no way I'll sleep now. I yawn, stretch, and then close my eyes. I measure my inhales and exhales for a count of three.

And then, I open my eyes and just get on with it.

I can't do anything else. I think because we moved so much, I have learned to adapt. Every new place came with new people and a new set of rules—different clothes or speech or interactions. Granted, nothing at all like a whole *other world*. Even when a new place felt exactly like that. I never quite fit in, but I could fake it. I need to know more. But adapt or die, right?

I pocket my phone and head down to Ellie's, hoping that she's already up. She meets me at the door, looks me over and then steps back so I can enter. "Hungry?"

I want to laugh at her. How could I eat with everything she told me? Then my stomach growls loudly, and I do laugh under my breath. Ellie ghosts a smile and hands me a plate.

"Ellie, I don't know what to think about… last night," I say and tear into the bread and salted honey.

"I dreamed of your mother," Ellie says instead of answering. "I dreamed she was trying to reach me, but my arms were not long enough to take her hands."

"Well, I couldn't sleep. Last night…"

"I will show you the next step in the pelts now."

"What? That's okay…"

She takes my plate. "You can learn. We can talk."

I just look at her, but she ignores me and walks out the door. Ellie has set up a table outside with a bench on one side. She leads me past this and into the shed. She pulls a sopping skin from a tub—rabbit?—and hands it to me. "Rinse that and then press the water out. Don't wring it."

"I don't—" But she's walked away. The fur drips as I take it to the sink, holding it straight-armed away from my clothes.

Ellie watches me. "Use the apron," she says, pointing to a blue oilskin apron hanging on the wall.

I put it on and, as if in a dream, prime the pump in the sink and sluice water over the pelt. Ellie brings another one over as I'm trying to gently press the water out of mine. The fur is cold and the skin squishes wetly under my hands. I gag.

Ellie ignores me, takes the skin, and tacks it onto a piece of smooth pine and holds it out to me. I don't want to take it, but she pushes it into my hands with a wry look. I hold it by the edges and breathe through my mouth, just in case.

Ellie leads me out to the table. "It's dry enough that we can do this outside," she says as she affixes the other pelt to another board and motions me to sit at the bench. She lays some tools on the table. There's a knife like she used at the tide pools, another that is completely white, both handle and blade, and two large seashells that kind of look like big clams. She hands me the white one.

"Is this…?"

"Bone. It's carved of one piece."

"I have some questions about last night."

"Start here and scrape along the skin. Be careful. The skin is still delicate. You just need to remove all the remaining flesh but without peeling too deeply." She shows me what she means and then turns to the other skin.

I scrape across the skin, and the knife pulls and snags. Disgusting. I lay my knife down. I am tired and confused and full of questions. My mind is still whirling. Ellie works swiftly and precisely over her pelt, her hands flashing down the board, flicking stray flesh to the side. It's gross but also kind of fascinating to watch her. A seagull wings by, interested. Without breaking stride, Ellie fixes it with a cold stare as it swings back. It banks and flies off cawing excitedly. My mouth drops open, but then Ellie turns that stare on me.

"You work, we'll talk."

My temper shifts inside me. "I think I deserve some answers. I mean, all of this is crazy." My voice rises. "There has to be some sort of…"

"Begin." Ellie's voice cuts in like a guillotine. Her eyes are just their normal blue green, but they still make me dizzy.

I break the gaze and focus on the pelt, my anger receding for the moment. I drag the knife again, trying to be gentle. Ellie starts to hum a complicated melody. I scrape the skin and listen to the song. It pulls at me and I follow the tune like a story—a journey—and the questions crowding my mind drop by the wayside. The song is some sort of quest. My quest. Traveling across the world to find something, something that I must have or my world will end. Something I need. I ache for the loss of it. The song brims in me like an over-full cup. And just as I am about to overflow, my anger returns—lancing the song. She is *doing* something to me.

"No." The knife comes down, point first into the table. Ellie's song cuts off. She seems surprised. "We have to talk about this," I state. My phone rings then. Afraid it's about my mom, I wipe my hands and pull my cell from my pocket and answer it by the third ring.

"Sorry it's early. Are you okay?"

"What?"

"Cam? Did I wake you up?" Macon asks.

"No. I'm fine, why?"

"You're not in trouble?"

"Trouble?" I'm trying to process what Macon is asking me. How does he even have my number?

"Cam? Was Ellie mad?"

"Oh, right. Uh, no everything is fine," I say. Ellie is peering at me curiously. I turn away. "Can I call you back later?"

"Sure. I'm going out with my dad now, but I'll be back this afternoon."

"Okay. Talk soon."

"Great," he says and hangs up.

I slide my phone back in my pocket and, in spite of everything, warmth spreads through me. I turn back and, on the table, Ellie has several finished pelts stacked up next to her. Mine is nearly complete, and I don't even remember doing it. How long was she singing?

"Go on. What do you want to ask?" she says, as she tacks down another pelt.

"What's with all the singing?"

"Music is life."

I laugh breathlessly. "I love music too, but I can't sing like you, where I forget what's happening or whatever. And last night, I heard so many voices. I wanted to go to them. It was like the noise I heard in the storms."

She sits up straighter. "You had already heard them? What did you hear?"

"It just sounded like the wind, and last night it was like that too, but there was so much more. Like they were all singing or talking at once. Like when you hear noise in another room, but you don't know what it is until you walk into there and see the TV on." I pause because Ellie doesn't have a TV. Maybe she's never seen one. "Anyway, was that it? I stepped into the sea and then I could hear? Are there people actually in the water?"

"I told you the sea is the portal. My world is not like here; it is suffused in the ocean. And sometimes the veil is thinner, and you can see more. Hear more. Sometimes we—they—visit the ocean. Sometimes you just have to call. Or sometimes they call."

"I don't understand. So the 'veil' was thinner last night?" I stop myself from actually making air quotes with my fingers, but they're still in my voice.

"I think it must have been."

"Okay. How did you get my earring?"

"It was given to me from the sea."

"What does that mean? It washed up?"

Ellie hasn't stopped working. She is quick and methodical. "Like that, yes."

"How?" It isn't like it could have floated here faster than Macon's boat. It isn't like it could float anyway.

Ellie shrugs. "How did you lose it?"

"It fell out in the water... No, something took it."

"So 'something' brought it here. You need to be careful in the water."

"What do you mean by that?"

"You don't know the ways. You could get lost." She is already done with the next pelt and adds it to the stack.

Looking at the pile, I think of something else. "What do you do that's different?"

"Do differently? With what?"

"I mean the skins. Jane said that you have a special process."

"It is just how I treat them."

"The stuff you soak them in?"

"No, not only the solution but how I handle them."

"What do you mean?"

"Camline, they are different because I am different. Everything I do is different because I cannot help it." She hands me the seashells. "Finish off with these."

I take the shells and brush them once or twice over the skin. "So because you are not—from here—you do this differently."

"Yes," Ellie says shortly and then steps behind me. She puts her hands over mine and moves them like a puppet to show me what she wants me to do to the skin. "Yes, Camline, that's what it is. I cannot help but be who I am, and it gets into everything I do." With her moving my hands, we finish the pelt in front of me. She untacks it and gathers the others. "We'll soak these again."

I follow her. "Last night your eyes... they were strange."

"The salt water makes them shine, come to life. Even the dullest land dweller can see a glimpse of our true heritage with salt in our eyes."

"The salt water did that? Your eyes always look like that in seawater?"

"And yours, Camline."

I roll my eyes and scoff. I think I would have noticed if I suddenly had crazy eyes besides... "No, I'd never even seen the ocean before I came here."

"Any salt water. Seawater has the most effect, but any salt could reveal you."

The penny drops. I see my mother's face in my mind's eye, feel her fingertips tracing around my eyes, singing softly, telling me to, "Hush, hush, don't weep..." Maybe it was Mom more than Dad who didn't want to see me cry.

"How come Mom didn't tell me any of this? Why didn't you tell me when I got here?"

"Would you have believed if I had not shown you? You would not come to the water. How could you see?"

"If I had known…"

"Your mother should have told you."

I agree, but I don't want to fight about this. "You—" I say, then pause before going on. "…aren't human. This is why everyone is scared of you? But how do they know what you are?"

"People are always afraid of what they cannot define and do not understand," she says, then continues. "You would do well not to discuss it, Camline. Most people may have a feeling that we are different. Only a few guess at the truth. Knowledge can be dangerous for us, for them. And to truly see us can have consequences."

Then a horrible thought comes to me. Last night after I fell in the water, a million years ago. "And does that… seeing our eyes like that… have an effect on people?" I ask, afraid of what she'll say.

"Yes."

"What exactly?"

"It depends on the person." She regards me closely. "To see into the real eyes of one of us can mesmerize. Enchant. Repel. Or drive to distraction."

Macon's interest takes on a new meaning. The remembrance of warmth dissipates, vanishes just like it never was.

Chapter 18

My phone is ringing, and it takes me several seconds to figure out what the noise is. I must have fallen asleep when I came back to Windemere after working with Ellie, too tired to think. I tried calling Mom, but she was sleeping. I'm still fumbling for my phone when it stops ringing. It's a Maine area code, but I don't recognize the number. I'm checking the recent calls when it starts ringing again, and I answer.

"Hey Cam!" Blue nearly shouts. "Wait, are you still sleeping?"

"No, I'm here. How are you?"

"Oh, I slept for ages and then ate All The Foods." I hear the capitalization her voice. "You should have stayed."

After everything I learned, I almost wish I had. I was halfway to normal hanging out with her. I say instead, "Yeah, sorry, I just had to get back."

"Did anything happen?"

"What do you mean?" I ask quickly, afraid she can hear something in my voice.

"You left with Macon and Bridgette. Now are they on or

off again? I am guessing off with the way he was mooning over you last night."

"Don't say that!"

"Calm down. I'm just teasing."

"Right." I try to force a laugh and change the subject. "You sound not-hungover."

"My extreme powers of regeneration. And you didn't see me earlier. My mom woke me at an ungodly hour because Macon called."

"He did?"

"Yeah, he wanted your number. Is that all right that I gave it to him? Did he call you at Ridiculous Hour?"

"No. I mean, yes, it's fine and he called, but I was up."

"Uh huh, like you were just now?"

"Ha. I was working with Ellie on those skins. He just wanted to make sure everything was okay."

"That Ellie hadn't skinned you too?"

"Blue!"

"I'm kidding! Sheesh. But really, was she mad?"

"Not so bad. Didn't your mom notice anything wrong with you when she woke you up?"

"Nah. I'm a notoriously heavy sleeper. Plus, my parents are pretty relaxed most of the time. The joy of being a late baby. Glad Ellie wasn't mad. You'll have to come stay for real some time."

"Yeah." Talking to Blue makes me feel better. It's just a regular conversation. No one is talking about mesmerizing people or being from another world or anything.

After we hang up, I call Mom, hoping she'll be awake now. Maria is back on, and she tells me again that Mom's temperature is normal and that I shouldn't worry. When she puts the phone up to Mom's ear, I say, "Hi Mom, I'm glad you're feeling better. I really miss you." I pause and then continue in a rush, "And I really, really wish you could talk to me right now. Ellie has been telling me things. I don't know what to think of it. I don't know what to say. It all sounds really crazy. I have so many questions. Why didn't you ever tell me any of this? I mean, what exactly did Dad know? Why didn't we ever visit the island? Why did you and Ellie fight? Am I going to…" I break off because I realize that Maria is calling my name.

"Cam, Cam. Take a breath. I don't know what you are saying, but I think you are upsetting your mom. What's wrong?"

"Nothing. I'm sorry. Just tell her I love her. I have to go."

I'M restless and can't settle so I grab my phone and head out. I don't know where I am going; I just walk in the opposite direction to Ellie's. I didn't mean to upset Mom. I don't understand how she could keep this secret. It's crazy. Hardy trees spike through the rough terrain. What does Dad know? There's no clear path I'm following—not on this walk and not in my head. Ellie is not… human. *I'm…* No, I can't even go there. When the ground starts to slope, I pass a trail that looks like it leads to the east side of the island toward Macon's. I stop for a moment, staring down the path. I can't go there either.

Windemere looks tiny this far away. The sun winks on one of the windows. This must be where they sometimes walk with Beau. I keep heading south until the trees give way to black rocks, and then the ground starts to climb again. The surf gets louder, but I can't see the ocean until I come to a sudden, sharp drop.

Directly below me, the water is dark and deep and

agitated. Foamy waves hit, shred apart on the rocks and then are sucked back into the sea only to crest and break again. I watch the violence of it, and my breath quickens. I can't let go of my fear. Habits are hard to break.

But I still need to get closer. I want to know if I can really see something—or someone—out there. Make sure this isn't an elaborate trick. Or that I'm not losing my mind.

Further off to my right, there is a break in the rocks, and the land tapers off toward the water. I make my way across toward the break and then start to climb down. Carefully placing my feet and hanging on to the rocks for balance, I pick my path, getting closer to the ocean. My jaw aches from clenching it, but I finally make it to where tiny tide pools have formed. From here, the waves break further out but fingers of water reach toward me each time the waves hit. I find a flat place where I can sit. I can feel the spray from here. The ocean goes on for miles. My mouth goes dry. I don't see anything unusual in the sea. No faces appear; I hear no singing. I shift until I can reach my hand down into a shallow indentation below me, worn smooth by the sea. As the next waves comes in, it fills with water that closes coldly over my hand and wets my sleeve. I brush my fingers over my eyes and look again.

It's like a filter drops over the scene. The sea is no longer dark blue with white crests. It has complexity and subtleties within its mass like I've never seen before. Emerald and jade green swirl with royal and sky blue around bone white waves and steel grey depths. My own hands have a slight pearlescent sheen like they had last night, and the rocks are a deeper black. I look out across the ocean searching for flashes in the water, for faces. Ellie said they were always there, but I only see water. I dip my hand again and press it against my eyes.

"Hello?" I call out, "Can you hear me?" I feel foolish.

Then I see a metallic flash further away. I scoot closer. A wave builds, and in it I see a face like a dark pearl surrounded by silver. Stormy eyes and sharp smile, looking at me as the wave comes in. I laugh in delight, and it comes out like music, startling me. The wave breaks, and I lose sight of the face as the sea pulls back. "Oh no, where'd you go?" I say aloud, disappointed.

A shy face pokes around the furthest rock. She looks to be about twelve or maybe thirteen years old. Her hair is chrome silver. When she sees me, she disappears behind the rock.

"Hi," I say. She peeks one eye around the rock. A wave breaks over her, but she doesn't seem to mind.

"I won't hurt you." I say before she disappears again.

She laughs like I have just told a joke, her sharp white teeth flashing. I sit back a little as she comes fully around the rock.

"I will not hurt you," she says. The words seem particularly placed, her accent odd. She looks at me curiously.

"Um, my name is Cam."

"Why are you there?" Another wave breaks over her head.

"I am just, well, I wanted to see one of you. Again, I mean."

"See one of who? Why are you up there and wearing those funny clothes? You look ridiculous." She laughs and it's like glass tinkling.

I glance down at my outfit. I look fine. I look normal. She's the one wearing something odd. Her dress or shirt covers her shoulders and arms and glistens like mica. The sunlight refracts off of it, casting colors over the rocks.

Stones clatter behind me, and I turn around to see Jane, all sunny hair and smiles.

I look back at the ocean, but the girl has disappeared. I dip my hand and splash water on my face and search the sea.

"Cam? What are you doing?" Jane asks me, sounding concerned.

I glance back at her, frustrated because she's scared the girl away.

"Whoa. Are you okay?" Jane has a slight sunburn across her nose, and her hair shines in the sunlight.

"I'm fine," I mumble.

"Are you sure you're all right? You look…" She steps closer.

"I'm fine," I say clearly. "Just drop it."

Jane smiles. "Okay, great." As if she had never been worried.

I blink and feel the salt water leave my eyes. Jane acts like everything is completely fine. Not at all like I just sea voodooed her or anything.

"Anyway, I did call out, but you didn't hear me. What are you doing down here?"

"I thought I saw something. When did you get back?"

"This morning. I was just out walking with Beau. Gotta stretch the legs. I'm glad I ran into you. I was looking through some old newspaper articles and found your grandfather."

"You did? What were you looking for?"

"Something completely different, actually. I did take a picture of it." She thumbs through pictures on her phone until she comes to a snap of a grainy picture of a newspaper article. The caption reads: *TOWN REJOICES*.

"What is this?" I ask, taking her phone from her. There is a picture of my grandfather, Oscar Alcott. I read on.

TOWN REJOICES: Local Man Returns Alive

Oscar Alcott, son of William and Sarah Alcott of Williams Point, returned safely following the surprise storm of last week. The young man seemed unhurt but confused. "Young Mr. Alcott is understandably shaken up after his ordeal. He simply requires rest," said Dr. Honeycutt, family physician. The spring storm ravaged the southern coast causing much damage, but with Mr. Alcott's fortunate return, no casualties.

"He was missing."

"Yeah, I guess for a few days. This article didn't really go into it much, but I found this too." She takes her phone back and flips to another picture. It's a handwritten page. "Here. This is the Coast Guard report. I found this first, and I got curious." She hands the phone back to me.

Incident Report: M. E. Jones

Vessel spotted off the coast of Osprey Island identified belonging to that of missing man: Oscar Alcott of Williams Point. Vessel appeared undamaged, but Mr. Alcott expressed shock when informed he had been missing for three days. He was agitated and addled and had to be restrained after trying to jump overboard. Vessel was towed into Williams Point harbor and family was notified.

"That's wild," I say, at a loss for anything more clever.

"I know, right? So, I think 'Osprey Island' was what this was called before people started calling it Shell. I think that was after your grandparents moved here."

"Where did you find these?"

"I was at the library in Portland. Isn't that crazy? I just recognized the name and then found the newspaper."

"Will you email those to me?"

"Sure. We better head up. The tide is coming in."

Jane is right. The little pool from earlier is much fuller. I search the waves one last time but don't see the girl or any other faces. My hands shake as I climb.

Chapter 19

As soon as I'm back at the house, I call my cell provider. Jane emailed the pictures before she left. Unless I want to wait until I'm on the mainland again to look at them, I'm going to have to get data on my phone. At least I can find out how much more it would cost.

The chipper guy takes my info and even though it's the whole reason I am calling, he seems surprised that I don't already have a data plan. They are running a special, and it'll only cost about ten bucks a month to get it started. Ignoring the worry that springs up about the money, I go for it. I can always cancel it later. The guy tells me that it should activate shortly.

I get off the phone and try Google right away. The phone says I have no connection. I pace around for a few minutes and try again, and this time the multicolored logo comes up. I check my email first and download the pictures from Jane.

Then I do a search for Oscar Alcott in quotes. A few things come up, but I am pretty sure he never had a Facebook page. I try again, adding Maine. Not much more. I try adding Williams Point. I get the Williams Point Gazette archive site but can't search with names. I start a new search and take out Oscar's name and just do Alcott and Williams Point. I find a land sale list. Blue had said that they had owned a lot of property, so maybe there's something there. I find a couple of sales from years ago with a William Alcott but no mention of Oscar.

Then I find something purely by accident. It's for a town meeting:

Meeting unfinished after altercation between Wm. Alcott and son. To be rescheduled.

The date, May 21st, is just a few weeks after the newspaper article Jane showed me. I go to the Gazette archive site again and search May 8th, and there is the exact article that Jane had. I scroll back a few days and see the forecast of the storm and then forward to see a picture of the marina the day after. I go to the 21st, but the town meeting isn't mentioned. I scroll through the online paper for a few minutes and am about to close it, until I see the announcements pages.

Marriages: Oscar W. Alcott (Williams Point) and Ellianna Shell.

They were married the same day that Oscar fought with his dad at the town meeting. The fight had to have been about Ellie, I'm sure. There were only two weeks between Oscar being rescued and him getting married. I wonder what his parents thought.

There are a few other announcements, and in each one they give the person's town. It says that Nicollette Leshane is from Brookland Cove, as are Russell Walker and Cole Tyler. Marie Burge and Jean Wheeler are from Williams Point like Oscar. Ellie is the only one without a home town. I guess they couldn't very well put "Alternate Plane, via Ocean."

It's interesting to read this in print, corroborating what Ellie told me. I wonder if she's seen these. I take screenshots of them both. I find the picture of me that Mom had written on and take that with me as I head back to the cottage.

I FIND her down by the tide pools, standing on a rock looking out to sea. As I get closer, she disappears from view.

"Ellie!" I call out. I can't see where she's gone. I'm making my slow way toward where I saw her last when she reappears over the lip of the pool. Her hair hangs loose around her shoulders and down her back. She climbs out, and I can see that her legs are wet. She stands and watches me come to her. She has an urchin in one hand and a knife in the other. She cuts the shell like she had shown me and flicks a segment of meat into her mouth.

"Camline, are you hungry?" She spears a segment and holds it out to me on the knife.

I shake my head. "I'm okay."

She shrugs and continues to eat. Her feet are bare, but she doesn't seem to feel the rocks below her.

"I found a picture of Oscar."

"In the album?"

"No, in an old newspaper. I have it on my phone. Do you want to see?"

She nods and looks intently at the newspaper picture. She touches his face on the glass. "So young."

"Is this after he met you? After he was missing?"

"He was not missing; he was with me."

She finishes her urchin and throws the shell into the pool. We start back to the cottage.

"He came to this island. He had been here before; I had seen him. But this time, I had to speak to him. This is where we met. He begged me to go home with him. I said no. The storm came, and when it had blown out, they came and took him away. It was for the best, I thought, but after he had gone I couldn't bear it. Something changed in me, in that brief time. My world seemed too small; I was too restless. I could not settle. When he came to me again, I could not resist, and I returned with him."

"And you got married?"

"Yes."

"I also found this." I show her the screenshot of the town meeting.

She looks at it for a few seconds without saying anything.

"Was it about you? The fight, I mean."

"Yes, they fought over me. It wasn't until your mother wanted to run off with someone that I understood how difficult it must have been for his father."

"What happened?" I ask.

"Oscar told his father we were to marry. Your great-grandfather, William, was suspicious of me. No one knew me; I had no family near, no past. He said I had 'dropped from the sky.'" She laughs at this.

"It was only a few weeks since you'd met?"

"I told you. I had seen Oscar before then, but he did not see me. But, yes, it was so quick. I gave up everything to come here—my sisters, my home, certain freedoms. It was worth it, to be with him, to have your mother. Your grandfather had to give up much as well."

"Because his family didn't accept you?"

"His father cut us off. It meant nothing to me, but it hurt your grandfather. They did not reconcile before William died. It was only us. Oscar was the only son and the last alive in his family. We didn't need much and had so little—some savings and the boat. We had already moved to this island."

"My friend said he built Windemere?"

"Yes, he liked to make things from wood. He liked to carve things."

"Like little boxes?"

Ellie smiles. "There is one in the house. I left it for you."

"It had a snail shell in it."

"I put it there. Something from the sea in something from the land. Like you." We're back at the cottage.

"I went down to the ocean today on the south side of the island," I say, and Ellie stops to stare at me.

"You went into the water?"

"No!" I shudder. "But I saw someone. A girl."

"In the waves?"

"She came to the rocks to talk to me."

"Did she try to harm you?" Her eyes narrow.

"No."

"What did she talk of? Did she ask for your jewelry? Did she want you to go with her?"

"What? No, it wasn't a long conversation. She just made fun of my clothes and asked me what I was doing."

"Your clothes." She seems puzzled, and then her face clears. "She recognized you?"

"What do you mean?"

"She saw you as a sister."

"I'm not sure, we didn't talk long. Jane scared her off."

"Jane saw her?" She seems to find this hard to believe.

"I don't think so. But something strange happened with Jane. I think I maybe made Jane do something. Is that even possible?"

"What happened?"

"Well, I was annoyed that she had scared off the girl, but Jane was just being nice and asking me if anything was wrong. I told her not to worry about it. And she stopped. Immediately. It was like she changed in an instant."

"Was salt in your eyes?"

"I guess so. I was using it to 'see' the ocean. But it's happened to me before. Recently."

Ellie doesn't say anything, just studies me like she's waiting for me to go on.

"I told someone, a guy, to leave me alone and he did."

"Not one of Rob's boys?"

"No, a different person. When I was at that party." I wonder if she's still mad at me about that. So much has happened since then.

"What happened." It sounds like a statement to me, and I hesitate. I can't read her tone.

"He wanted to talk to me, I guess. He kept following me around and wouldn't leave me alone. But then, he did."

"Because you commanded him?"

I laugh. It sounds so ridiculous out loud. "Sort of. But I didn't have any salt in my eyes. I'd need to, to make anything happen, right?"

"Usually. You were inside a house?"

"Outside. In Brookland Cove."

"Perhaps that was near enough to the water for there to be salt in the air. Camline, this is why you must be careful. You do not want to have unintended consequences." She reaches out and touches me between my brows.

Unintended consequences. The phrase lands hard in me, touching on a memory and making my next question even more difficult to ask. "Wait. Is it possible, can we affect other things… even if it's not a command? Like a wish?"

She gives me a measuring look and finally says, "It is possible. Are you talking about something specific?"

"No. Just curious," I mumble. Old guilt reveals itself in new light and solidifies, weighing on me even heavier than before. All my fault. Maybe a lack of positivity wasn't even the issue with Mom. I can't. I lock away the thought, shove it down.

Because another thought is rising, taking center stage. Unintended consequences. Macon's face as he looked at me, as he told me he wanted me. There was definitely seawater involved there.

What did I do to him?

Chapter 20

I'm not much for talking after that conversation, and Ellie must sense it because she tells me she doesn't need my help today. She sends me off with stew, which I can barely stop myself from drinking on the way back to Windemere. As I open the door, I do sneak one sip and lick my lips. I set the stew down and touch my fingertips to my mouth. My lips are soft and supple, and I can't remember when I last put on lip balm. I haven't even opened the new one I bought the other day.

A quick look in the mirror tells me that I don't look any different besides my hair growing too fast and my suddenly not-dry lips. My eyes are the same mixture of blue and green and look so much like my Mom's that missing her cuts right through me.

I call the facility again, but Mom is sleeping. There's been a shift change and Lupe isn't ever as chatty as Maria. But she lets me know that Mom's temperature is completely normal, and all is fine. That's one thing that I don't have to think about now.

Other worries crowd my mind, competing for attention. I

check the time. Macon said he'd be back in the afternoon so he should be home now. That's one thing I can make right. That I should make right. I mean, if I did *do* something. I can just back off and then he'll be free. Right? I have no idea.

I finish my stew first and agonize over what to say. It would be easier if I didn't still remember what it felt like to kiss him. I choose his number off of my recent calls. This morning feels like a long time ago. Last night, like a dream. The phone rings so many times that I am about to hang up when he answers in a rush.

"Hey." I can hear the smile in his voice.

"Hi." I want to smile too.

"So. Miss Ellie was okay?" His voice is pitched low, like he doesn't want anyone else to hear.

"Yeah, everything's okay. But I wanted to talk to you…" I trail off.

"Hang on." I hear voices in the background which go muffled after a door bangs. He must have gone outside. "What is it?"

"Last night. I think I might have made a mistake."

"What do you mean? At the party? Theo was out of line."

"No. I know that. I mean after."

"Oh." He sighs. "With me."

"I just… I mean, I don't know what got into me. It's funny, really. I shouldn't have, well, I don't really…" I am babbling, and I cannot even stop it.

"Cam, just tell me what you want to say." He doesn't sound mad, just a little exasperated.

"I think I just need to focus on settling in here without making waves." The pun is not lost on me and I stifle a sudden, crazy laugh.

He laughs a little too. "Might be too late for that."

"I don't want that!" I say too quickly, too loudly. I get

control over myself before continuing. "I just don't want to cause any trouble."

"Trouble? With who?"

"Um. Bridgette? Your mom?" I'm flailing.

"Cam, neither of those people have anything to do with us. Whatever happens."

"But—"

"You don't like me."

"I like you, I do." This is the whole problem.

"But not like that?"

"Well—" I am a crappy liar. "It's just that—"

I hear the door again, and someone call his name. He shouts back, "Be right there!" Then back to me, "Hey, I have to go. Can we talk tomorrow?"

I agree and hang up. I've never broken up with anyone before. I guess I still haven't. Is there really anything to break up here? Seriously, it was only one kiss. Or two. Three? Warmth uncurls like a lazy cat inside my chest and stretches to my fingertips. It did feel nice on the boat. Maybe I don't have to do any more than this.

THE NEXT DAY, as I empty my pockets, I find the photo of me on the porch, the one that Mom wrote on. I forgot to ask Ellie about it. I slide it back in my pocket. I pour some salted nuts into a bowl, and I get online on my phone.

I search "sirens" and get a lot of "mermaid" hits although I read that they are different creatures. Greek mythology describes sirens as half woman, half bird and they drowned in the end. Mermaids are everywhere. Some sing, some are evil, some are good, most are really pretty, and some are just pretty scary, but they all have one thing in common: a tail. Ellie was very particular about not having that. They all live in water, too. At least at one point—some start off there, longing for land, and others long to return.

I look further. Selkies are seal-women who shed their own skin to walk on land. Ellie does have a way with skins, but she's not a seal. Naiads are nymphs that live in fresh water. So do melusines, but they sometimes have wings and often not one, but two, tails. Lorelei is a rock on the Rhine river named for either a woman who bewitched sailors to their death or a brokenhearted woman who fell to her death because she thought she saw her love in the river. Cheerful. I don't know what I'm expecting, but there's nothing here that describes Ellie. Maybe if you took little parts of each story, there's something. There's nothing about another realm.

I get dressed and head down to see her. She's not in the cottage. I don't see her down toward the ocean, either. I walk around the cottage to the shed and hear her humming. She's over the tubs, dipping her fingers in one and then another. She's not humming, really, but singing very softly. I can't make out words, but she reminds me of Mom talking to the house plants we occasionally had. Her voice is beautiful, and my music soul rises to hear it. I don't fall into the song though. I am outside of it. Listening and appreciating but not drawn in. Ellie spreads her hands wide across the tubs, finishes her song and bows her head for a split second before she meets my eyes. Her mouth quirks into an almost smile.

"What were you doing?" I ask.

"Treating the hides."

"By singing?"

"Yes. You heard the song."

"Yeah." Duh. I am standing right here, but that tells me nothing.

Ellie's eyes narrow like I said it out loud, and I almost feel embarrassed.

"It is good for you to hear the songs and remember them."

"I don't know about that, but it was really pretty. What does the singing do?"

"It wakes," she says simply and walks past me.

I hurry after her. "Ellie, I found pictures that Mom sent you. Pictures of me."

"Yes?"

"I didn't know that she was sending them."

"You are of me too, Camline. Your mother wanted to show me how you grew." Before I say anything, she goes on, "Pictures are a wonder. Don't you think so? It preserves a moment in an instant. You can never recreate that time, but it is there for always."

"I guess so. I never really thought of it like that. I found this one." I show her the picture from my pocket. She takes it, flips it over, then hands it back to me and stalks off inside the cottage, banging the door.

I follow her inside. She's at the stove stirring, the spoon clunking against the side of the pot.

"Ellie?"

She bangs the spoon down on the counter. "I did not *win*."

"What does she mean by that?"

Ellie presses the palms of her hands into her eyes and sighs. "I wanted her to come back and bring you. Not send you and then stay there with no one."

Ellie looks at me with eyes that are multifaceted, the color changing. Tears—I realize—she has tears standing in her eyes. "Ellie? Are you okay?"

"Don't worry," she says.

And suddenly, I'm not worried at all. About anything. Everything is going to be fine. Nothing's wrong. It's not wrong that Ellie's hands are balled in fists or that her face is contorted, veins standing out at her neck. Wait. Ellie never looks like that.

"Stop that!"

Ellie looks at me, surprised, and then releases her hands with a breath. "I did not mean to get so upset."

"That was weird." So, this is what it feels like to be on the receiving end of the whole "salt in the eyes" thing.

"You are very strong, Camline."

"Evidently not," I mutter, and she laughs out loud. It sounds like bells.

"You have a lot of your father's influence in you, but you have more of your mother and me. You knew what was happening, and you were able to fight it. You did the same with my song when we were working."

I feel a flash of anger. "So, what were you trying to do to me? Why do you keep trying to make me do something?"

"I do not." She says it evenly. "I am who I am. Just like you are. You cannot fight it because it's inside you, who you are."

I think of Macon again. My anger fizzles. "Ellie, could I have done that to someone without meaning to?"

"Possibly."

"If I did do something to someone, how can I stop it?"

"Something you meant to do?"

"No!" I burst out. "I mean, I don't think so." I try to qual- ify. "I'm not sure." Maybe my stupid crush on Macon made me unconsciously *do* something.

And even worse, I'm afraid I have done it before.

In a box I dare not open, a memory niggles at me, pulling my attention. If I could have done something without even realizing it, without intention, then what could I have done with conscious thought? It's too horrible; I slam the box shut again, push the memory as far down inside as it can go.

Ellie is still talking. "If it is something that you want to undo, just follow the same route. Command it be not. I cannot believe your mother told you nothing."

"Well, she didn't. And she can't now," I snap. My chest tightens and my throat starts to close. I breathe deeply and try to get myself under control. Maybe if I could cry, it wouldn't hurt so much. Frustration takes over and I say in a rush, "I don't want this! I just want a normal life."

"That is one thing you cannot have, Camline."

Chapter 21

As I leave Ellie's, my phone chirps. It's Macon.

Can u meet?

OK, I text back. I think for a second and then type: *I'll come over.* I see the three dots that show that he's writing.

OK c u

The screen goes dark, and I see my reflection in the glass. No time to change.

Well, at least not my clothes.

I hurry back to Windemere and straight to the kitchen, searching through the cabinets until I find a small empty glass bottle with a top. I pause and then dig through my bag for a pocket mirror. I throw on my jacket and run south until I meet the cliff and then find the break in the rocks where I can make my way to the ocean.

My mouth is dry, and my heart is thudding in my chest. I know it's not just from running, and I steel myself to climb down. I am so careful as I make my way across the wet rocks to where the waves splash, but my sneaker slips off a slick rock and I fall, catching myself but landing hard on my left hand. The healed cut on my palm splits back open. It hurts, but I ignore it and continue down to the surf.

After I fill the little bottle and close the top, I set it to the side and pull out the mirror. Leaning back down, I cup some of the water in my hands and hiss as the salt hits the wound. I shake my hand until it stops stinging. Then, using only my right hand, I try again. The water is cold. I take a deep breath and splash it directly into my face. Salt bites for only a second, and I open my eyes. The rocks and ocean are more vivid like before, but I don't see anything—anyone—in the sea. Doesn't matter because right now I'm more interested in what I'll find in the mirror.

Beads of water hang from my lashes, which are shot through with just a glimmer of metallic sheen. My skin shines like I've overdone it with the highlight powder. But my eyes. They are insane. I can't land on a specific color—blue, indigo, green, grey—chasing and swirling like the wind with thunderheads in a storm. I stare until they settle, until they are just the blue green I know. Ellie said that the salt would make me see "true," and that people could see some of what we are. I don't know if what I'm seeing is the salt affecting my eyes or if I'm seeing what it does to them. I wonder what Macon saw.

I climb back up, favoring my left hand, and then run until I finally make it to the woods path. I slip into the coolness of the trees, mind buzzing with what I need to do. It's strange to me to think I have to worry about making an impact. Since Mom made me promise to go to Ellie's if or when she got too sick, I feel like all of my decisions have been made for me. At least the really big ones. It didn't matter what I thought about moving 2,000 miles away from Mom. Where I can't be there to make sure she's okay. Or what I thought about living on a flipping island.

I pat my pocket that holds the little bottle of seawater. I am going to be sure. I have to make this right with Macon. I may not be able to make every decision for myself at the moment, but I won't take away anyone else's ability to, either. I'm so deep in thought, and hurrying to make up for the time I've lost by going to the ocean, that I don't see Macon until he calls my name.

"Cam!"

I stop short. He is down the path in front of me. He waves and trots toward me closing the gap.

"I was checking to see if you got lost," he says with a half-smile.

"I had to do something first. Sorry."

"I'm just joking. I was hoping to catch you here. I want to show you something." He nods his head to the right. "Come with me."

I allow myself to be led away from the path. I catch a glimpse of emerald and smile as we break through the trees. "The clearing!" I say it too loudly, for here it is church quiet. "I love this," I say in a hushed tone this time.

"You know about the meadow?" he asks, matching my pitch.

"I found it the first time I came over to your side of the island. It's really peaceful here."

"Yeah."

We walk further in, and I look to the sky to find the sun. It glows dully from behind a large, dark cloud.

"It's so quiet," I whisper.

"That's why I like it. It feels like we're somewhere else. It feels like home."

"Oh yeah?" It's a great respite, but it doesn't feel like home to me. But then, I don't know what does feel like home. Home was always wherever my parents were. Now that we're all in different corners of the earth, where should that be? I guess I have to make my own home. I just don't know how.

"Are you okay?" he asks me.

"Yeah, fine."

"Sure?"

"All good." I change the subject. "This place is beautiful."

"I come here sometimes to think. I thought you'd like it."

"I do." We walk to the center of the clearing and sit. I feel the bottle of seawater hang heavy in my pocket.

"Where's your dad?" Macon asks suddenly.

"Uh, I don't actually know. He's usually not allowed to give a lot of details."

"So that's why you don't live with him, then." He says it smiling.

"Well, it does make it a bit difficult." I mean to sound funny, but it comes out sour.

"You two aren't close?"

"Not really. We used to be, I guess. We used to go on camping trips. It was fun."

"That's cool. Where'd you go?"

"We went out into the desert usually, but sometimes we'd go to the woods. He knew—I suppose still does know—all these survival tricks. Like he could shoot a bow and arrow, knew how to find water, and which plants were edible. Not like we really had to use them, though. We always had tents and brought food with us, so we didn't have to hunt or anything."

"I've stayed out here a few times."

"Really? On your own?"

"Sure. Or with Jack. Sometimes, I don't even use a tent. I just feel good here. Like the trees are guarding me."

"Huh." I hadn't thought of it before but his hazel eyes are like a tree canopy, bark brown and leaf green mixed.

"So, if you didn't hunt, did you take, like, freeze-dried meals?" he asks.

"Yeah, or even regular food that we would cook out there. Potatoes wrapped in foil in the fire, that kind of thing. And Dad was always so chilled out. He never got mad at me there."

"Mad at you?"

"Yeah." I see his expression and go on. "Wait, he wasn't, like, angry all the time. Just sometimes. Maybe he was frustrated or something. And he and my mom fought."

"What was he frustrated about?"

"I don't know. Me? Mom?"

"Was this when your mom got sick?"

"I don't know, around that time. Yes. At the start of it. She wasn't even too bad. He didn't like to see her sick." Why did I bring this up? I don't want to talk about my dad. Or camping. I don't want to think about what I did on that last camping trip. What that meant for Mom.

"So, your mom now lives in a care home."

"Yeah. And I hate it. I hate that she's there, and I'm not there to help."

"What could you do for her?" I look at him sharply and he goes on, "That didn't come out right. I mean, what could change by you being there?"

There's the crux of it. "Nothing. There's nothing I can really do. Just be there so she knows she's not alone. So she knows that I would do anything I could to help her. To say I'm sorry."

"Sorry? For what?"

Crap. I didn't mean to say that out loud.

"It's not your fault she got sick."

"Yeah. I don't know." Guilt nudges me, flattening my breath. The memory in the box rattles.

"Cam." He puts a hand on my shoulder. "Of course it isn't."

I can't look at him. "Macon. You don't know everything." I cover my face.

"Of all the things I do know, though, I am absolutely certain that you didn't make your mom sick."

"I know. But—" The word hangs in the air. But what if I did? I don't go on. I didn't know then that I had some sort of powers. It's unbelievable. I laugh into my hands.

"Hey, are you crying?"

I drop my hands and look at him with dry eyes. "No, I'm definitely not."

"Of course. No crying."

He hugs me then, and I feel equally safe and stupid. This wasn't supposed to be how this conversation went today. I pull away, and he leans back.

"All I can say…" He looks troubled. Then he half smiles and states with absolute certainty, "That sounds like it sucks."

"It does." We both laugh then. It releases a knot in my chest and makes me feel the tiniest bit better. Macon is different from anyone else I've ever known. Like with what he just did. He can change the whole conversation with just a funny comment. He has a great laugh. I love it when he really smiles, full teeth and crinkly eyes. It's so honest and happy.

He reaches for my hand. I let him. "Hey, what did you do?"

He takes my hand in both of his and spreads it out, lightly touching where I reopened the cut. Only it isn't open. There is dried blood, but the cut has nearly closed again. Macon traces around it and the lines of my palm. My breath stutters, but then my head finally catches up and I pull my hand away.

"Sorry," he says. It's almost like a question. "This isn't what you wanted to talk about."

"No." I feel terrible, but I might as well get on with it. "It wasn't." He's watching me, waiting. "I think you're great…"

"I think you're great." He moves toward me again, but I rock back.

"Wait." I fix my eyes on the top button of his shirt. "You're a great guy, but I have to figure my life out here."

"What does that mean?"

I am a terrible liar, so I tell him something true. "I don't want any entanglements here."

"What? I don't get it. I like you, Cam. I thought you liked me too."

It's time. I have to do it, and I have to make it stick. I turn slightly away and take off the top the bottle without him seeing. I dip my fingers into the water, and gently press them to my eyes. I feel the nip of the salt and turn back to him, my eyes downcast.

"It's like I said on the phone. I do like you."

"But?"

"You're a great friend, and I don't want to mess that up."

"What would get messed up?"

"You don't have to like me, Macon," I say quietly.

"What are you talking about? I just said that I like you." He sounds like he's getting annoyed.

Just do it, I tell myself.

I finally look at him.

"We're just friends. Okay?" I lay out each word clearly, my gaze fastened on his. He doesn't say anything for a couple of seconds, but his eyes don't leave mine. I'm afraid to blink. His skin is flushed, and he has a slight glow, but his straight black brows are pulled low over his eyes.

He nods slowly. "Okay. I get it." He shifts a little away from me and raises his palms as if in surrender.

"Great. Okay. Cool."

"Friends." He holds out a hand to shake.

"Friends," I say. His hand is warm and rough in mine. He smiles, but it doesn't quite reach his eyes.

I did it. I broke whatever it was that made him like me. I freed him. I should feel great.

Chapter 22

I call Mom when I get back to the house. I want to tell her what happened and have so many questions for her, but I swallow everything and keep my tone light. I hear her breathe in response, before Suzanna takes the phone back.

"Okay, Cam, it's lunch time, so we'll have to hang up," she says to me. "How's life for you? Make any new friends?"

"Sure have," I say brightly, and say goodbye.

I call Blue after. She asks me if I want to hang out the next day.

"I'll check if anyone is heading that way," I say.

"I have the day off. I'll come to you."

"You don't mind coming out here?"

"Nah, we'll have a picnic on the beach or something. Maybe Jane's around. And Jack and Macon could come."

"I don't know if that's a good idea."

"Why? Anything going on with you and a certain Stone?"

"Nope." We're friends. We could hang out as friends. "I think they're out on the boats."

"Well, whatever. We'll see."

BLUE SHOWS up with Diego and Luke the next day. I haven't seen any of them since the party. She'd texted me her ETA, and I had gotten up early to let Ellie know that she was coming to the island. From Ellie's porch, I can see that Blue's hair is now insect green. The boys are laughing and fooling around as they come up the path. I walk down to meet them.

"I brought strays," Blue says, handing a cooler to Diego.

"Okay. Are you sure you guys are allowed here?" I half joke.

"S'all good," says Luke, as he puts a finger to his lips in a "shhh" motion, and Diego swings the cooler as if to hit him. Luke yelps and jumps back.

"They are incorrigible. The whole way here was like this."

The guys quiet down as we get closer to Ellie's. She comes outside as we are passing her door.

"Lucas. Diego. And Bluebell." She nods to each.

"Hello, Miss Ellie," says Blue and the guys murmur hellos as well.

"Where will you go, Camline?" Ellie asks me.

"We're having a picnic, I think."

"Have fun. And have care," she says to me.

"I will," I say, and I mean it. We head up the path.

I turn to Blue. "Bluebell, huh?"

She makes a sour face. "Yeah, perfect name for a cow."

"I like the hair."

"Thanks. It was time for a change. You're wearing the earrings."

I touch my fingers to the pearls and feel the delicious jolt they always give me. "Yes. I love them. Thanks again."

"No prob. They look so good on you."

Everyone piles into Windemere.

"Wow," says Luke, "you really are all on your own."

"I've never been inside here before," says Diego.

"None of us has, genius," Blue says with a sassy smile.

Diego's face drops and he says with mock seriousness, "I think your hair is going to your head."

I show them around, and they look at everything wide-eyed. Luke gets his phone out and starts texting, and Diego is looking at the books in the living room while Blue and I head to my room.

She kicks my mostly full duffel bag. "You could stay awhile, you know."

I shove it under my bed with my foot. "I know. I am. I'm gonna unpack soon." I grab a hoodie.

"This was your Mom's room?" she asks, heading across the hall. I nod and she looks around. "Nice."

Then Blue and I raid my cupboards. She finds the cookies that Jane made me buy and adds them to her bag. I get a packet of salted peanuts too.

"He says to meet them off the 'south path.' Does that make sense?" Luke asks me.

"Who?"

"The others," says Blue. "The Stones and whoever else they round up."

"Macon says there's a great area off the path between here and their side," Luke says.

"I know where the path is, but I haven't walked it yet."

"We'll just go there and then head east," says Diego. "I might know what he's talking about."

The weather today is supposed to be good-ish. Meaning it's not going to rain according to the new weather app I downloaded to my phone, so I leave the slicker behind.

"I can't believe you get that place all to yourself," Luke says as we leave.

"I know," Blue chimes in with longing in her voice.

"Oh, come on, your parents are so relaxed, you can do whatever," says Diego.

"Not always, D. They're still there making sure I eat vegetables, do homework, and all that. And I was grounded forever after I got my tattoo."

"Oh yeah, I remember that," says Luke.

Blue and Diego continue to tease each other and exchange jibes as we head south. Luke is texting and walking at the same time until he nearly trips over his own feet. Diego jokes about his gracelessness. I laugh a little to myself; Luke catches me and then looks sheepish. It's fun. When we get to the path, we turn toward Macon's side of the island. Blue and Diego lead the way and Luke hangs back a bit and finally puts his phone away.

"Don't you ever get wigged out in the house by yourself?"

"Sometimes," I admit with a shrug.

"Do you get bored?"

"Not really. I don't mind hanging out on my own and I help my grandmother sometimes, too."

"I can't even imagine what that's like. To have Miss Ellie as a relative. Your Nana."

I don't even comment on that. Ellie is no Nana. "How does she know all your names? I mean, when did you meet her?"

"We've all been out here at least once or twice. Some-times a lot more if your family likes to stay in the cottages."

I'd forgotten about the cottages. "But why do people come to stay in them?"

"What, because it's not that far from the mainland?"

"Well, it isn't."

"Macon's one of my best friends. And it's just totally different out here. It's like a different world from town."

I can't argue with that. I hear a shout and see Jane waving. I raise my hand and then see that Macon is standing next to her and right behind him, Bridgette.

Chapter 23

It was going to happen sooner or later with a place this small. We all say hi, but Bridgette gives me an inscrutable look before following after Macon. He leads us down toward the ocean where a sandy beach stretches between the ever-present rocks. Jane has brought some blankets, and I help her spread them out.

"Did you get my email the other day?" she asks me.

"Yeah, I did. Thanks. It was really interesting to see that."

"See what?" says Blue.

"Just an old newspaper article," I say.

Jane pulls out her phone and shows the picture to Blue. Bridgette comes up and looks over her shoulder.

"Your grandfather. Oscar Alcott. My grandmother knew him." She smirks like she knows something.

Blue rolls her eyes. "All of our grandparents knew each other." She starts swiping through Jane's pictures. "Is this where you were? It looks kind of boring."

Jane laughs and takes the phone and navigates to another set of pictures.

Bridgette is still standing next to me. "My grandmother was Annette."

"Okay."

"Annette Dupuis."

She is clearly waiting for a reaction, but I have none to give. "I've never heard of her."

"They were going to be married."

"Who?"

"Annette and Oscar. She told me the whole story. But your grandmother showed up and, well, you know what happened."

Blue laughs out loud and I glance at her and Jane; they've moved away and aren't listening to us.

"They fell in love instead," I say to Bridgette.

"That wasn't all. *You* know that."

I am starting to feel uneasy. "I have no idea what you're talking about."

Bridgette shrugs and tosses her pretty hair. "I *know* about you." The same words she said to me the other night. This time they actually mean something to me though.

Macon walks up then. "Hey, Cam."

"Hi." I don't know if Bridgette's words or Macon's presence is more disconcerting. I don't think he heard our conversation, but I feel like I should say something more to him. I just stand there, mute.

Bridgette turns to him. "I brought your favorite, Macon." She pushes him toward one of the blankets. "We can speak more later, Cam," she says over her shoulder to me.

I wonder what Bridgette thinks she knows or if I even want to find out. Ellie said we shouldn't talk about it. No one would believe her if she did blurt out that Ellie is basically an alien. But all the sly looks and knowing nods, all the comments about "island girls." I'm still figuring it all out. I don't want to fuel the fire of gossip. I don't want everyone to look at me like I'm the alien.

"What's going on with her, now?" asks Blue.

"No idea."

We unpack food and share it around. I set myself as far from the surf as possible, enjoying the warm sun on my face. Diego tries to juggle fruit, much to Blue's hilarity. I sneak little peeks at Macon as he chats with Luke and Jane but keep catching eyes with Bridgette.

It soon gets warm enough for me to take off my hoodie. But it's warm enough for everyone else that they want to go down to the water. Blue rolls up her black stretchy pants to her knees and pulls my hand to try to get me to go with her. I tell her maybe later, and Macon gives me a look. But he's quickly distracted by Luke goofing off.

I close my eyes and lie back using my hoodie as a pillow and listen to the others shouting and laughing as they get further away. I can hear the waves break, but they are far enough away that the sound is almost comforting, rhythmic as breathing. Seagulls caw to each other as they wheel through the sky. I smell salt and taste it on my lips. I feel heavy and relaxed, like my body could melt right through the blanket and into the warm sand.

I DON'T KNOW how long it's been, but it gradually dawns on me that the sound of the waves has changed. The soft slap of ocean on sand has morphed to a thunder crash on rocks. I feel water seep into my sneakers and into the bottom of my jeans. I sit up, scrabbling back, heart pounding. I can't see anyone anywhere, but the sun has disappeared and the tide has risen at an alarming rate. I smell ozone, like after a thunderstorm.

The sky swirls with colors, like Ellie's eyes. I jump to my feet, the world spinning for a moment, or maybe it's just my head. Suddenly the tide retreats, but it isn't going out; it's just feeding into a giant wave. I see it build, far out from shore. It's enormous, taller than a building, and heading straight for me. I want to scream, but I can't gather enough oxygen.

And I can't move.

My feet have sunk into the sand. I hear my mother's voice call to me. The wave rises up over me like a giant. It hangs for a breathless second and starts to fall.

"CAM!" My eyes fly open to meet sky blue ones. "Cam, what were you doing?" Bridgette is staring at me; she looks almost scared, but her mouth is downturned in something like disgust.

I shake my head and look around. I'm at the water, and I gasp as a tiny wave splashes my feet. Wet seeps into my shoes. I stumble back a few steps. "I don't know."

"You were *doing something*, weren't you?"

"I think I was dreaming."

"Really." She says it like she doesn't believe me.

I rub my eyes. I can't quite shake the dream, the wave about to fall, my mother calling me. I could hear her so clearly. I look around again as if she's going to appear. No one else is here.

"You know that you could really hurt someone with your power?" Bridgette continues, "I don't want it to be any of my friends. I don't want it to be Macon."

I'm fully awake now. I study her face. She's serious. I see the others now in the distance making their way back toward us.

"I don't want to hurt anyone," I say.

I swear Macon is looking right at us.

"I'll tell him everything. How you're trying to trap him."

"Trap him? That's ridiculous." Is that what would have happened to him if I hadn't let him go?

"I know more than them." She motions her head toward the group. "My grandmother told me everything."

The others are getting closer. I really don't want to have this conversation now. Ever.

"What your grandmother did to Oscar Alcott."

I stare at her, my mind ticking. Bridgette's voice is insinuating, but Ellie is adamant that we have to be careful. She didn't do anything to Oscar. Did she? No. She let him go. He returned on his own. She said *he* called to her. This is just probably just... gossip. Stupid small-town gossip. Little towns and their little worlds. "I don't believe that she did anything to Oscar." My words are chips of ice, and more certain than I feel.

Bridgette's eyes widen and she takes a half step back, clutching at her necklace. She holds up her pendant. "I have this!"

Her pendant is made of two stones—one red, the other black. "Yeah? It's pretty," I say and move to touch it.

"It's protection. From you."

"What?"

"Red jasper and jet." She says it like she just scored something on me.

I'm totally confused. Ellie said nothing about stones affecting her. What could a rock do? My bewilderment must appear on my face, because Bridgette looks less sure of herself.

"It's red jasper and jet," she repeats. "Together."

I shrug. Blue is leading the pack, and she's almost in hearing distance.

Bridgette glances at the group and then hisses softly so only I can hear, "It protects against witches."

I can't help myself; I burst out laughing. Full belly laugh. "*That's* what you think? That's as far as your imagination goes?" I wrap my fingers around Bridgette's necklace, pull her a little forward and hiss right back at her, "I'm no witch." I let the pendant drop. I laugh again until my anger fizzles and the others walk up.

"What's so funny?" Blue asks.

"Uh, Bridgette just made a joke."

"Really?" Blue looks her up and down. "You have a sense of humor?"

Bridgette's pretty face is blotchy with red. I wonder if she's embarrassed. She should be. "She told me something funny about small town life," I say.

"Ugh, never mind, I don't need to know. I live it, I don't have to joke about it," says Blue as she roots around in one of the bags and pulls out the cookies. "Want one?"

"I'm good."

Jane snags a couple of cookies but then says, "Okay, play-time's over for me. I have to send a report to my advisor. Thanks, guys!" She marches off to the east.

The rest of us sit down on the blankets, and Blue passes around the cookies while the others rummage in bags. Bridgette sits far from me and stays quiet. I wonder if all small towns have a go-to witch insult, or is it just this close to Salem? Luke teases Bridgette about something that I can't hear, and she rolls her eyes but smiles. Guess she's back to normal, whatever that means. Blue complains that Diego has taken the last chocolate cookie. He holds it in his teeth with half of it sticking out.

"I'll split it with you," he says, or tries to, around the cookie. "Here."

"Nice try." She makes a face. We all laugh.

Luke tosses me a bag of chips.

"Dill?" I ask when I see the front of the package with a smiling egg—Humpty Dumpty.

"They're good! Try them."

He's right. They're great. I munch them and try not to look at Macon too much. Bridgette spreads something on bread and passes it to Blue. Luke and Diego start pelting grapes at each other until Blue snags one out of the air and tosses it high before catching it in her teeth. Then they all take turns trying to toss them in one another's mouths. Macon pulls out the peanuts and looks right at me. "Can I have some of these?"

"Sure. How'd you know they're mine?"

"Extra salt," he says, pointing to the front label. He smiles and I have to look away. He seems fine, normal, friendly. Like a friend. I try to ignore my disappointment.

Chapter 24

When we've snacked again and the sun hides behind clouds, we gather our cooler and bags and fold up the blankets. Macon and Bridgette head off together. I tear my eyes away from their retreating backs and feel annoyed. The rest of us head back toward Windemere.

"That was fun," I say to Blue. The guys are a way ahead of us.

"Yeah, stick with me, kid." Blue says in a funny 1930's accent, "I'll show ya the world."

"Ha. Hey, what's the deal with you and Diego?"

She side-eyes me with a grin. "I don't know. I've known him forever, but lately something's different, you know? What's up with you and Macon?"

"Nothing. We're friends."

"I think he likes you."

I shake my head.

"No, really. Even if he showed up with Bridgette."

"You think they're back together?" I hate the sick feeling that settles in my stomach as I say this.

"Mmmmmmmmmm, nah."

"Did you invite her?"

"Hells no. She's too uptight."

"Well, someone did, right?"

We catch up to the guys, and we all head back into Windemere. We throw the trash away, and just as they're about to leave, Blue finds the album on the coffee table. It opens to where the picture of Ellie and Oscar is stuck between pages.

"Oh wow, amazing."

Diego and Luke crowd around her.

"That's Miss Ellie?" asks Luke.

"Cool," says Diego.

"Yeah." I feel shy about them looking at the album, but Blue is already closing it and setting it down.

"We should go, peeps," she says.

I walk with them down to the dock and say goodbye, promising Blue that I'll let her know the next time I'm coming to the mainland. Luke and Diego help stash the cooler and bags and prep the boat to take off. Blue is at the wheel.

Ellie comes out as I'm walking back.

"Have you news of your mother?" Her voice is a little higher than normal.

I pat my pockets and realize that my phone is still at the house. Again. "What's wrong?"

"I thought I heard her call me," Ellie says.

I think back to my dream on the beach and feel cold. "I don't have my phone."

She walks with me back to Windemere, and I find the phone forgotten in my room. There are messages. Suzanna asks me to call. Then another message, this one from Maria, only a half hour ago, asking me to call. I dial the facility and get transferred back. Maria answers.

"Dr. Barry is here and wants to speak with your grandmother. Could you get the phone to her?"

I reluctantly pass the phone to Ellie. "Yes?" she says. There's silence as she listens. "No, there is nothing." A pause. "I see. What will you do next?" Another silence. I'm itching to grab the phone from Ellie. "Yes, she is here." She finally passes the phone back to me.

"Dr. Barry?"

"No, it's me again."

"Maria, what's going on?"

"Your mom's temp is up again."

"What is it?"

She hesitates and then says, "104. Dr. Barry was hoping that your grandmother might be able to provide some information from when your mom was a kid."

"What information?" I ask. Ellie is staring at the wall.

"For example, childhood illnesses or accidents and that sort of thing. Anything that might give a fuller picture of her past health."

"Oh. So, what happens next?"

"We'll keep treating the fever and run some tests."

"Okay. What kind of tests?"

"We'll do a CT scan, to start."

"That's like an X-ray?"

"It's more involved and will give us more information than a regular X-ray. If that doesn't show anything, we may do a different sort of scan in the nuclear medicine department."

I don't know what nuclear medicine is, but it doesn't sound good. "Oh, okay. When does she go for the first one?"

"Immediately."

Maria says to call later, and I make a noise like assent, but I don't reply. I can't talk over the word sticking in my head.

Nothing happens "immediately." They must be really worried.

I drop my phone. My chest tightens. I feel like I can't breathe. There isn't enough air in the house. All the air is gone. 104? That's too high. The memory I've tried so hard to keep down bursts out of the box and fills my mind until the edges of my vision blur. Cold sweat breaks out across my neck. I can't get any oxygen past the lump in my throat. I'm going to suffocate. No air.

Then I feel Ellie's hand on my shoulder. I suck in a breath and turn to her. Somehow, I let her take me into her arms.

"It's my fault." I choke out the words.

"Nothing is your fault, Camline."

"It is! I didn't know, and I'm so sorry!" I feel sick. I can't breathe. I pull back from Ellie, but she holds me tighter, strokes my back and hums. I can feel the song vibrate through her chest and seep into me. I let her hold me, surrender to the song until I can get control of my breathing. Then I pull away again, and she lets me go far enough that she can look in my face.

"Camline. Why did you say that?"

I bury my head in my hands. I am afraid. The pressure builds again in my chest and behind my eyes.

Ellie gently moves my hands and tilts my chin toward her. "Camline, tell me." Her voice is as gentle as her touch.

"I think it was me. I think I'm the reason that Mom is sick." The words catch in my throat; it's hard to speak. Ellie just looks at me, her eyes soft, waiting. Somehow, I go on. "I've never told anyone this. We were camping, me and Dad. Mom was at a lake. This was in New Mexico but before we lived there. It was the last trip that Dad and I took. Things hadn't been very good at home." Now that I've started, I can't stop myself—words just fall out of my mouth. "Mom started to have problems. And they were always fighting. But on this trip, he was happy. He wasn't mad about anything. And I remember him laughing at some silly joke I had told. We'd been gone for two days, and Mom was going to meet us the next day. But there in the woods… no one was mad at anyone. And I… I just wanted it to stay like that. I thought, what if she didn't come back? What if she wasn't here? If something just happened to her and—"

"Oh Camline," says Ellie sadly.

"I know, it's terrible. Because she did come back, of course, and they fought more and more. And then she got sicker. He left." I put my hands over my face. It's hot with shame.

"You did not do anything."

"I thought it! I put it out there. I couldn't keep positive. And now… You said yourself that there could be 'unintended consequences' and that we have to be careful."

"Not like this."

"But what if it was like a wish? I didn't mean it! I'm so sorry."

"Camline, look at me." I do. "You did not make your mother ill. If you had the power to wish her sick, then surely you could wish her well again. If it were that easy, then I would have done it myself."

"But what about being careful?"

"You do need to be careful. You could have an effect on a person, of course you could, because of who you are. And you must take care because you know so little. But you cannot direct the Fates or play God with a simple desire for peace in your home." She pulls me back into her arms, holding me for a breath, and lets me go. I straighten up, a little embarrassed and feeling very young. Then she says again, "You did not do this, Camline."

I want to believe her, but I don't know if that's possible. "They're going to run some tests," I say instead.

She shakes her head. "The tests will show nothing. What's wrong with Serena will not be on a test by your doctors."

"Why not? Ellie, if you don't think it was me, what is happening with my mother?" My voice breaks on the last word.

"I'm not sure, child."

"But you have an idea or you wouldn't have said that about the tests. What is it, Ellie?"

She sighs, leads me into the living room to sit down and opens the album to the picture of Mom on the beach. "Your mother chose your father and followed him to a desert." She touches her fingertips to Mom's face in the picture. "Away from her kind, away from me. She forgot who she was."

"If that's true, then what if she came back?"

"I don't know," she says in a small voice.

"If there's hope. If she could feel better, be better. If being near you could help her in any way." The realization of this hits home. "We have to bring her here. She's getting worse. These fevers are new."

"I have tried, Camline. She is stuck. I hear her and I call to her, but she does not hear me. I think she waits for your father."

"Like you wait for Oscar?" I feel sick.

"Yes, but your grandfather didn't try to dissolve our union."

"But... Dad isn't coming back." As I say it, I know it's true. Even if he came back from overseas, we would never be the happy family that we used to be. "Maybe if we try together. We have to try something. Please Ellie."

"It's not me you have to convince."

Chapter 25

Ellie leaves to get food from her cottage while I call to see if Maria will put the phone up to Mom's ear. If I could talk to her, maybe I could convince her. But they've already taken her for the CT scan.

I hang up and can't relax. I pace from the kitchen to the bedroom and back again. I stand for a long moment at the doorway of Mom's old room. Then, head back to the living room for the photo album.

Starting from the beginning, I run my eyes over the photos of my mother, Oscar, and Ellie. The wedding picture of my grandparents takes on a new meaning, and I search their faces for clues to the deeper story. Oscar certainly looks besotted with Ellie here. Is it more than that? Ellie doesn't look like she's controlling him. She looks… new. There is determination in her regard, and an unsettling wildness.

Ellie walks in then, carrying the stew pot.

"Were you careful? With Oscar?" I've said it before I can think twice. It just pops out before I can stop it.

Her mouth drops open and her eyes narrow. She sets the

pot on the stove. "I never once tried to use my power on your grandfather."

She sounds certain, but… "Ellie, how can you be sure? What if it was unintended? You said you called to him."

"And he called to me. We loved each other, Camline, don't doubt that. He pulled at me even stronger than I would have called him." Her face is sad but honest, and I believe her.

"I'm sorry. Someone was talking about his ex today, the woman he was going to marry."

"Oscar was never going to marry Annette Dupuis. That was her plan, not his."

"Oh." I wonder what Bridgette would think of that.

Ellie's attention has shifted to stirring the pot on the stove.

I go back to the album, turning to the picture of mom on the beach. Then I flip forward to the one where she's with me on the bike to compare them again. The difference in her eyes in these two pictures is so stunning. Obviously, Mom is older in the second one, but she hadn't changed that much. Her hair is still long and there are no lines on her face. She barely has any lines even now. It's just her eyes as she looks at the camera. What changed so much in her life to create this difference? Was it me?

I pass my hand across the page and feel a catch where I reopened the cut on my palm. It's just a dark line now with the edges slightly raised. Nearly healed again. So fast. Just like the first time I cut it on Macon's boat. That had been a lot worse; there had been so much blood. And Jack was surprised I hadn't gotten stitches. Ellie had thought it had been bone deep. I'd thought that too, until the doctor said it wasn't that bad. Ellie said I'd "bathed" it. And then after working with the hides, it was pretty much gone. Until the other day when I reopened it, when I was getting seawater…

Where did I put the bottle? I glance at Ellie and the countertop next to her. The bottle isn't there. It's not on my dresser or nightstand, either. Only when I move my jacket and I feel how heavy it is do I realize that it's still in the pocket. There isn't a lot left. I feel foolish, but I have to try. I take the bottle to the bathroom sink and set it on the side. I press the edges of my cut, and it aches but is still closed. I push until it pulses with pain, and a little blood wells up. I am slightly afraid I've lost my mind as I pour a little seawater over it. There is a little tingle, a burn. I tip out the rest into my hand. The blood stops, and my palm starts itching. I rinse it. All that is left is a light red line, even the edges have smoothed.

I rush to the kitchen.

"It's more than just being near here, isn't it? The actual water affects us," I blurt out, holding up my palm. "I just used it on my hand. Look."

"Yes."

"Then it could help Mom."

Ellie creases her forehead. "She's been gone so long. She may not be able to… She may be more of the land now. I don't know."

"I don't believe that. I was never 'of' here and it works on me. And I am only a quarter, Mom is half."

"You are strong, Camline."

"So is Mom. I didn't even have that much water to try just now. If I put more on it, even the red would go away, wouldn't it?"

"I think so."

Hope flutters inside me. "It helps me, so it could help her."

"I have been giving it to you as well, Camline."

"The seasickness drink?"

"Yes, but it is also in the stew. You were so removed from the water, you needed more. You were drying up."

I lick my lips and touch my fingertips to them. They are still soft.

She must guess what I am thinking because she says, "Yes, that was one sign. Also, you crave salt."

"But I always have." That hasn't really changed since being here.

"You missed the sea without ever knowing it."

"If I was 'missing' the ocean, then maybe Mom is too? So maybe this water could help her. We have to go get her."

Ellie shifts. "I can't leave here."

"We can't just abandon her there without trying. You have to go. I'm not old enough. They won't release her to me." Ellie turns away. "I need you to go." Ellie won't look at me. "Please. For Mom."

She finally turns, face stricken. "It isn't that I will not; I cannot." She folds in half and sinks to the ground. "I would have gone to her. Convinced her! She must make the decision. I can only sit here helpless. I know she is in pain. I hear her when she calls to me, and I can do nothing. She no longer hears me."

I touch her shoulder and she stands, squeezing my hand, and continues. "I cannot leave here. I'm tied to this place. I am not from this land. If I leave here, I die."

"But you left before—" She's not making sense. "You said that you had been to the mainland."

"Only with Oscar."

"What did he have to do with it?"

"I made a choice to leave my world and be with him. With him, with our connection, I could leave the island. Without him, I am tied here—to this island. I gave up the right to leave with my choice to stay. That was my price—to stay with him forever. Now that he is gone, I can never leave."

I feel like I am sinking under the weight of her admission, but I'm not completely ready to give up hope, even if right now it lies curled and cooling. It's not fair. But when has anything been measured by what's fair? I don't know what to do, but one thing is certain—I can't sit idly by. It's up to me.

"I'll go. I'll bring the water to her myself."

Chapter 26

"Will you help me?"

"Of course. I will do anything, everything, I can do." Ellie presses a mug of stew into my hands and holds it there as if to underline how serious she is.

I take a gulp of the stew and set it down. It's warm and delicious as it travels down my throat. Island restoration. "I should take some of this with me."

I ask Ellie to find me some canisters while I type airline addresses into my phone, looking for flights that might match up to my timing. I note costs and find three that could work depending on how quickly I can get to Bath. The nearest airport is Portland, nearly forty miles away from there. But first I have to get to Bath. I text Macon.

Ellie ladles stew into an airtight canister, while I log into my bank and transfer money from savings into checking. I only hesitate for a second before I hit confirm. This is exactly the kind of just-in-case I was saving for. With Dad's extra deposit and my savings, I should have enough for what I need.

I dump my clothes out of my duffel and repack it with just

224   DANIELLE BUTLER

a pair of jeans, a couple of shirts, and my toothbrush along with my ID, wallet and bank card. I can hit an ATM in Bath. I plug in my phone and iPod so they can charge while we go to the beach.

We walk down to the ocean, and Ellie waits on the sand while I take off my shoes and roll up my jeans. I'm going to do this myself. I take the bottle from her. My heart starts to thud and I get a chill across my neck, but within one breath, I'm moving. Propelled by my resolve, my bare feet slap the hard-packed sand and then splash in the first edges of the waves. I barely flinch. I don't stop until the water swirls around my calves. I dip the bottle into the seawater.

As it fills, I search the waves but see nothing. I brush my wet fingers over my eyes and look again. I hear the voices first. Then I see a shimmer of movement and a spark of silver. I take a couple of steps forward and as the next wave crests, I see the dusky pearl face of the girl I spoke to on the other side of the island.

"Hi," I say.

She stands up out of the water. "Come play." She reaches her hands out.

I take another step. Her eyes are incredible. Even from this distance, I can see the swimming colors. I hear Ellie call me, but the girl's pull is fierce. I want to do as she asks. Talk to her and find out more. I have so many questions.

But Mom.

I have to get to Mom. Thinking of her fills me with renewed purpose. I shake my head. "I have to go. I'll come back as soon as I can."

The girl drops her hands and seems disappointed. She slips back under the waves.

Ellie joins me. Her expression is hard to read, but she

clasps my hand. "They will find you fascinating and want you to go with them. You did well, Camline. You are very strong."

It's the third time she's said that to me. I don't know if she's right, but I cling to the compliment. I need to be strong.

I put my shoes back on my wet feet and feel time pressing on me. Ellie clutches the bottle to her breast, whispering, as we hurry up the path. I gather my things at Windemere; Ellie tucks a wad of cash in my pocket. I accept it with no complaints. As I am about to take the seawater bottle from her to put into my bag, Ellie holds up a hand. She lifts the lid and whispers directly into the water. I can't hear what she says. The water seems to shimmer for a second, or I'm seeing things.

"I think that could help even more," she says as she hands it to me. Her gaze is steady and she seems filled with guarded hope.

"What did you do?"

"A mother's blessing to fortify it."

It feels significant. "Thank you."

"Journey safe." She surprises me by lightly kissing my forehead.

I sling the bag across my shoulder and make for the forest path. Macon hasn't texted back. But someone will take me to the mainland. They have to. In the forest, fallen pine needles dampen my footsteps. I'm hyper-conscious of the sound of my breath. I pick up the pace.

When I break through the trees, Beau is outside and barks at me until I shush him and hold out my hand. He snuffles my fingers looking for treats, tail wagging. Anne peeks her head out.

"Cam? What are you doing here?" She steps onto the porch and someone comes out behind her, flipping glossy hair back. Bridgette.

"I need to get to the mainland."

"Now?"

"It's an emergency."

Bridgette and Anne exchange a couple of sentences in French. I wish I hadn't taken Spanish. Then Anne just looks at me for a moment like she's deciding whether to believe me. Macon steps outside. There is someone else behind him. I think I've interrupted their dinner.

"Cam?" He walks down the steps toward me. "What's up?"

"I texted you. I need to get to Bath. Or to the mainland at least."

"I didn't get it. Are you okay?"

"I'm fine. It's my mom."

"I'll take you."

"Wait a minute, Macon," says Anne. "I'm not sure that's a good idea."

Rob comes out of the doorway then and touches Anne's waist. She looks back at him and something unsaid passes between them. She purses her lips, looks at me, and then back at Macon, her expression softening.

Rob says to Macon, "Take my boat. It's faster."

"Thanks," I say to Rob. Then to Macon, "Can you go now?"

"Let me grab a coat." He disappears inside.

"Come on in, Cam," says Anne. She's polite but not exactly warm.

I enter the house and see that I was right, they were having dinner. Jane and Jack are chatting over a half-finished seafood meal. When Jane sees me, she gets up.

"Hey, where'd you come from?" she says with a big grin. Then she must see something in my face because she asks, "What's going on?"

"I have to go. It's my mom. She's gotten worse."

"Oh no, I'm so sorry. Are you headed there now?"

I nod. Bridgette just watches me like I might suddenly burst into an evil cackle or ask for eye of newt.

Jack gets up too. "I hope everything will be okay." He pats my shoulder.

"Do you want something to eat, Cam? Or you could take something with you?" Anne asks me. She sounds like a mom. My mouth drops in surprise, but I quickly try to cover.

"I'm okay." A lump burns in my throat. "Thank you."

Macon comes back then, wearing his green jacket. "Ready?"

I say goodbye to the others and follow Macon to his dad's boat.

I WAIT on the dock while Macon preps the boat. "Thanks for this."

"What are friends for?" he says with a half-smile.

Right. Friends. That's cool. Macon is a good friend to have. So why does it kind of hurt to hear him say it this time? He finishes his prep and reaches to help me aboard. His hand is as warm as mine is cold. He gives me a life jacket, which reminds me that I still have his blanket. I slide my arms into the jacket but before I fasten it, Macon pushes away from the dock and I hold on to the bench with two hands.

"What's happening with your mom?"

"We're not sure. It's not good."

"Damn."

"Can you take me all the way to Bath?"

"Yeah, of course. I could take you all the way to Portland,

but you'd probably get there faster over land. How are you getting to the airport?"

"Bus? Or maybe a taxi."

"I think the last bus has already left. Cab will probably be faster. There's a taxi stand near one of the public docks. We'll head there."

"Okay." I feel like even the cells of my body are pushing me on.

"You just want to be there for her?"

"Yeah. But I also need to give her something."

Talking about it, I check my bag again. I feel my clothes and toothbrush. I didn't bring toothpaste or any other toiletries. It doesn't matter, as long as I have the real necessities. I feel the canister of soup but not the bottle of seawater. I remember putting it in there. I have to have it. I stand and start frantically pulling everything out of the bag onto the seat.

"What's wrong?" Macon asks.

Just then my hand closes over the bottle, and I lift it out.

"What is it?" He pulls back on the throttle and the boat slows.

He starts toward me, and then the weight of the stopping boat catches up to us and we roll forward with the force of our inertia. I stumble. Even Macon loses his footing. The bottle slips from my fingers and topples to the side of the boat. I lunge for it. The bottle balances for a second on the edge and then as the boat rolls again, as if in slow motion, it drops over the side.

No! I'm up on the side of the boat just in time to see it start to sink. I gasp. I'm surrounded by ocean but lost the bottle with Ellie's blessing. My hope for Mom. One second passes. One and a half. I *have* to have it.

So, I jump in after it.

The shock of the water as it closes over my head jolts me, and I close my eyes tight. I'm sinking. I've lost my life jacket. It's somewhere on the surface. What have I done? I don't know what I was thinking. But I need that bottle for Mom. I try to open my eyes, but they don't obey. I can't see anything and it's dark and I'm *under water.* Panic wells. I don't know what to do and start to thrash, but I'm still sinking.

I thrust my hands out, still trying to find the bottle. Fingers entwine with mine, and I open my eyes. I'm looking into the multifaceted eyes of the girl from the water. She smiles her sharp smile. Her teeth are so white. The light under water is strange. There are so many colors and patterns. It isn't dark at all, but different things are highlighted like how colors change under a black light.

"Come with me," the girl says. I see her lips move, and I hear her. The sound is coming from a long way off or as if it's inside my ear. I can't tell. It's layered and complex. I clutch her hands tightly, but we're still sinking.

"Here," she says, and lets go of one of my hands. She reaches out and makes a motion in the water like she's sweeping a curtain aside, and we step into somewhere else.

Chapter 27

We're outside. Somehow. Somewhere. The light is muted and the air is damp as if someone is constantly spritzing water into it, as if it's almost still liquid. I gasp, pull in a lungful of thick air. I don't know how to describe the sensation. Then I realize that I hadn't been breathing under the water, and I didn't drown.

Unless I did.

I pinch myself and it hurts. Not dead then. I lick my lips and they taste salty. I push my wet hair back off my face and tuck it behind my ears, or try to, but it floats in the strange air. My heart is kicking. We're in the shelter of slick rocks that rise up to the side, curving around us like a shallow cave. I can see the sky beyond, and it's wide but indistinct like a watercolor painting. There is light, but I can't see where it's coming from and everything looks filtered like I'm looking at it through the thinnest gauze. I hear voices or music in the distance. Someone is singing—or maybe a whole choir—the air is alive with it.

I can't get my bearings. "Where are we?" My voice has the same layered quality.

"We're home," the girl says.

"I don't live here." The voices are coming closer.

The girl shushes me and pulls me down to crouch deeper into the shelter of the rocks. The rock is solid but the ground is soft, spongy, beneath my knees. I feel like I might sink into it. Something flies, or swims, in the distance. I get an impression of feathers or scales, dark but with the rainbow surface of oil and a tail divided into two. I can see something like trees or foliage clustered together, moving gently. They look like filigree. The voices pass us by, but I can still hear song and sounds in the distance.

"You came back." The girl is smiling. "You live in the Other-side?" She asks it like I'm the one who is a mythical creature.

"Do you mean where we were before? Uh, yeah."

She runs her fingers down my arm, which is shining with that pearly cast again. Pale to her dark. She looks at my face curiously. Then tugs on one of my curls.

"Is that why you cut your hair?" she asks. Her own silvery hair swims around her face, like it's caught in a breeze. It turns in soft waves and spirals, looking like Mom's in my dream.

Focus. I cannot sit around discussing hair right now. I look around for the door or whatever. "I can't stay here. I have to get back to the boat, to my friend. And I have to find the bottle I dropped." I can't see where we came from. My brain is having trouble processing. I take a deep breath, and it's so strange in my throat, in my lungs. I can't freak out right now. I have to get back.

"You can stay," the girl says.

"I can't. Please. It's really important. I need to get back. Did you see the bottle I dropped?"

"I found this." She pulls it out from a pocket or fold in her iridescent dress.

"That's it. I need that."

"But I want it. I found it."

"It has seawater—special seawater—in it, and I need it for my mother." I reach for it, but she pulls back.

Her eyes turn sharp and cunning. "Trade me."

"With what?" I say. I haven't exactly brought anything with me. "I mean, yes. But what can I give you?"

"That." She points to my ear.

I slip the pearl earring out of my ear and hand it to her. I'd have given her anything, but I'm still a little sad to let it go. She gives me the bottle and greedily inspects her prize.

I clutch the bottle to me. "Now, how do I get back?"

"I could take you." She says it slowly, and like she might not.

I can feel frustration and anger bubble inside but tamp it down as I meet her stare. Macon must be freaking out. He'll think I've drowned by now. The girl's eyes flick to my other ear. It's harder to hand over the second earring, but I do it without hesitation. She claps her hands and then stops to listen for a second. Then she twists the earrings up into her hair like decorations. I hear voices approaching again. She raises a finger to her lips to make me be quiet.

"Who is that?" I whisper.

"My sisters. They will be angry."

"Why?"

"They said I could not."

"Couldn't what? I have to get back." I'm getting frantic, my nerves clawing at my throat.

"They'll say I called you. But you called to me and I was only curious."

"What do you mean? I called you?"

"On the rock, you called out. I went to you."

I don't know what she's talking about at first. Then I remember the day I went looking for the faces in the waves. I said hello. Maybe she means that. None of this matters right now. "Look, I have to get back."

She listens again and then nods, heading back to the mouth of the shallow cave. She seems disappointed. "There is a portal here." She gestures. "See?"

All I see is empty space. I don't have time for this. And then I do see it. A distortion, like a heat shimmer on an Arizona highway. The girl sweeps her hand like before, like opening a curtain. Hanging there is a cross-section of ocean. It looks totally different from where we are now. A fish swims toward the window but changes course in a flash as it gets close, then swims away. It's incredible... like a dream.

We step through the window and cold water wraps around me. It presses against my skin, fills my ears, and opens my eyes. I watch the sea around us with its patterns and shades. The girl pulls my hand upwards, and I slide through the water after her, still clutching the bottle. I'm worried that the boat will be too far away from where I went in or that Macon has come in after me and then we'll both be lost. We surface, and I'm surprised and relieved to see that we're right next to the boat. It's so bright. And dry.

"Cam!" Macon shouts. He's at the side of the boat looking over and throws a floating ring on a rope to me. I grab it and slip my arm through it. I feel a tug as he pulls it closer. Behind me, the girl is pushing me too. When I'm at the boat, Macon reaches out one hand to me, the other holding the rails. I'm afraid that I'm going to be too heavy for him at this angle, but I leverage my foot against the side of the boat and then the girl gives me a last push upwards. I come over the side onto the boat floor in a rush of water.

Macon helps me stand, but he's looking past me, right at the girl in the water.

"Forget me," she commands.

Macon doesn't move. His mouth is open in shock and his eyes are wide. He glances at me, and I am struck again by how much I like his face. He looks lit from within.

"Cam, are you okay?" I nod, but his eyes are already fastened back on the girl. He's about to throw the ring to her.

"Forget me," the girl says again and slips under the waves.

"Wait!" He leans over the side of the boat and stares for a few seconds. The girl is gone.

"It's okay," I say, tugging on his sleeve.

"Cam? What the hell is going on?"

I'm totally at a loss for words.

"You… Did you fall? Did you jump? And then you pop right back up, with another girl?"

Why isn't he forgetting the girl? She was clear. I could feel the power in her voice. Maybe he couldn't see her eyes. So, I try. I can still feel the salt in mine. I lock eyes with him and say very clearly, "Macon, forget her."

"Uh, no. I don't think so. Where did she go? Who was she? What was she?"

I try again. "Don't think about her,"

"Cam, say it however you like, but I'm not going to forget anything."

"You… You won't?"

"No, how could I? There was a person in the water with you!"

"Wait." I brush my still-wet hands across my eyes. Everything is enhanced, the salt is still there. "Give me my bag," I command.

"In a sec, Cam. What is going on?" He just stares at me.

Then his face changes as he really looks at me. "You lost your earrings. And your eyes look different."

I blink, and then again, until I am sure my eyes are clear. He's not affected! I don't know why, but it doesn't work on him. I couldn't have made him do anything inadvertently if I can't even do it on purpose. If the girl couldn't even make a dent.

"That's amazing," I say and hug him.

He jumps back a little. "Whoa. Cold!"

"Sorry!" I'm still soaking wet. "Got a towel, maybe?"

He gives me one that smells of ocean and fish. I stop his questions by asking him to turn his back so I can change my clothes. The cash that Ellie gave me is wet, but fortunately my phone was in my bag, not in my pocket. It's cold and my teeth are chattering by the time I get dressed again. "You can turn around," I say as I am bundling my wet things into a pile and laying out my jacket to dry. "We have to go. Please."

"Cam, you've got to tell me what's going on. Who was that girl? Where did she go? What was going on with your eyes? Am I dreaming?" He says the last to himself and pinches his arm, just as I had done, and I laugh. It comes out like a melody. His eyes fasten on my face, pinning me as neatly as Ellie's stare.

"Macon…" I start. "I don't know what to tell you."

"Tell me everything, Cam."

"I don't even know everything. I can tell you what I know, but I have to get to my Mom. Please, can we keep going?"

"Okay." He gives me his coat—over my protests—and another life jacket. He makes sure that I clip it on this time. Then he starts the boat, checks our direction, and we head off. "Talk to me."

I watch him for a long moment. "Can you keep a secret?"

"Yes." Sure and final.

"What gossip have you heard about my family? What superstitions?"

"I don't care about gossip, Cam! And I'm not superstitious."

So, I tell him.

I tell him what I learned about Ellie, about myself. I show him my hand and tell him about the water's effect on me. I leave out the salt-washed eyes bit, but I tell him about when I met the girl, whose name I still don't know, and tell him where I went when I went under.

"Hang on. That's not possible," he interrupts.

"I know it sounds insane."

"No. You didn't have enough time to go anywhere."

"What do you mean?" The *timing* is what he finds unbelievable about everything I just said?

"You fell in and by the time I got to the side of the boat, you had come up and she was there."

"No, I was gone ten minutes, at least."

He shakes his head. "It was less than thirty seconds, Cam."

I'm at a loss. "I don't know. Maybe time passes differently there?"

"I suppose if we're going with a whole other... what? Another world?"

"Another realm, anyway. I know it sounds crazy, but you can feel the difference there."

"Fine. Another realm." He laughs like he can't believe he's saying it. "Wow. Okay. So, maybe time does pass differently there."

He's maneuvering the boat up through the long fingers of land that stretch out from the mainland. I'm standing next to him, balancing in spite of the bumps and rolls of the boat. I don't feel sick at all. And right this second, I am not even a little bit scared of the water.

When we arrive at the dock, Macon ties up the boat and climbs onto the dock with me. "I'm sure I can find it." I say.

"I know you can. I just don't want to say goodbye yet."

I flush. He's so nice, and I had tried to control him. But I couldn't. That's the important thing right now—it didn't work on him. So maybe this means he really did like me.

"Are you freaked out by what I told you?" I ask.

"No. And yes."

"Okay."

We get to the taxi stand and there a few people ahead of me. There's a guy in a suit and a family. The little kid is running back and forth between his parents.

Macon continues in a low voice. "What you told me is unbelievable." I start to say something but he takes my hand, and I forget my words. He goes on. "It *is* unbelievable, but I know that you're telling me the truth."

"How do you know?"

"I just know that you aren't lying."

"Okay," I say slowly. A cab comes, and the couple with the kid piles in.

"Cam, you are not like anyone I've ever known. And I like that about you. There's a lot I like about you. Even if you just want to be friends. No, let me finish. I like how you care about your mom and how you made sure Blue got home that night. You're so independent. You're different, and I'm glad we're friends, I am. But I do like you." His cheeks are stained with color. "You don't have to say anything."

The next taxi arrives and picks up the businessman in front of me. I am conscious of Macon's hand in mine. "Macon." I lean forward. "I— I—" I'm searching for the right words.

A car horn sounds. I'm next for the taxi, and the driver is getting impatient. I let go of Macon and throw my duffel in the back of the cab. I start to take off his jacket.

"Keep it. I'll take yours back to Ellie."

The taxi driver bumps his horn again. "Kid? You comin' or what?"

"I'm coming. I'm coming!" I jump in the car and close the door. Macon is saying something and I roll the window down. "What?"

"Check the pockets. There's something for you in there. And… just come back, Cam."

"I will," I say, and the truth of the statement wraps around me like a blanket.

Chapter 28

As the taxi speeds off toward Portland, I settle back in Macon's coat. It smells like him. I feel around in the pockets and come up with a hard, square object. It's a puzzle box. A new one, not the carved one from Windemere. It's sanded smooth and glides in my hands as I play with it. A shushing noise and a clink come from within. I give it a shake to hear the sound. I can't find the catch. I try to remember what Macon had done with the other one to open it, but I can't figure it out. A secret-keeper. That's what he called it. I wonder what Macon would have kept just for me.

I need to focus on the trip ahead. It's not going to be easy. I ask the driver how much longer until we get to the airport and check flights again with that estimate. Like the last time I traveled across country, I don't know what's waiting for me on the other side. But this time, nothing is set up and everything is up to me.

I call the facility and ask Lupe to put the phone up to my mother. She doesn't want to. She says Mom is resting. Her temp is still up, hovering around 102. I ask about the CT scan, but she says she hasn't talked to the doctor yet. I hang up and kick the seat in front of me. The cabbie looks over his shoulder at me but doesn't say anything.

At the airport, I head straight to the counter and ask about the next flight. The first has already stopped boarding, but there's another in an hour and a half that only has one stop. I buy an open return flight, grateful for my dad's monthly checks, the recent windfall deposit, and my own thrifty nature. It puts a huge dent in my balance, but I still have some in savings and Ellie's cookie jar money in my pocket. I don't care. I can't believe that all it takes is a little money and I can be by Mom's side in less than twelve hours.

I go to the magazine shop and buy several tiny products— mouthwash, basic contact lens solution, and a few empty travel-size plastic bottles. I have to get everything I need to take into three-ounce amounts to have a hope of getting it through security. I take it all to the bathroom. I find a dry washcloth in my bag and have an idea. I put it into a baggie and pour the contact saline solution over it. Ellie said any salt water would work.

Then I empty everything else down the sink and run the water as hot as it will go. I wash the travel bottles thoroughly. Then I lock myself in a stall and refill all the bottles, some with seawater, others with Ellie's stew. I stuff them into the standard quart-size clear baggie. It won't close properly. I am not sure I will get this all through as hand luggage, but I have to try. I don't dare check the bag. My whole plan rests on the contents of these bottles.

The security line is relatively short, but the officers are taking their time with each inspection. A man ahead of me is the fourth who's been pulled out of line. I take the washcloth out and dab my forehead and eyes, then zip it back into my bag. I feel the sting of salt. I take off my still-damp shoes and Macon's jacket and lay them with my bag and phone in one of the grey plastic containers. I move up, keeping my eyes low. I go through the metal detector with no trouble and wait at the end for my things to come through.

They hold my container and run the belt back to look at something again. I shift my weight from one socked foot to the other trying to look at ease. My stomach sinks when a uniformed officer holds up my bag and asks whose it is. I raise my hand, and he motions me to join him at a table.

His focus is on the bag as he says, "Take out your liquids, please, miss." He is officious and unsmiling.

I take out the baggie. "This needs to be able to close," he says and pokes a bottle for contact solution. "What is this?"

"Saline." I'm so nervous I almost giggle. I'm telling the truth after all.

He must hear something in my voice, because he finally looks at me. I hold my breath. He cocks his head.

"Everything's okay." I say.

He closes his eyes, then opens them and smiles, his face changing, looking younger. "Yes. You have a great trip, miss."

"Thanks." I wait until he moves away before stuffing my things back in my bag and wriggling my feet back into my shoes. I keep my head down and go to wait for my flight.

The first leg is uneventful and boring. I try to flip through magazines but can't concentrate. I put my earphones in and my iPod on shuffle and stare out the window at clouds that look like cotton candy.

During the layover, I pace until I see an airline officer looking at me a little too closely. I call the facility again, but the nurses don't have any more information. Mom is still running a fever, but it's not as high. My chest tightens. I can't even think of eating, but I buy a bottle of spring water. Just a few more hours and I'll be with Mom. With this layover, I'll get into Albuquerque really late or very early depending on how you look at it. Not exactly visiting hours.

My flight is called. I wish I had the power to make the plane go faster, but no amount of seawater could do that. I listen to music and drum my fingers on the armrests until I notice that I'm annoying my seat mate.

We finally land. The ticketing offices and tourist shops have all closed for the evening. There are only a few people meeting loved ones or collecting luggage. I forgot how dry it is here in the high mountain desert. I drain the rest of my spring water. I'm jittery as I organize my taxi and settle in for the twenty-minute trip to the facility. I check my bag again—and then again—to make sure everything is there. I give the cabbie so many monosyllabic answers that he stops trying to make conversation. Now that I'm so close, I have a ball of nervous energy coiled under my breastbone. I'm excited to see Mom. I'm scared to see her. I'm trembling with hope.

We finally arrive and I pay the driver with still-drying bills. I stand at the top of the path leading down to reception. To my left, the windows of the dining hall are in darkness. It's so late. I tell my feet to move, but I'm rooted to the spot. I close my eyes and pray, hoping someone is listening. Then I walk down to the door.

Chapter 29

No one is at reception. I bypass the sign-in sheet and head straight to the east wing. I pass a couple of aides I don't know. One checks his watch. I walk like I belong and nod at them. It's so late. I know I won't have much time. I slip into Mom's room and close the door. There's only one bed in here. The night light is on, casting a soft glow on the ceiling.

My breath rushes out at the sight of her. She looks so small in the bed. She's lost tons of weight since I saw her last. Why didn't they tell me? She's wasting away. Her eyes are closed, her breathing shallow. An oxygen feed loops from her nose to hook behind her ears. I walk around the bed and put my hand on her arm. Her skin is hot and so dry. I can feel her bones beneath it.

I shake her gently. "Mom, it's me. Wake up."

The overhead light switches on. "Cam!" It's Suzanna, and she doesn't look pleased to see me. "What are you doing here?" She briskly crosses the room. "Don't wake your mother. She has to rest. You shouldn't be here. Come back in the morning."

Mom just lies there, unmoving.

Suzanna takes my arm. "Come on, you need to leave her."

I shake her off and scuttle closer to the bed. "Suzanna. I got here as soon as I could. I've been traveling. Just let me be with Mom." My voice is firm. I want to reach for the seawater or even the saline washcloth, but I don't dare look away from Susanna. And I need to save it for Mom.

"How did you get here? Where's your grandmother? Is she here? Did you run away?"

"No, she knows where I am. I'm supposed to be here. Just give me a little time." I strain to put power in my voice even without the water.

Suzanna is unfazed. "Where is your grandmother, Cam? I want to speak with her."

I pause, and she narrows her eyes. "She's in Maine. She couldn't come," I admit.

"Get her on the phone."

"I can't. She doesn't have a phone," I snap at her. Anger fueled by frustration and fear builds. "And I'm staying." I take Mom's hand.

Suzanna huffs and I hear a squeak as she turns on her rubber-soled shoes. The door closes as she leaves. I only have minutes.

"Mom. Mom! You have to wake up." I fumble in my bag and pull out a little bottle. I don't know what to do with it. I sprinkle some on her head. I pour some more and then squirt some on my fingers and rub them across her lips. Then across her eyelids. I dribble more onto her lips, trying to get it into her mouth.

But it's not working. Nothing is happening.

I hear voices in the hall. I need more time. I push a chair under the doorknob. My chest is tightening, and my throat starts to close. "Mom..." It's hard to get the word out. It's hard to breathe. Maybe she needs more water on her. I pour a whole three-ounce bottle on her head and finger-comb it through her hair. It seeps into the pillow and droplets run across her face, but she doesn't move.

I fight my growing panic. People are right outside. They are talking loudly, pushing and banging on the door. The chair stutters across the floor. Suzanna sounds mad as she calls out for me to open the door "right now." Once they get in, they'll make me leave. They'll call social services. And they won't be able to reach Ellie, and even if they do, she can't come for me. Where will they send me then? I won't get another chance to wake Mom.

I pour more water across her face. "Please."

There's a flicker of movement under her lids, like she's dreaming, but she doesn't open them.

"Momma…" I bathe her lips again in seawater and press my head against her hand. The tightness in my chest is like a band of fire, cutting off my breath. I call her again, the sound lengthening until from somewhere I hear humming. It's the complicated melody of Ellie's song. It's coming from me. I didn't even realize I knew it.

The door rattles, and Suzanna calls out again.

Mom touches her tongue to her lips.

The sound of Ellie's song soaks into me, coursing through my breath, binding to my blood, twisting and untying at once. I can't stop it. It fills me. The band across my chest tightens until I think it will snap me in two. Then it frays and breaks apart. And as it does, my eyes fill with years of unshed tears, blinding me.

Then everything comes into knife-sharp focus.

Mom is shining like a pearl, her blue green eyes wide.

The door bursts open. An orderly grabs me around my waist, bodily lifting me away from Mom. I shout. Suzanna has gone straight to Mom. She touches her hand to the wet pillow.

"What have you been doing to her?" She moves as if to wipe her face, but Mom grabs her hand. Suzanna freezes. Mom is focused on me, or on the guy holding me.

"Take your hands off my daughter." Her voice is like a croak full of breath. It's the most beautiful sound I have ever heard.

THE ORDERLY DROPS me to the floor, and I rush back to Mom's side and into her feeble arms. Suzanna stares like a startled fish.

"Leave us." Mom's voice is weak, but the command is clear.

"I'm calling Dr. Barry," Suzanna says as she exits, pushing the orderly in front of her.

I can't stop crying. Mom is so beautiful. She is so frail. I haven't heard her voice in so long. Then I remember. "I have some of Ellie's stew."

Mom smiles at the tiny bottles as I shake them out of the baggie. I have to help her drink. After two, she seems to gain a little strength back.

"Cam, how did you get here? Why are you here?" Her voice scratches, and she coughs.

"Mom, you know why." Tears slick my face. "I need you to come back with me."

Mom takes another sip of stew. "I think maybe it's too late, Cam." Her voice is quiet, resigned.

"How can you say that? You're *talking*. Look how just a little water affects you."

"Yes, but—"

"No. Mom, no 'buts.' I hardly know anything. You should have told me! If I'd known… You should have come with me. We should have gone when you first got sick. And… you didn't tell me… I didn't know that we could have an effect on people or maybe even events."

"What do you mean?"

"I'm so sorry, Mom." Fresh tears flow.

"Honey," she gathers breath, "what are you talking about?" She puts a hand over mine.

Guilt weighs my head. "I couldn't keep positive, Mom. Not all the time. I couldn't. And then… I did something." I'm not sure I can look at her, but I have to tell her. "That last trip with Dad. I thought that if you didn't come back—if you weren't there—it might be better. If something happened to you, things might be easier."

"Oh sweetheart…"

"I'm so sorry. I'm so, so sorry."

She struggles forward and touches my face. I glance at her for only a second. "Cam. I need you to listen to me." Her voice fights for strength. "And hear me." I nod, miserable, and study my hands. "Look at me, Cam." I do. Her face is set, stern, almost angry. "You had nothing to do with me getting sick. You didn't wish it into existence."

"But—"

"No 'buts,' Camline. You were a little girl looking for calm in a brewing storm. I'm sorry I didn't realize how much you were seeing. But it wasn't you. You do not have that power. Whatever you've discovered about seawater and compelling a person, it's not the same."

When you believe something for so long, it's hard to let it go. Even if it hurts to hold on to it.

"Ellie said that too, but—"

"She was right." Mom holds my face in her hands and says it again, "This is not your fault."

"Then why? What happened? Is it because you were away from the sea?"

"I don't know." She leans back against the pillows again, looking exhausted. "Momma thought I should go back to the island, but I didn't listen. I don't know if it would have changed anything or not. And after your Dad left, it got worse, and it seemed impossible for us both to go."

"But this is helping you," I say, gesturing to the plastic bottles.

"It may just be temporary."

I press another bottle into her hand and help her hold it. "Drink more. Mom, you have to be well enough to come back with me."

She shakes her head. "I don't want you to get your hopes up. We don't know if it would make a real difference."

"You have to try."

"I don't know if I can."

"That's ridiculous! Yes, absolutely yes, you can! You can at least try. I can help you, but you have to make the decision."

She smiles sadly. "Look at you, my daughter, my precious, strong girl."

"Mom. I don't even know where to start... The things I've learned... You should have told me."

"I wanted to. But I also wanted you to have a normal life. Your dad was so adamant that he didn't want you to grow up like that."

"Like what? Like you? What you are, what I am?"

"He didn't want you to grow up... fanciful... believing in fairytales."

I half laugh. "Mom, we are the fairytale."

"I know. I don't know how much he believed or guessed. He wanted us to be a regular family. I wasn't sure how much you would be like me. You hated the water."

"I was scared."

"I know, and I couldn't break that in you. Your eyes would change when you cried."

"Is that why you commanded me?" I know now that's what it must have been. "It *was* you. You sang to me."

"I was trying to protect you. I was trying to make you normal."

"I'm not even sure what that means anymore. But when you got sick, why didn't you listen to Ellie? Why didn't you go back home?"

She falters, sighing, resting her head back.

I give her another bottle of stew. "Drink that. I need you to be strong. Suzanna will be back any minute. She thinks I ran away. The doctors will come. They'll make me leave."

"I wanted your father to…"

"Dad doesn't have anything to do with this. He isn't coming back, Mom."

She seems to shrink a little, and she turns her face away from me. "I know." It's so quiet, I almost miss it.

I'm still crying. It's like I have saved up for this my whole life. Dad leaving still hurts. "He wasn't strong enough to stay for you, for us. He just left. You don't do that to people you love. You don't forget them. You stick it out. No matter how hard it is."

"You're right."

I wipe my eyes on my sleeve. "So you have to try. You have to try for me."

Her eyes are full and sad, but also maybe proud. "She was right. You needed her."

"I need *you*. You need her. She sent a wish in the seawater and it *is* helping. She needs you too, Mom. You have to come."

She closes her eyes. Pain etches along the lines of her face, but her voice is strong when she finally says, "We'll go back. We'll go back together."

Chapter 30

They pull a bed in for me because I refuse to leave. Mom rests and dozes, but I can't sleep. I stay by her side watching anxiously and holding her hand. Every time she moves, breathes or sighs, I jump. I am terrified that she'll slip away again. *Stay with me, stay with me, stay with me.* Over and over in my head.

When morning comes, Dr. Barry shows up. She called a specialist, and they all stand around amazed at how Mom is doing and subtly claiming responsibility for the turnaround. Mom's awake and making plans. She informs them that she will be returning with me to Maine. They caution against it; they want to run some tests, but they can't force her to stay. She's a miracle. Lucid and commanding as we pack her things and check her out. She gets them to agree to lend her a wheelchair and gets us a ride to the airport. It only takes a drop or two of seawater.

At the airport, I book our tickets to Portland. Then we'll make our way back to the island from there. I'm exhausted but full of gratitude and expectation. Mom is still really weak, almost brittle. I buy more saline for the washcloth and give it to her to hold while I feed her the rest of the stew. I only have one more little bottle of seawater to get us back. Then she'll be surrounded by it. Maybe the water and Ellie and Ellie's songs and my own hope can work together to heal her completely. It's possible. Anything, everything, is possible.

I still have so many questions. I want to ask Mom if she's gone through to the other world. I want to ask Ellie about it too, and about her sisters. I want her to tell me everything.

I check my phone and have messages. Two are from Blue. The first is asking me if I am coming to town soon. The second is frantic, and she wants to know if I'm okay and if my mom is okay and if I am coming back at all ever. The next is from Macon checking in and letting me know he told Blue where I was. I text Blue that I'll call her soon. I mull over what to text Macon and decide to do it later.

I wheel Mom to our gate. She rests as we wait for our flight, and I play with the puzzle box that Macon made. I twirl it in my fingers and with sudden clarity see exactly how to open it. A touch and a push and the catch springs open. A few grains of sand fall out. Inside, on a shallow bed of sand is a tiny snail shell carved of wood. Its delicate whorls spiral tightly, and it's so fine. With it is the tiniest bottle with a minuscule cork stopper. It's full of liquid. I uncork it and sniff. Seawater. I laugh. He's given me a little piece of the island in a box. I scroll through my phone to his number and dial. He answers on the first ring.

"Cam?"

"How'd you know it was me?" I can't keep the smile from my voice.

"Caller ID."

"Right." Duh.

"But I knew without looking. I just knew it was you. Are you okay?"

"I am, Macon, I really am." He doesn't sound like he thinks I'm weird or crazy. He doesn't sound mesmerized. He sounds perfect.

"Good. It's really great to hear your voice. Where are you?"

"I'm with my mom. We're at the airport. I'm coming home. We're coming home."

EPILOGUE

When we're seated and in the air, I finally sleep.

I wake up to find myself on the plane but it's moving too slow, so I leap through the wall and sail through the clouds and air as fast as thought until I'm standing in front of Ellie's cottage. She's baking bread, faced away, bent over the stove. As I look in on her, I hear her sharp intake of breath as she straightens and turns toward the window.

But I'm off through the trees and over the clearing until I'm passing Macon's house. Beau barks and wags his tail furiously as I go by. I hear Anne tell him to be quiet. I go on until I'm over the ocean. I see colors in the waves and glimpse a face here and there. But I don't stop to hear them sing.

I don't stop until I come to two boats out together. On one, Jack and Rob are hauling in traps. Macon is by himself in the other boat. He's standing, surefooted in the little craft, his hair tossed in the breeze, concentrating on a net, moving it through his hands and checking it. I am right in front of him, watching him work. He looks up then, straight into my eyes, surprised. He smiles his slow smile. "See you."

THANKS FOR READING

I hope you enjoyed *Watermarked* as much as I've enjoyed sharing it with you.

If so, would you be willing to leave a rating or review (on Amazon, Goodreads, BookBub, etc.)? Reviews are the best way to help other readers discover new authors. I am sincerely grateful for every one I receive.

WANT TO KEEP IN TOUCH?

Join my Readers' Group to be the first to know about fun news and info, new releases, and giveaways. Just pop to my website www.daniellebutlerwriter.com and sign up. I'd love to see you there!

ACKNOWLEDGMENTS

There are so many people who helped make this book a reality, I'm bound to forget to name someone...sincerest apologies in advance. I am grateful to all my friends and family who pushed me and encouraged me along this path and to the readers who picked up the book and gave it a go.

A huge thank you goes out to Christina Albetta, Paige Beeman, Cami Bourquin, Bryn Butler, Taylor Glenn, Jane Hoskisson, Jean Kneller, David McIntosh, Iren Merdinyan, Ben Plotkin, and Emma Smith as my earliest readers—I am indebted to your feedback and forgiveness for very rough drafts. Thank you to Joanna Farrow for her insights into story and whose suggestion to "play with the POV" was a key to changing the whole feel of the book. Thank you to Elizabeth Luce for her questions and observations in a later draft that made me think and refine. Also thank you to Helen Bell for cups of tea and tips on indie publishing in the UK.

Special mention and gratitude must go to Christina Garner an early/late/and in between reader and sounding board whose support through the many permutations of the book has been as invaluable as her encouragement in this foray into indie publishing.

Thank you to my fellow writers Abigayle, Alexis, Angela, and Cherry at the Retreat West character retreat for their great conversation and keen perception. And also to Debbie Flint and Retreats for You for the excellent food and creating a sublime place to work. Thank you to Amanda Saint for leading the retreat and for making time to do the final edit and pushing the book to be the best I could make it. Thanks to Andrea, Bre, and Michelle at Three Points Author Services for proofreading and for catching errant British vocab and references in this American story.

The extraordinary cover was done by the incomparable Jennie Rawlings of Serifim who found a way to visually express the heart of it.

Massive thank you to my extended blended beautiful family whose encouragement, teasing, support, and craziness influence my every day. I wish my grandmother, Hazel, and my dear sister, DeJuana, were still here—I would have loved to have shared this with them.

Finally, my most heartfelt thanks goes to Matthew Lange who always has my back and will stop everything to listen to me read something aloud when I need to clarify my thinking.

ABOUT THE AUTHOR

Danielle Butler has spent most of her life making up stories. From the rich and multi-layered lives of her Barbies and anthropomorphised stuffed animals, through her work as a long form improvisation and stage actor to development producing for film and TV—it was all about What Happens Next. American-made, she lives the exPat life in the UK with her husband and various pets in a little house on a very old river.

daniellebutlerwriter.com

facebook.com/DanielleButlerWriter

twitter.com/DSButlerWriter

amazon.com/author/daniellebutler

goodreads.com/danielle_butler

THE STORY CONTINUES...

Read on for a sneak peek at *Landbound*, Book Two in the Watermarked Trilogy...

CHAPTER 1

With "salt-washed eyes" I can "see true" and make people do what I say. At least that's what's supposed to happen.

"Try it again." Macon flicks water at my face, and I laugh.

The sun is high overhead in a blank blue sky. It's like summer. I mean, technically it *is* summer, so it should feel like it, but weather on an island in upper New England is changeable. The dry sand we're sitting on is warm enough that I don't mind when the edge of an icy wave reaches for my toes.

"C'mon, try it again!" He leans his head back and narrows his eyes like a challenge.

"Okay, okay." I hop up and splash down into the surf until the water eddies around my ankles. Yep, right into the water. Something that wouldn't have been conceivable just a few months ago. Even just sitting close, I'd be fighting a panic attack. Now I can walk right into the ocean. I have made my small peace with it.

I cup sea water in my hands and splash my face. Salt hits my eyes and the day turns even brighter. The sand glints in the sunlight; the ocean stretching away is multi-shaded, the depths darker and wave crests whiter than bone. My skin shines with a pearly cast, and I know my eyes swim with colors.

Macon smiles at me. He's so beautiful that for a moment I forget what I'm supposed to be doing. I do see Macon's true beauty—like a glow from within—but I can't make him do anything. That part of my newfound siren power hasn't worked on him yet, but we keep trying. I haven't really used it on anyone else since I got back to Maine. I don't know why he's so insistent, but at least he didn't freak out when I told him I had tried to control him before. I mean, I thought at the time that I was releasing him from any inadvertent thrall I had over him... but still. I'd have been mad if I thought someone was taking my choices away. He gives me a "get on with it" look.

"Go get me a snack," I command, feeling the salt in my eyes, the force of my will. Nothing. "Get me a towel." Macon just looks at me, grinning. I dip my hands again and wet my face. I lock eyes with him. "Kiss me."

In a second, he wraps one arm around my waist and pulls me close, his face a breath away. Then he leans in and I am caught up in his embrace, his mouth on mine.

When we break, I am out of breath. "That worked?"

"Well, no, but I didn't want to waste the opportunity."

I shake my head but can't help laughing.

"I'm going to have to go," Macon says, looking at his watch. "I'm supposed to help my mom."

"Where does she think you are?" I try to keep my tone light.

"She knows I'm with you. I just promised that I'd be home by two." I don't know what my face betrays, but he puts his hands on my shoulders as if to underline his next words. "She likes you. Or she will once she gets to know you better. It's fine."

"Yeah, I know."

He doesn't look as if he believes me, but he doesn't say anything more about it. It's as if a cloud has covered the sun.

"I want to run by the clearing really quick on my way."

The clearing isn't exactly on the way to his side of the island from here, but it feels like home to him. It's one of the most peaceful places on the island, so I can't begrudge him. I guess it's a recharge for him, the way Ellie's sea stew is for me.

"I'll see you in the morning. Meet you at your dock."

"I'll be there." A school day. Hurrah. The year has just started, and I'm still finding my way in the new school.

"Oh, I almost forgot. I made you something." He holds out his hand in a fist, hiding whatever it is.

"You did?" A pleased flush warms my face. "What is it?" I slide my hand under his, and he places a small figurine in it. It's a little, carved seahorse about two inches tall. Really intricate. He's managed to carve even the little spines decorating its back and the tight spiral curl of its tail. It has a cute snub nose and the wing-like fins are so fine, I imagine I could see through the edges. He's smoothed it well, but it still looks like new pine and carries the scent of the forest. "This is really good. It must have taken you ages."

"You like it?"

"It's beautiful. I love it."

I launch into his arms giving him an exaggerated thank you smooch. He smiles against my lips. Then he really kisses me again.

Too soon, he steps back and gives me a rueful half-smile. "Okay, gotta go. See you."

I say goodbye, and he heads east. I watch him until he

goes over the rise and then turn back to the ocean, slipping the seahorse into my pocket.

I walk a little way into the surf and splash my face again. I search the waves but see nothing and no one. Since I brought Mom back from New Mexico, I haven't seen the girl from the water again. I met her on the rocks on the south side of the island, and later she took me to the siren world— Araem, Ellie's world—for a few moments. I don't even know her name. I remember her face like a dark pearl, her silver hair, and sharp smile. I've dreamed about her a couple of times, too, but no sightings.

I haven't seen *any* faces in the waves. I was sure we heard singing the first night we got back but nothing since then. It's as if the other sirens have disappeared. Ellie says sometimes they go quiet. I don't think my grandmother would outright lie to me, but I'm sure she wasn't telling me the whole truth. What a surprise.

I've tried to get her to tell me more about Araem and those she calls sisters, but she only gives little snippets of stories. To be honest, it seems to make her sad, so I haven't pressed her. When we needed to get Mom from New Mexico, she told me that she wasn't able to leave the island—not since my grandfather, Oscar, disappeared. That makes no sense to me, but she won't say much more than that. Mom has told me what she remembers about that world, but she hasn't been there since she was a little girl. She remembers that the ground was soft and that someone taught her to paint colors in the air. I probably remember more from my short visit.

Still, the last couple of months since I got back have been pretty decent. And not just because I kind of have a boyfriend. Dang, how did *that* happen? I'm not complaining, not really, just feels… surprising. No, that's not the only thing, not even the best thing, if I'm honest. Mom has been doing good, really good. She has to use a cane and gets tired easily, but she's out of her wheelchair. And considering the state she was in back at the facility in New Mexico, even being *in* the wheelchair was a huge improvement.

Seeing her with Ellie has been an education. They held each other for five whole minutes when we got back, both crying. It was beautiful. But before long, I guess they remembered why they hadn't spoken for years. They aren't fighting now really, but let's just say that I'm glad that we are living in the house, Windemere, and that Ellie stayed in her cottage. Everything is pretty good.

I just need to make sure it stays that way. Keep positive. Make sure Mom stays healthy, that she doesn't get too stressed out. I need to focus on that. It's way more important than quiet sirens, I know. We can make our new life here work.

My phone chirps, but I don't check it. It can't be Macon texting me; he'll still be walking back. It could be Blue, but I know she's at the café this afternoon. Jane finished her research here and left a few weeks ago to go back to college in California. Besides, she was camping this weekend somewhere, as she said, "No phones can find me." Mom and Ellie were working on some hides when I left them. They won't be done quite yet. And Ellie sure doesn't send phone messages anyway.

I'm trying to time it perfectly so that they'll be finished before I get back, and I don't have to help with the hides. I just want to spend a few more minutes enjoying the walk, the heat and sun soaking into my skin, salt drying on my lips, and listening to the seagulls chattering at each other above me. I take a deep breath of sea air and along with the ocean, smell pine trees. The breath of the island.

My phone chirps again as I'm climbing back up toward

the house. My stomach churns. Persistent, that's for sure. I stop, annoyed, and finally pull out my phone. It's an email, not a text. This must be the fourth message this week.

"Cam, honey, you coming?" Mom calls me from outside our front door.

I wave and pocket my phone again without opening the email. I know I don't have to be on high alert every time he writes, and I'm not trying to ignore him, per se. It's just things are so good right now...

"What's up?" Mom asks when I get close.

"Nothing." I shrug.

"You have that look. That 'I'm gonna tackle everything myself' look."

I smile at her grumpy impression of me and try to see past it to gauge how she's feeling. She must guess what I am doing because she rolls her eyes.

"I'm fine. Stop watching me like that. Go get cleaned up and you can help me with the dinner prep."

I spot one of Ellie's baskets on the ground. "You went fishing?"

"Momma did while I was working on the skins." She purses her lips.

I don't ask why they divvied up the tasks but hurry off to the bathroom to wash my hands. Then I head across the hall into the small bedroom that I took over when we got back. I'd never really moved into the other one anyway. It's easier for Mom with her cane to be in the room connected to the bathroom.

In the privacy of my room, I pull out my phone and check the email.

Cam—this is getting ridiculous. You need to write me back. I tried calling the house, and the number is discon-

nected. I tried your cell. Your Mom's number isn't working. Where are you?

"Cam?" Mom is at my door, and I fumble the phone trying to put it away. "You all right?"

"Mom!" I groan her name and make a silly face at her, mock-rolling my eyes just as she'd done to me, phone safely in my pocket again. "I'm fine."

"Careful, your face'll freeze like that."

"Yeah, yeah. Let's go see what we're having for dinner."

I haven't told her about the emails. That Dad is finally wondering where I am. I will. Just not yet.

CHAPTER 2

I check my bag and pockets again, making sure I have my notebook, phone, lip balm, books, snack, and all that. I usually manage to forget something, and it's not like you can just jog home to get it. My fingers slide across a tiny bottle of sea water. I'm not planning to use it; it's just in case. I don't know "just in case" of what. It makes me feel safer, more comfortable, to have it with me. I also have the little seahorse Macon carved for me. I run my thumb over the whorl of its tail and smile.

Macon glances back at me from the driver's seat of the boat. "Come on up."

He slows the boat gently, while I make my way to him. He's been teaching me how to pilot a boat. I had to take a safety course online first, though. I settle into the seat, take the wheel, and put my hand on the throttle but don't yet increase the speed. Instead, I search the horizon while we float. I study the lapping waves looking for any flashes, any faces. I strain my ears but only hear the slosh of water. There's nothing out there. Listening to the sirens' songs, seeing their other-worldly skin and eyes, visiting Araem... It almost feels like a dream.

"Cam?"

"Yeah, I have it." I toss a smile at him. "All good."

I push the throttle forward and speed up. I take us all the way until we see Williams Point in the distance. I don't yet feel comfortable docking. Macon says I'm going to have to learn sometime, and I will. But today is not that day.

We pass Blue's café on the way to the high school, and she barrels out the door wearing an acid green coat and trying to hold three bamboo to-go cups. Macon grabs the door, and I take a dripping cup from her.

"Nice coat. Where'd I put my sunglasses? Is this for me?"

"Ha ha, and yes, so be more grateful to be served by my awesome fashionista self. One for you, too." She hands a cup to Macon.

"Goddess," I say, then take a big swig.

"That's me." She grins and flips her currently magenta hair. It kind of clashes with her loud coat, but because it's Blue she somehow pulls it off.

Macon thanks her, and they chat and joke the rest of the way to the school. I must be a little quieter than normal because at one point, Blue bumps me with her shoulder and tells me to "join the party." I laugh and make some silly comment, but my words are as empty as the sea was this morning—and has been for weeks. Macon catches my eye, but I just shake my head.

My new high school is completely different from the others I've gone to and also totally the same. I'm pretty sure the full school population is less than the last graduating class of my school in Albuquerque and you couldn't take Costal Navigation 101, but I swear it smells the same inside. It's a thing with public schools. I'm convinced they all use the same cleaning products or something.

Macon touches my elbow before he takes off to his first period class. We're not big on PDA, so no sloppy kisses in the hallway like the senior couple that always seems to be making out by the entrance to the girls' bathroom. Still that small touch sends a zing up my arm. I tell him I'll see him later and say goodbye to Blue, wishing I had first period with either of them.

Instead, I get to have it with Bridgette—Macon's overly pretty ex and the one person in our friend group who seems constantly suspicious of me. She doesn't look over as I enter the class, but I see her perfect nose wrinkle a little as she smooths her glossy, dark hair. I ignore her and go to my seat toward the back. I don't have time for whatever drama might be simmering there. With the curriculum differences from the southwest to the northeast and me missing loads of school last year due to Mom's sickness, I'm behind in a few classes. I had to test to get into this English class and still have a backlog of required reading to catch up on.

It actually isn't as bad as you might imagine—Bridgette, I mean. Since I shot her down when she labeled me a witch on the beach that day and tried to ward me off with a necklace, of all things, she hasn't said much to me. She makes comments, of course. Sharp, subtle remarks as if she's trying to get me to admit to something or get other people to realize something about me. She's been around at a few get togethers I've been to over the last couple of months. Snarky cracks and definite side-eye shade aside, she's been civil to my face, at least.

I get my notebook out and listen to Mr. Owens talk about *To Kill a Mockingbird*. I've already read it. Or rather, I listened to it. I got it from the library on audiobook last year.

Sissy Spacek was the narrator, and I was entranced with how her southern accent made the words sing. I had to look her up because I didn't know who she was. Mom was appalled that I didn't know the original *Carrie* and the million other parts she'd played.

Mr. Owens is a really good teacher. He asks interesting questions, doesn't try to be "cool" and never talks down to us. Today, though, as I lean my chin on my hand and listen, I can hardly hold onto his words. His voice is calm and almost hypnotic. He's talking about the setting being like a character, but his voice is getting lost in the sound of waves.

The ocean has turned tide, and I can hear how there's a little bit more water in each crash. Each wave bringing the sea to land, pulling back, then falling forward again, rhythmic as breathing, as blood flowing, as a heartbeat.

Suddenly, I am at the coast, on the sand, watching the ocean come in. I see a flash that could be sunlight on the waves but might be something more. I hear voices, far away but distinct, calling out. Finally! Lightness floods me, as a weight is lifted from my heart, sending effervescence through my veins. I could almost cry. I hear my name, the voice urgent, pleading with me. But I can't see anyone. I try to call back, but no sound passes my lips. The weight settles back through my body, a creeping dread. I reach out toward the surf, but there's an invisible barrier stopping me. I hear my name again, and try to push through the surface blocking my way. It's smooth and cold, like glass.

"Cam, Cam Vale!"

I jump. I'm in the classroom, hand pressed against the window, looking at a ghost of myself in the reflection. My heart is hammering inside my chest.

"Cam?" Mr. Owens is standing next to me. I can literally feel the entire class staring. Excellent. "Are you okay?"

I look up into Mr. Owens' face, embarrassed. He looks confused and strange, his brown hair has so many colors in it that I have never noticed, and his dark eyes are a richer chestnut color. That's when I realize that my cheeks are wet. I look away and blink rapidly to clear the salt from my eyes.

"You were staring out the window as if something was wrong. You didn't hear me?"

"I— I thought I saw something," I say. My face is in flames. "I'm sorry, it was just… nothing."

"Well, sit back down." He furrows his brow at me. "All right everyone, show's over. Lilly, how does Harper Lee describe the heat in Maycomb?"

Back at my desk, I wipe my face and try to concentrate on what Lilly is saying. I breathe in and out, timing my inhale to four counts and then exhale the same. I haven't had a panic attack in weeks, but I feel the buzzing in the back of my head as if one's close.

I glance up and most people are listening to Lilly, doodling in their notebooks, or trying to slyly text, but Bridgette is staring at me, eyes narrowed. She turns away pointedly when she sees me looking.

Landbound, The Second Book in the *Watermarked* Trilogy, is out summer of 2020.

Made in the USA
Coppell, TX
05 March 2021

51336426R00166